The Children

The Children

Ann Leary

ST. MARTIN'S PRESS • NEW YORK

THE CHILDREN. Copyright © 2016 by Ann Leary. All rights reserved. Printed in the United States of America. For information address St. Martin's Press, 175 Fifth Avenue, New York, N.Y. 10010.

www.stmartins.com

Library of Congress Cataloging-in-Publication Data

Names: Leary, Ann, author.
Title: The children : a novel / Ann Leary.
Description: First edition. | New York : St. Martin's Press, 2016.
Identifiers: LCCN 2015048744| ISBN 9781250045379 (hardcover) | ISBN
    9781466844025 (ebook)
Subjects: LCSH: Stepfamilies—New England—Fiction. | Brothers and
    sisters—Fiction. | Family secrets—Fiction. | Domestic fiction. | BISAC:
    FICTION / Contemporary Women. | FICTION / Family Life.
Classification: LCC PS3612.E238 C48 2016 | DDC 813/.6—dc23
LC record available at http://lccn.loc.gov/2015048744

Our books may be purchased in bulk for promotional, educational, or business use. Please contact your local bookseller or the Macmillan Corporate and Premium Sales Department at 1-800-221-7945, extension 5442, or by e-mail at MacmillanSpecialMarkets@macmillan.com.

First Edition: May 2016

10 9 8 7 6 5 4 3 2 1

Dedicated, with love, to my mother, Judith S. Howe

The Children

ONE

One August morning in 1956, Whit Whitman sat down to a breakfast of soft-boiled eggs and toast with his grandmother Trudy. They dined outdoors on the wide front porch of Lakeside Cottage. Whit's father had an early golf game that morning. His mother and sister had gone for a sail on the lake. Although he was only eight at the time, Whit would always remember what he and his grandmother talked about during their breakfast. First, Trudy had described her displeasure at finding the family cat on her bed when she awoke. She had thought it was her sweater and was alarmed when it sprang from her hands. Then they had discussed the weather.

"Isn't it cold for August?" Trudy asked.

"Not really," said Whit. He wanted to go sailing and was bitter about being left behind to look after his grandmother.

"Won't you and your father want to plant bulbs this afternoon? Or is it too soon for bulbs? Didn't we just plant the tomatoes?"

Whit answered in a dull monotone. It was a bit soon for the bulbs. The tomatoes had been planted in May.

"Oh, didn't we have the loveliest tomatoes last night?" Trudy asked.

"Yes, Gran."

"Weren't they perfectly ripe, dear?"

"Yes, they were."

"The roses, have they been cut back?"

"I don't know, Gran," Whit said, squinting out at the lake in search of his mother's boat. (Here's the point in the story where I always see the two white birches, gone now, against a flat blue sky, and the lake spread all around them like a pool of shimmering silver.)

"It's too soon to cut them back. They're still blooming," Trudy scolded, as if it had been Whit who suggested cutting the roses back in the first place.

"Would you like to walk down to the garden, Gran?" Whit asked.

"No, dear, thank you," Trudy said. "But if you'll excuse me, I think I'll just go upstairs and die now."

"Gran, not die," Whit corrected her. "You mean *lie*, not die."

But Trudy had meant die. She walked up the back stairs to her bedroom. She used the servants' staircase behind the kitchen because she found the carpeted front stairs harder to manage. Then she folded back the quilt on her bed, pressed herself against the cool sheets, and died.

"It was her time. She was eighty-nine years old," Whit would explain years later, his eyes sparkling and sometimes streaming with tears in the telling. (Whit was unable to laugh properly without crying.) "Still, it was the way she did it—so polite. Well, she was a Farmington girl, after all. One doesn't just die."

Whit was my stepfather. My sister, Sally, and I grew up in his house, and we often begged him to repeat this story to us when we were little girls, usually interrupting him with demands for details.

"Did she really try to wear the cat?"

"Was her body stiff when you found it?"

"Did it smell?"

Trudy Whitman wasn't the first to die at Lakeside. Her mother-in-law, Ruth, died here twenty years prior. According to family legend, Ruth had spent much of her ninety-third summer in bed because she had some kind of heart problem. One night, a rabid raccoon ate its way through the window screen and leaped up on her bed, snarling and spitting blood-tinged foam everywhere, so old Ruth Whitman beat it to death with her book. Ruth didn't contract rabies from the animal, but instead enjoyed several weeks of renewed vigor, dressing each evening for dinner with very little help from the maid. One night, after tasting her dessert, she said, "That German cook has finally stopped using too much sugar in the rhubarb. It's quite good." Then she astonished her family by appearing to forgo utensils and eat her pie from the plate like a dog. In fact, her heart had stopped. She had died, and that's just where her face had come to rest, there in the German cook's rhubarb pie.

Whit loved telling family stories, their general theme being that Whitmans are gritty and combative, they live long and then die when they're good and ready—not a moment sooner. So it must have come as a shock to him to learn that he had cancer at age sixty-five, though it was anybody's guess how he reacted, as he kept the diagnosis to himself until just a few months before he died. Then he told only our mother, Joan, who neglected to inform any of us kids until after he was gone.

"It's what Whit wanted," she had said at the time. It seems that he didn't think he was going to die as soon as he did. Perhaps he thought the rules of cell division, malignancies, and whatnot, like so many other boring rules, simply didn't apply to him. Maybe he thought he could opt out of the whole cancer scheme that his doctor had laid out before him. In any case, he did die, less than a year after his diagnosis, leaving Lakeside in a sort of limbo.

Lakeside Cottage is still owned by the Whitman estate. It was left to my stepbrothers, Perry and Spin Whitman, but Whit requested that Joan be allowed to live here for the remainder of her life. It's all part of a family trust. Sally and I aren't part of the trust, being Maynards and not Whitmans.

Sally lives in Manhattan now, but I live at Lakeside with Joan. I'm twenty-nine. I know—I'm a little old to live in my mother's house. I like it here, though, and not just because it's free, as my stepbrother

Perry is always hinting. I work at home. I have a blog, and I'm also thinking of writing a book about Laurel Atwood. Maybe a sort of memoir.

It's hard to understand what attracted Spin to Laurel, and vice versa, without understanding the Whitmans. You need the whole picture. I stupidly told Joan about the book idea the other day, and now she keeps insisting that she doesn't want me to write about her. "Go ahead, tell the story, just keep me out of it," she'll say, and then she'll remind me of the time she ran the Boston Marathon, or the time she won the regional women's amateur open tennis championship.

"Whit's marriage was over when we got together. People forget that," she'll announce suddenly, as if I had asked. "In any event, if you're going to write about me at all, I think it'll give a more rounded perspective if you include the fact that I went to Princeton."

"Okay, well, I'm really focusing on Whit now," I told her the other day after she offered another writing prompt involving her triumphant goal in a field hockey match sometime in the 1970s.

"Whit? What on earth has Whit got to do with it? He was already dead when Spin met Laurel."

I don't leave our property in the day much anymore, but when I do, I stay close to home. I often walk in the woods. I like wooded paths. I like the dark. I can go anywhere in the dark, I just don't go to strange outdoor places during the day very often. Fields, roads, parking lots, open places like that make me anxious. Vast indoor areas like shopping centers are tricky because of all the people, but at least there you can grab a wall or a railing or something. In open outdoor places, there's nothing you can hold on to, nothing to anchor you to the earth's surface. I was always a homebody, a "house mouse," as Whit used to say. I think it's just part of my nature, but over time it's gone from a quirk to something more.

Three summers ago, not long after Whit died, I stood on the

town beach of this lake one afternoon and was suddenly undone by its vast, yawning strangeness. I think that's when I first got this sense of needing to grab hold of something. The ground would have been fine. If I could have crawled back to my bicycle from the lake's edge, I would have. But there were people at the beach, watching me with all their eyes. I walked away slowly, looking down, each footstep placed deliberately, heel-toe, heel-toe, so as not to scuttle sidelong before the entire group like a crab with no shell. I walked back to the cool shade of the tree where my bike was resting. Once I caught my breath, I pedaled home.

Another thing—I don't drive, but I've always been able to ride my bike on roads that I wouldn't dream of walking along, especially during the day. Of course, at night, it's different. I can ride anywhere at night, as long as the weather's not too cold.

Joan says I need to learn to adapt. I think she's wrong. I think my problem is that I'm too adaptable. Have you ever seen a large cat fold itself into a tiny shoe box? Or the way a bat wraps its vast wings around its torso until it's no bigger than a prune? A grown rat can squeeze through a hole the size of a dime. I'm like that. I'm like a contortionist that way. I must have softer bones than most people. I can deflate myself into the tiniest recesses and be quite comfortable there.

"It's a beautiful day, Charlotte," Joan said this morning. "Why don't you go outdoors and enjoy the nice weather?"

I don't have to go out to know that it's a beautiful day. I don't have to walk on the grass to feel it cool and damp beneath my feet. We had a thunderstorm an hour ago, and the lake is almost black. In a moment, the light will shift and it'll be steely and blue. I don't need to go out to know that; I can see the weather from here. Now the evenings are getting warmer. I'll be able to walk down to the lake in the moonlight tonight. I'll watch my legs sawn off at the ankles, calves, knees, and finally the thighs as I wade into the dark water. When I'm cut off at the waist, I'll lie back and float like a spirit. I swim only at night now.

TWO

Not everybody has heard of Laurel Atwood—I have to keep reminding myself of that. Not everybody watches reality TV and reads tabloids. The funny thing is, when we first met Laurel, she acted as if she had never watched TV or read anything but books—important books, important literary *works*, as she liked to call them. And she didn't read magazines like everybody else. She read quarterlies. She was a writer. She had just gotten her MFA from USC and had received a six-figure advance for her first novel. Her agent had sent the publisher one chapter and an outline. That was all they needed.

Her accomplishments didn't sound so far-fetched when we first heard about them—the book deal, the training for the Olympic ski team, all before her twenty-seventh birthday. Of course, we didn't learn about everything at once. Laurel has a way of unveiling herself little by little. I think she tried to give herself a more human scale that way. Spin was always like that, too, before he met Laurel, but his motives were the opposite of hers. He wouldn't tell people about his accomplishments because he didn't want people to envy him. Laurel does.

Kindness always came naturally to Spin. He got that trait from his father. Whit was actually a very kind man, but he could come off a little gruff if you didn't know him. I'd known him since I was two years old. That's when he and my mother got together. Of course, I didn't really understand what was going on between them at first. Apparently, no one did. They somehow managed to keep it a secret for over a year. But in the summer of 1988, just before he turned forty, Whit Whitman fell in love with our mother, Joan.

Connecticut had a major heat wave that summer; people still talk about it. The Fourth of July fireworks were canceled because of the fire risk. Some people had their wells run dry. Lawns were brown, streams evaporated, and local farmers watched their tomatoes roast on the vine, but Whit's memories of those days remained vivid, if not entirely accurate, and in every one of them, the grass surrounding Lakeside was greener and the gardens more alive with color than ever before.

Whit had no recollection of any dry spell that summer because he was always drenched. His clothes clung to his damp skin all day, and each night, he'd leave his wife, Marissa, alone in the house with her drink, her book, and her disdain, and he'd stride, nude and "savagely alive" (his actual words), out across his lawn to the lake. There he'd float on his back, sometimes for hours. He'd search the sky for the Dippers, Big and Little, for Polaris, Orion's Belt, and the other twinkling constellations that had fascinated him in his boyhood. Now they fascinated him once again. Whit said there were times that summer when he felt that the muscles in his chest weren't equipped to sustain his swelling heart. His every waking moment pulsed with thoughts of Joan.

It was a thorny situation. Whit was the first to admit that. Joan, though still quite young, had Sally and me, and wasn't divorced from our father yet. Whit was also married and had his son Perry, who was then about seven. The thought that two families were about to be dismantled was agonizing to Whit, but the thing that tortured him most wasn't his guilt, it was the humbling knowledge that midlife affairs like his were so common. His love for our mother was anything but common. I know this because he would sometimes shout this information, spittily, at Sally and me—especially if he was into his gin. His love for Joan was the most extraordinary thing he had ever experienced. Suddenly, all was illuminated. He had lived his life thus far as a sort of affable, obedient pet—first to his mother and father, then to his wife. Whit had always done what *others* had wanted him to do, not what he wanted. College, law school, marrying his first serious girlfriend, joining his father-in-law's firm in Manhattan (he would count these off on his fingers for us, like crimes), it had all been expected of him, and he fiercely resented the expectations of others.

Whit had never been in love before. He saw that now. His marriage to socially striving Marissa was nothing more than a dull, ill-conceived alliance. It was a sham; there was no other word for it, and it had been from day one. Within weeks of his first tryst with Joan, Whit knew that life was shorter and more exquisite than he had ever imagined, and what was left of it, damn it, he would spend with her.

The surprise of Marissa's pregnancy, almost a year into the affair, complicated things, but it didn't alter the course Whit had set for himself. For the duration of his wife's pregnancy, he stayed in their town house on the Upper East Side. Two months after Spin was born, he moved out for good. He moved up here to northwest Connecticut, to Lakeside Cottage, where his family had spent their summers for four generations. Once we moved in with our mother, Whit had the house winterized so we could live here full-time. Perry and Spin visited every other weekend, certain holidays, and one month of the summer.

This house is huge. It's old and drafty. In order to cut back on energy costs, Whit would close the heating ducts in the boys' rooms when they weren't here, and he'd often forget to open them until after they arrived on wintry Friday nights. So there were the cold beds and, over time, another kind of chilliness that developed between Whit and his sons, especially Perry. Marissa had remarried and remarried well. Her new husband, Peter Sommers, was wealthy, like Whit. Probably not quite as wealthy, but he actually worked. Marissa and Peter held a certain contempt for Whit. Perry picked this up early on, and eventually he absorbed it himself.

Richard "Whit" Whitman (or "Idle Rich," as Marissa had taken to calling him) was a little eccentric. But he wasn't really idle at all; he just stopped earning his own money after he met Joan. He had to leave his job at his former father-in-law's firm, but instead of starting his own practice or joining another, he retired and lived on the interest of an enormous trust that had been left to him after the deaths of his parents in the 1960s. Whit wanted to devote the rest of his life to the pursuit of things that *really* interested him. He was really interested in American history. To be more specific, he was interested in the history of American bluegrass music.

To be most specific, Whit was interested in banjos.

You could call it an obsession—most people did. He played the banjo. He collected rare banjos. Eventually, he built banjos—beautiful five-string banjos that he carved by hand in a workshop he had set up in a shed behind the old boathouse. Until he became very sick, until those last few months, you could find him working in that shed almost every day except Sunday. Whit sold many of the banjos he made. He had a little mail-order business, and eventually enthusiasts from all over the United States sought his instruments. He was a bit of a legend in the banjo community, but, well, it was the banjo community. It barely existed in the Northeast. In the grand scheme of things, I guess, it barely existed at all.

The Whitman money is old family money, mostly steel money. Whit's uncle Leander Whitman was the ambassador to Sweden during the Eisenhower administration. A John Singer Sargent portrait of Whit's grandmother used to hang over our living room mantel. Perry took it after Whit died because (he said) we never lock our doors. We don't lock the doors because we don't have much crime here, and even if we had, nobody would have known it was an important painting, because you could barely see the thing. On the mantel below it were always stacks of books, gloves, old dog collars, banjo strings, and guitar picks. Whit hated throwing anything away. He hated new things. He always drove the most beat-up car in this town—a rusty old Volvo. He was very thrifty, and so was Spin, at least before he met Laurel.

Laurel, we learned from Spin, was also a member of an important American family. Her great-great-uncle was Ernest Hemingway. Laurel grew up in Idaho. That's where her family is from—Ketchum, Idaho, where Hemingway lived at the end of his life.

In fact, Idaho is where Spin first met Laurel. Spin taught science and music at Holden Academy, the boarding school here in Harwich, and it was during Christmas break of last year that he was skiing at Sun Valley. He and Laurel first met at a lodge at the top of the mountain. She was with some old friends of his from Dartmouth. I don't know how she knew the Dartmouth group; I don't know how Laurel manages to insinuate herself into everything, she just does. Apparently, the friends wanted to hang out in the lodge and have another beer. Laurel and Spin decided to get in a little more skiing before the lifts closed. Spin had just bought one of those helmet cams, and he turned it on for their first run together. I've watched this video so many times that I have almost every second of it memorized. I keep looking for clues. Sometimes I find them.

For example, the other day I realized Spin says something right after the two-minute mark. I called Sally immediately. It was several hours before she called me back.

"Look at two-oh-four," I said.

"I can't," Sally said. "I'm at work."

"Write it down. Two minutes and four seconds. It's right after she comes flying out from behind the trees and almost collides with him. He says something."

"I'm not watching it anymore."

"I thought it was just a sort of grunt. For the longest time, I thought he was just grunting, but he says something. He says a word, I'm certain."

"Okay," Sally said. "Listen, Lottie, stop watching it."

"I can't."

"Yes, you can. It won't change anything."

"Also, at the beginning, she turns and flashes that smile at him. But it isn't really him she's smiling at. It's the camera, up on top of his helmet."

"Yeah, I know," Sally said. She was smoking a cigarette, I could tell. She told me she had quit.

"He was always so cautious, that's what gets me," I said. "We used to make so much fun of him. I mean, I know he's a great skier, but the way they were speeding through those trees . . . They were flying. He would never have done that without her, he was trying to keep up with her."

"Okay, stop now."

"Just call me after you look at it."

"No."

"Watch it when you get home. See if you can see what he says."

"No."

After we hung up, I watched it one more time.

It starts with just some shaky whiteness. Spin is messing around with the camera, fastening it to his helmet. Then the world swings into view as he lifts the helmet up onto his head. He's near the ski lift. You can hear the whirring of the motors, the clanging of metal, all those muffled sounds in that rare air at the top of the snow-covered mountain. For a second or two, there's a glimpse of the steep white slope below and the wooded valley beyond, but then he's turned away from the slope and facing Laurel.

She's bent over, brushing something off the top of one of her ski boots for the first twenty or thirty seconds, and then she whips her head up and smiles at the camera. She's wearing goggles. All you can see is a silver helmet, the blue-tinted goggles, the long, wavy blond hair, and that perfect smile, and somehow you have it all. As many times as I've watched this, I'm never prepared for her beauty in that instant, when she faces Spin and we see her for the first time. It's the moment when I feel I can see her most clearly, when I can finally see her for who she really is. But the strange thing is, you really can't see her face at all. What's most noticeable is the reflection of Spin in her goggle lenses. There he is, twice, smiling from each lens.

"I'll race you down," Laurel shouts.

"Okay, you start," Spin shouts back.

"Oh, you think I need a head start?"

"You might," he says.

And then she turns, stabs the snow with the tips of her ski poles, and she's gone.

She's fast, skipping along the tops of the moguls. It's a little hard to see here, because it's so bouncy, but she's wearing a bright yellow parka, and we never let her out of our sight, perched as we are on Spin's head. He's finally gaining on her when, suddenly, she cuts into the woods. He cuts in after her. This is the great part. This is the reason Spin sent us the video the same day that he took it. It makes your heart race. He's carving little lines into some deep, untouched pow-der, speeding down a steep, heavily wooded trail. It actually looks fake in parts. Sally noticed that when we first saw it. It looks animated, like a video game, the way the trees are whipping past.

First they're in among the evergreens and you can hear Spin laughing. He quietly curses once, when he snags a branch with his arm. He stays up, though. He's behind her, and then he's not; she cuts out of sight and he's slaloming his way around the trees. The ever-greens are gone. The trees have become just trunks; they're in the deciduous trees now. If they had stopped, Spin would have been able to identify each tree for Laurel. He can tell a maple from an ash, just by the pattern of the bark. Even in the dead of winter, he knows one tree from another. He can closely estimate their ages; he probably would have if they had stopped. But they didn't stop. Spin must have regretted that gentleman's head start he'd granted her. We all laughed about that later, when we watched the video together. He had under-estimated her.

Suddenly, she flies out from behind some trees on the left of the screen and almost hits Spin. This is the 2:04 mark I was telling Sally about. He says a word, and then he's skiing very fast behind Laurel.

"She waited until we got to the bottom to tell me she was on the U.S. Olympic team," Spin told us a few months later, when we all watched the video together.

"Short-listed," Laurel corrected him. "I wasn't on the team. I was short-listed. I tore my meniscus during the trials."

So modest.

Spin definitely says something around the two-minute mark. I don't know why I hadn't noticed it before. I watched it. Then I watched it again.

"I'll get you," he says. Or maybe it's "Look at you."

It's really something, seeing the world from Spin's perspective. I think that's why I keep watching it. You can hear his breath in that video. You can see the tips of his skis pointing left, right, left, right, then straight down the mountain.

Spin always made everything look easy. You should have seen him play tennis when he was a kid. You should have seen him play the guitar or the banjo. Spin made the varsity hockey team at Holden his freshman year, but he'd been skating here on the lake with us from the time he could walk. That's how I like to think of him now—the way he was before he met Laurel. Out on the lake. Often alone. Practicing stick handling and shooting, his hockey stick snaking along the ice, flicking the puck this way and that. There's a calmness that's specific to a frozen place such as a lake or a ski slope. The cold air traps sound. A skater's edge on crusty ice sounds like the only thing on earth. I can still see him now, gliding backward, skates crossing one over the other so effortlessly. And that thin amber light you get here on the lake on winter afternoons. On weekend mornings, we always had pickup games in front of the house. The loud clacks of the hockey sticks, the triumphant cries, the angry objections and laughter, Whit's roaring protests. We haven't played hockey on the lake in years. Kids play at the other end of the lake now that we're all grown up. The ice freezes here first, but nobody skates on this side of the lake anymore.

When he was at Dartmouth, Spin wrote his thesis on the negative effects of invasive species on New England lakes and ponds. He did much of his research here on Lake Marinac. He majored in environmental sciences, with a minor in musical theory. He was the only one of us who was truly gifted musically; the rest of us had to work at it, even Sally.

The afternoon of Whit's funeral service, after everybody had finally left our house but the family, Sally kept playing the same melody on her violin. It was Bach, or something grim like that. Over and over and over again. She and I were sitting on the porch swing as she played. I put my hand on the body of the violin for a moment. My intention was to get her to stop, but then I felt the long whine of the bow running through the instrument and into the tips of my fingers. The vibrations went all through me. I felt the pull of the bow across the strings and wished I had learned the violin or cello. We spent a good part of the afternoon like that. Sally weaving the bow up and down, me with my hand touching the body of the violin. It was Spin who got us out of our funk. He brought out one of Whit's banjos.

The banjo is a happy instrument. Even if you play along with a sad song, as Spin did that day, the rolls that accompany the chords do something. They add humor. Soon Spin had Sally on some other melody altogether. It was a Celtic-sounding thing. Some kind of reel, one of those fiddle and banjo songs you hear on Saint Patrick's Day. They went round and round with it and were becoming extremely amused with themselves. I walked down to the lake and dove into the cold water. I swam out to the float. I could hear their song from there.

THREE

S he's into yoga," I reported to Sally the day we learned that Spin had asked Laurel to marry him. We were all completely surprised by the news of the engagement. Spin had met her that January. Now it was April and they were engaged? I work on my computer—I'm on it all the time—so I checked out her Facebook, Twitter, and Instagram accounts as soon as he told us. I called Sally to fill her in.

"Lots of yoga," I said.

"Does she do it for fitness or is she into the whole energy thing, or what?" Sally asked.

"I don't know," I said. "She's just doing poses. Standing on her hands, with her legs up in the air. That kind of swastika legs pose? Over and over. Oh, here's one where she's standing on one foot, pulling her other foot over her head. From behind. Like a figure skater."

"What?" Sally asked. "Why?"

"She's flexible. Some are selfies, with a mirror."

"Oh, okay, as long as it's just a showing-off thing," Sally said. "As long as she's not one of those positive-light, quiet-energy, serene, contemplative fuckwads. One of those people who talk about blessings and gratitude all the time and meanwhile, they're so bitter and angry and self-absorbed, they literally suck the energy out of every room they're in. As long as she's not that."

"She doesn't really write much on the posts. It's mostly photos. Thousands of followers. She's got over ninety thousand Twitter followers."

"I wonder why so many?" Sally said.

"She has a beautiful body, maybe that's why," I said. "I guess from all the yoga."

"I don't care how many followers she has as long as she doesn't talk about being *present*. About having thoughtful, present mindfulness. I hate that."

"Lots of selfies. Some are just her face."

"Is she smiling in them?" Sally was on a break at a recording session and couldn't look.

"Yeah, most of them."

"Good, then she's not trying to look all soulful. I hate that. As long as she's not into *mindfulness*," Sally repeated.

"I do hope she's not boring," Joan said later that same day, when I told her about all the yoga. "Yoga people always seem so, well, tedious, don't you think?"

"No," I said. It bothers Sally and me how judgmental our mother can be.

"Don't they always have those glazed eyes?" Joan persisted. "Missy Wentwood is obsessed with yoga, and she always has that little smile and those glazed eyes. Like she's in a cult or something."

"I think that's Missy's medication," I said. "I don't think yoga does that to you."

"I just hope she's not one of those people who bores everybody, like Perry's Catherine," said Joan a little later. She had actually come up to the attic, where I work, to say this to me. My mother will go out of her way to be a snob. She makes an effort—you have to give her credit for that.

Sally came out from the city almost every weekend during the short period of time between our learning of the engagement and our meeting Laurel. Spin usually joined us for Sunday dinner, and we'd act very casual when he spoke of her. Later, after he'd left, we would dissect every tidbit that we'd been able to glean from him. One night, Joan cooked linguini with clams, and Spin mentioned that Laurel was allergic to shellfish.

"Oh no," Joan said, her voice conveying a deep sadness, but not because she pities people who have food allergies. Joan doesn't believe in food allergies. She thinks people have them to get attention. "I'll be careful never to make them when she's here," she said, leveling her eyes across the table at Sally and me when Spin looked away for a moment.

Good Lord, is what her gaze said. *This is even worse than we imagined.*

Joan worried that Laurel was "needy." "High-maintenance." Joan disdains this trait in a person more than any other. And though she isn't the cuddliest person, and Spin isn't actually her own son, Joan adores him. She always has.

The plan was that Laurel would move into Spin's campus apartment with him once the school year ended. The wedding was planned for sometime during the summer. Holden Academy doesn't like having unmarried faculty or staff living together as couples on campus, so that, we assumed, was part of the urgency. But we were a little bit worried. Everything was happening so fast. They hadn't known each other long. Most of the time they were together, they were apart. They had met only a few times after the ski trip. Spin flew out west for a couple of long weekends, I think. But they e-mailed and texted every day, and Spin said that through those communications they learned more about each other than they would have in many hours of face-to-face conversation.

I could see his point. When you talk to a person, the surroundings often distract you. You can become too absorbed with the other's appearance—the person's beauty or blemishes. When you're reading texts and e-mails, you're able to focus on what the other is saying. At least that's been my experience. Recently, most of my exchanges with other people have been via e-mail and Facebook. And I've met a lot of people online whom I consider to be my very good friends, though we've never actually met in real life. I met many of these people through my blog.

I started the blog a couple years ago, and this past January I was voted one of the Top Ten Mommy Bloggers by *The Huffington Post,* which boosted my already high daily page views and brought in a good amount of advertising revenue. No, I'm not actually a mommy; that's why I can't reveal the name of the blog. People think it's real. I'm supposed to be a snarky suburban housewife. I never show photos of Mia, my four-year-old daughter, or Wyatt, my six-year-old son, because I want to protect their privacy rather than exploit them like certain famous mommy bloggers whom I could name. Lots of people follow me just because of that—the fact that I go out of my way to protect the privacy of my children. Instead of photographing them, I write about the adorably crazy things they say. I include rage-filled thoughts aimed at the sancti-mommies at Wyatt's school, and sometimes at my adorable but clueless husband, Topher. That's all I'll say. And I'm not Charlotte Maynard. I have a different online name, a variation of which is also the name of my blog. I have many more Twitter followers than Laurel. Sometimes I wish I could use my real name so that people would know what a following I have.

Advertisers are paying me now. One is a diaper company, and I don't want to out myself. I frequent online parenting discussion forums; that's how I learn terms like *sancti-mommy,* and about vaccination controversies, preschool problems, and kids with special needs. Wyatt has a rare genetic disorder. It's a miracle he's alive. I'm able to joke about it, even when he has setbacks, which readers say they love about me—the fact that I can always find humor, no matter what tragedies this life might throw my way. Don't judge. The blog brings joy to many people; every day I get hundreds of e-mails and comments telling me so.

My point is this: I think you can get to know a person very well even if most of your interactions are online. I said this repeatedly to

Sally whenever we spoke of Spin's engagement. She was a little worked up about the fact that they were already engaged and we hadn't even met her yet.

Sometimes we'd tell Everett Hastings our latest discoveries about Laurel, and he'd have fun at our expense. Everett lives in the old carriage house on the property. He's a dog trainer by profession, but he works around here in exchange for his rent. We've known him all our lives. His father, Bud, was the caretaker before him, so Everett grew up here. He's a year older than Sally. Everett doesn't go on Facebook or anything, and he didn't understand how we felt that we knew her so well, based on what we had seen there. He thought we should reserve our judgment until we had met her. "There'll be plenty of time for hating her once you've actually been introduced in real life," he said one warm spring night when he, Sally, and I were out smoking a joint at the end of the dock.

Sally protested. "Who hates her? I don't hate her. I've never met her. What are you even talking about?"

"Just don't use up all your contempt before she gets here," Everett said, and laughed.

"We're not haters," Sally said. "She's odd. But we don't hate her."

"Right," Everett said.

That first week or two, we did judge her a little harshly, but that was because we had only been looking at her recent Facebook updates. One day, I decided to look back on her timeline, and what I learned changed our opinions completely.

I discovered that she'd had a terrible white-water kayaking accident in 2004. It had destroyed her career as a skier, ruined her chances for the Olympics. She had been with her sister; they were teenagers at the time. They had been caught in some rapid water and both kayaks had flipped. Laurel was thrown against a rock and fractured her spine someplace up near her neck. It was a miracle that she could even walk, let alone ski as well as we had seen in the video. Unfortunately, the sister had drowned. Laurel had chronicled her recovery on her blog. That's how she had developed the large following on Facebook and

Twitter. She had to put off college for a year for all the rehab. No sooner was she back on her feet than she was working tirelessly to help others with spinal injuries and also with grief over the loss of a loved one. She had experienced both at such a young age. She went to college there in Idaho, and when she wasn't studying, she volunteered her time working with veterans returning home from Iraq and Afghanistan. Eventually, she went to Afghanistan with a veterans group. She also kept a journal, and it was this journal that had caught the attention of the MFA program at USC and, later, the publisher.

We were in awe, my mother, Sally, and I. We had judged her too severely. The yoga was no longer seen as show-offy. It revealed her strength and resilience. It gave others hope. Sometimes, in the comments, people would post things like, "I had a C3 fracture two years ago, and you are my inspiration." Laurel would respond by asking where they were doing their rehab, or what kind of fracture it was. "Water therapy," she would say. Or, "There's a study at Johns Hopkins involving stem cells. PM me for more information, I know the doctor who's heading up the study."

We, like her many online followers, were humbled by Laurel's heroism and fortitude. Joan still found her "a little braggy." Sally and I told Joan that she was a snob. Sally, Joan, and I talked about her, wondered about her, praised her, criticized her, and argued about her. We were proud of her one day, and making fun of her the next. Some of her posts were a little too self-congratulatory and she used outdated acronyms like LOL and STFU all the time. And her sense of humor seemed off at times. She overshared about Spin, too—posting the weirdest stuff about how they're soul mates and how she knows him better than she knows herself. She didn't use his name, though; she called him "the Professor." Perhaps that was why he didn't object to her posting about his apparently insatiable sexual appetite.

"Teachers at prep schools are not professors," Joan said when we showed her one of Laurel's posts. The post had revealed, in very graphic detail, that our Spin was an oral-sex virtuoso. Sally and I were at the kitchen table, laughing uncontrollably while reading it. Joan asked what was so funny. I turned my laptop and showed it to her, just crying with laughter. Joan put on her reading glasses, read it coolly, and then removed her glasses and made the remark about how prep school teachers are not professors.

So, we were a little fascinated with Laurel, to put it mildly. We devoted so much time to the idea of her that we were bound to be disappointed when we finally did meet her in person. But she didn't disappoint.

It was the second weekend in June. A Saturday night. Joan had gone off to a dinner party. Sally was going to the Pale Horse Tavern to meet some old friends. Everett was sitting on his porch, drinking a beer and playing with his dogs. He has one dog, a Jack Russell named Snacks, and that week he had two others staying with him—a pair of young Australian shepherds who needed some training. I was in the driveway, having just said good-bye to Sally, when Everett gave a low, long whistle. I pretended I didn't hear him. I'm not a dog.

Then he called out to me. "Lottie? Babe?"

I turned and could see, even from my considerable distance, he had that grin going. He was all horny and high. I could smell the weed from where I stood.

"Come on, babe, come over here," he said. I shook my head no and turned to our house.

Then he added, "Babe, pleeease?"

Two minutes later, I was in his bed.

I'm in love with Everett; I might as well get that out of the way. I've been in love with him for years, really. Since I was a kid. He's always known it. He hasn't always felt the same way about me. He had been seeing other women in recent years. He was open about this. We weren't really in a relationship anymore, so I acted as if I didn't mind about the others. We still hooked up now and then. Not that often. Once a week. Two or three times, tops. Basically, whenever he wanted. I know, it wasn't an ideal situation.

Joan thought I should meet other guys. "You're just stuck on Everett because you never leave the property. Get out a little more, sweetie. You'll never meet anybody but Everett if you never leave the house."

I didn't like her to know how often I went to Everett's at night, so I usually snuck over when she was out, or waited until after she'd gone to bed.

That night, after Sally left and Joan was at her dinner party, after Everett lured me into his lair and I had his skin against mine, his lips on my throat, I almost cried. I don't know why; I just always got a little teary in that final moment when I felt his heart pounding against mine and we were suddenly both so still. He had no idea.

That was one of our first really warm nights of the summer, and Everett suggested we go for a swim. I sat up and looked out his window. It was almost dark, the evening sky was faintly streaked with pale pink clouds, and the lake was as still as glass. Every sound had paused, as it does at dusk, when the daytime birds and insects have clocked out and the peepers and owls haven't started up. I believe I could have heard Everett's heart beating in that moment if I'd listened hard enough.

"Come on, first swim of the summer," he said. He turned my face so that he could give me those big, pleading puppy dog eyes.

"No," I said. "Let's stay here where it's warm." I was tracing this cowlick he has on the left side of his forehead, where the hair turns into a little swirl. I love touching it.

"C'mon," Everett said, and a few minutes later, we were running across the beach, the three dogs racing alongside. I screamed from the cold when we dove into the lake.

Our spot on the lake is a little inlet. It's a cove protected on one side by our house and yard, and on the other by some wooded land that Whit deeded over to the town's land trust years ago. We often swim nude. Nobody can see us from the road, and in the evenings, there's usually not anybody out on the water. And when I say "we" swim nude out there, I mean all of us. Whit and Joan used to infuriate Sally and me with their nude strolls down to the lake after dinner. "Well, don't look at us if we're so hideous," Joan would say, laughing when we would scream at them to cover up. Later, when we were in high school, it was a tradition among our friends to take off our clothes and jump in the lake when we had been partying.

There's a float that's anchored about twenty yards off the beach. Everett and I liked to swim out to that float, and when the weather was warm, we'd sometimes carry on again there, the float rocking us, sometimes gifting us with splinters. But that night, we just lay there on the dock, stargazing. It was the first night of the new moon—you could see the bright little crescent resting in the arms of the old moon. The stars were bright against the glossy black sky, and we whispered their names.

I always look for Polaris first. That's the North Star. Everett looks for Sirius, the Dog Star, which is the brightest star. Most people think the North Star is the brightest, but Sirius is brighter. Whit taught us that. Polaris is the most important if you're lost, though. It's due north; it's a good star to know. Whit taught us how to identify all the constellations when we were kids.

"First find Polaris—it's right there at the tip of the tail of the Little Dipper. Now look east," he'd say, and we'd follow him across the Milky Way, shouting out the names of the stars.

Osiris! Capella! Vega!

It became a contest, when we were kids, to see who could find the most stars and constellations. So, that night of our first summer swim, Everett and I were lying on our backs, taking in the astral landscape, when we heard the dogs barking. We watched them race from the beach to the driveway, blustering friendly woofs, tails wagging.

"Is that Joan?" Everett asked. "Why's she back so soon?"

"No," I said. "It's Spin's Jeep."

We saw the headlights go off and heard the driver's door open. I jumped back in the water. Yes, I'm comfortable swimming nude with Sally or Everett, but not in front of my stepbrothers. Everett dove in after me and grabbed me playfully from behind, cupping my breasts and kissing my neck.

"I'll go get you a towel," he said.

"Hurry, it's getting cold," I said.

I watched him swim to the beach and I smiled at his muscular back, and, well, the rest of him from behind. You really can't help but smile. Everett doesn't work out. He's never been a gym guy, but he's always been in great shape. In addition to the dog training, he sometimes helps his uncle, who's a stonemason, building patios and stone walls. He also took up rowing not long after Whit died. Whit had an old wooden rowing scull left over from his Harvard days, and Everett rowed every morning, in the early dawn, when the lake was still smooth. I watched him walk across the beach, wave at Spin's car, and call out to him. Then I noticed that Snacks was barking more angrily at the car, and I saw Everett turn away from her. He gave me a sheepish look and scooted off to his house like a little boy who'd been caught running around naked. I was laughing. What the hell had gotten into him? He and Spin were like brothers; they had seen each other nude many times. And then I saw, in the dim yellow glow from our porch lights, that it was a woman who had climbed out of the driver's seat. She was facing Everett's screen door, which had just slammed shut behind him. "Hey, hey, cuties, it's okay," she said to the dogs, and they stopped barking and just circled her, sniffing and wagging their tails.

I had started swimming in toward the land.

"Hello?" said the woman. She must have heard my little splashes. I stopped moving. I knew who she was. I could only see her silhouette, there on the lawn. The light from our porch created a golden aura all around her. I couldn't see her face or make out what she was wearing, but I knew she was Laurel Atwood. Snacks barked again, and Laurel leaned over and scooped him up in her arms.

"Hey, hey! Careful, he bites," Everett said. He had come out of his house wearing jeans and no shirt. He was carrying a towel.

Laurel giggled as Snacks licked at her chin. "Is that right?" she said.

"I've never seen him act like this with a stranger," Everett said. "*Never.*"

"Well, he doesn't think I'm a stranger. I'm Laurel, by the way."

"Oh, of course, yeah," he said cheerfully, reaching out to shake her hand. "I'm Everett." He said it like she hadn't just seen every inch of him.

She lowered Snacks to the ground, flipped her long hair back, and took Everett's hand. "Oh, hi, yeah, Spin told me all about you."

The water was cold. My teeth were chattering.

"We thought you were coming later in the week. Where's Spin?"

I squatted there in the shallows, wearing nothing but the icy lake. The bats had come out of their winter hibernation and now one was swooping down over the cove. Soon summer would really be here, and the lake would be warmer than the air at night. Now the air was warm, but the lake was freezing.

"He had some final—I don't know, I guess he called them evaluations or something. I was bored, so he told me to take his car out for a drive. Oooh, your hands are freezing."

Everett just stood there grinning like an idiot. I coughed a little to get his attention. He didn't hear me.

"Great to finally meet you," said Everett.

"I decided to take a little drive around the lake, when I recognized the house from some of Spin's photos. I pulled in to say hello, see if anybody was home. Guess I should have called first."

"Nah," Everett said jovially. He had now wrapped the towel, *my towel,* around his shoulders. I guess he was chilly. I was sure that I was hypothermic, but he seemed to have forgotten all about me. "Everybody just stops by around here," he continued. "We're pretty casual."

"Everett," I said, through clattering teeth from the icy shallows. I didn't say it loud enough. Again, nobody heard me.

"Yes, I saw that. *Very* casual!" Laurel laughed.

Everett laughed and looked down at the ground and then back up at her, the way he always does when he's flirting. "Yup, we don't get all dressed up around here. Sometimes we don't even get dressed at all."

"Is it a proper nudist colony? Are clothes frowned upon, or what?" Laurel asked. "I don't want to shock or offend by being the only one wearing clothing. I'm not a clothes-ist or anything."

"Ha, ha, ha, clothes-ist," Everett repeated, laughing and glancing down at the ground again and then back at her.

Oh, hahaha, Everett. My brain still seemed to be able to formulate rage, so I knew I wasn't thoroughly hypothermic. I had read that when you freeze to death, a sense of euphoria sets in. I was still noneuphoric; that had to be a good sign. I was pre-euphoric.

Laurel laughed again and Everett laughed again. Laurel commented on the weather and Everett commented on the weather. Everett asked her about her flight, and finally I screamed at the top of my lungs, "Everett!"

They both jumped, and Everett dashed across the beach and into the water.

"Jesus, babe, sorry," he said. "I forgot."

I snatched the towel from him and wrapped it around myself. He forgot. Forgot all about me, freezing in the lake. He smoked way too much weed. He did shit like this all the time.

Laurel said, "Oh. My. God." And here's something I've forgotten to mention. She does that annoying thing with the single word as sentence on her blog and her Facebook posts. That thing people were doing five years ago because it was funny then. She often places a period After. Every. Word. I had no idea that the people who do this online actually do it in real life when they speak.

"I. Am. So. Sorry!" Laurel said. "I thought I heard somebody out there. You must be freezing."

"No. I'm. Fine," I said, deciding to speak her weird language. I was shivering under the towel. Everett was rubbing my arms up and down to warm me, but I shrugged myself away from him. Spin and Sally knew about Everett and me; that's probably why he was being so casual. But I didn't like others to know. We had just met this Laurel person, and here he was practically humping me on the lawn. I tried to pull my thick, wet hair away from my face, but my fingers were getting caught in the tangles.

"I'm Charlotte," I said, turning to face Laurel, and then I almost dropped my towel when I found myself *in her arms.* She had actually pulled me to her and was hugging me.

"I'm so, so, so glad to finally meet you, Charlotte," she said, pressing her warm cheek against mine. Her arms were still around me. I was clutching my towel to keep from being in a naked embrace with this stranger. It was insane. Who does that? Who would hug an un-clothed stranger? I knew that if I looked at Everett, he would crack up, so I stared off into space. Later he told Sally that I looked like I was in a "fugue state." Of course they were both stoned and helpless with laughter when he told her about it. Sally wouldn't have been laughing if it had happened to her.

"Let's go inside; I need to get some clothes," I muttered into Laurel's bosom. Finally, she released me. I walked toward the house, pulling my towel tightly around me. Everett and Laurel followed.

"Oh, so clothes *are* allowed," Laurel said. "It's an optional thing, then."

"Yup," Everett said. "Totally your call."

Laurel laughed, Everett laughed. I pushed the screen door open, and if Everett hadn't caught it with his foot, it would have slammed in his face.

I pulled on a pair of sweats and a T-shirt and brushed the hair away from my face. When I went back downstairs, Everett was alone in the kitchen. He was poking around in our fridge.

"Hey, Lottie," he said. "Think it's okay if I have some of this pie?"

"Where'd she go?" I asked. "Where's Laurel?"

"She left. She said she wanted to come back and meet everyone to-morrow with Spin. Said to tell you good-bye. What is this pie, strawberry? Strawberry rhubarb, or what?"

The kitchen windows were suddenly flooded with light. A car had just pulled into the driveway, and a moment later, Joanie was in the kitchen with us. My mom "cleans up good," as Whit used to say. She's so active with her tennis and running and gardening that she usually wears no makeup and pays little attention to her hair. But when she does put on a dress and some lipstick, as she had done that night, you can see why she was always popular with men. She keeps her blond hair shoulder length, she's never colored it, and now silver streaks surround her face, somehow making her pale blue eyes even bluer. She does have some fine lines around the eyes—she's spent so much time in the sun over the years—but she doesn't have the saggy skin or jowls that some of her friends now do. So, she looked quite pretty that night, and because she was a little tipsy, she was in a playful mood.

"Hey, Ev! Lottie! What a beautiful night, huh?" She tossed her purse onto the kitchen table and squatted to receive our Labrador, Riley, who came bounding into the kitchen. Riley is really Joan's dog. My dog—Whit's old dog, Scruggs—had died two winters earlier. Scruggs was a great dog. Riley's a moron.

"Who's a good boy? Who's a good boy, Riley? Who's Mommy's favorite boy?"

"Hi, Joan," said Everett. "Mind if I help myself to a little of this pie? HEY, Riley, OFF!"

My mother had gotten Riley too worked up, as she often did. He had knocked her back into a sitting position and was gnawing on her wrist. The minute Everett gave the command, Riley let go and sat down, his tail wagging apologetically.

"No, not at all," Joan said, jumping to her feet. "I was hoping somebody would eat it so it wouldn't go to waste."

"Ev," I said. "Do not eat that pie." I tried to grab the pie plate from him, but he's tall, and he grinned mischievously as he lifted it above my reach.

"I'm hungry," he said.

"I made that pie two weeks ago, maybe longer. It needs to be thrown away. Joanie left it out on the counter overnight last week, twice."

"Don't be ridiculous, it's perfectly good," said Joan.

"You'll get sick. You'll get food poisoning," I said, but it was no use. They laughed at me, and Joan handed Everett a fork. Neither of them believes in food poisoning. Joan thinks salmonella is a "myth." She tells us that it's a myth every Thanksgiving when she shovels hot stuffing into the turkey the night before she cooks it, then touches all the vegetables without washing her hands. Everett will eat anything, and Joan has a terror of throwing away uneaten food. They have, actually, sort of disproven current food-storage safety protocols. They've always gobbled up anything that's not attracting too many flies, and neither of them is ever sick.

Joan looked at Everett and then looked at me. She saw my wet hair and his. She saw what was going on. Like I said, she didn't love the noncommittal thing we had.

"What have you two been up to tonight?" she asked casually. She grabbed a fork and sat down next to Everett. He moved the pie pan over so she could reach it, and they both ate the foul old pie with gusto. "Looks like you've been in the lake," Joan said, her mouth full.

Yes, she'd had a little wine.

"We had a visitor," I said, leaning back against the counter.

"Oh yeah! Joan—damn, this is good pie—guess who just left?" Everett said.

"You know, it's those strawberries from the farm stand that make it so yummy, Everett. It's worth it to make the extra trip. I always buy fresh when I can; it makes such a difference," Joan said. Because it was her trip to the farm stand, not my baking, that explained the pie's deliciousness.

"Laurel," I said.

Joanie froze.

"Laurel Atwood was here," I said.

"NO!" said Joanie. "Laurel and Spin were here? I wish I'd known they were coming."

"It was just Laurel," Everett said. "She was driving around. I guess Spin's working. She just stopped by to introduce herself."

"Well?" Joan asked. "What was she like?"

She looked from Everett to me and then back at Everett. He was grinning and shrugging, shoveling the pie into his mouth.

"We barely said hello, but she seems friendly. She's coming back tomorrow," I said.

"How strange that she just showed up like that," Joan said.

"I think people do that in Utah," said Everett.

"What?" Joan asked, laughing at him. "Utah? She's from Sun Valley, which is in Idaho, Everett."

"Oh," he said. "Right."

"I've always been great at geography," Joan added, taking one last bite of pie.

FOUR

I get paid to do a blog post every day. It doesn't matter how long it is; I just have to post something so that the diaper people think they're getting their money's worth. I knew I wouldn't have much time to blog over the next few days, so I explained that I was sick, that some sort of plague had nearly annihilated my family. First little Wyatt woke up with a fever. He's always the first to catch any cold or virus, due to his compromised immune system. Then Mia caught his bug, and now Topher was rolling around on the couch, acting like he was dying. That was yesterday. Now everybody else was recovering and I was puking my brains out. I asked my blog readers if they knew the symptoms of Ebola. I was pretty sure that's what I had, since I had consulted with WebMD. Within minutes of posting the entry, I had four comments. Two were from regular posters, two from people whose screen names I didn't recognize. They each had amusing stories of how they had solved their own medical mysteries by using the Internet as their diagnostician.

I posted a comment from Kate Madison. She told me she was going to drop off some soup at our house later. Kate is one of my sock puppets. When I started the blog and began accumulating a lot of followers, I worried that readers might become suspicious. I worried that they might want proof that I was who I said I was, proof that I actually was a suburban mom. So I created JennyPenny, MrMom, and Katemadison. These are my IRL people, the people I'm supposed to know in real life. Jenny and I went to college together. Mr. Mom and Kate have kids who go to school with Mia. They live in my town. They're always careful to be discreet about where we live. We all want to protect the privacy of our children. The truth is, I never really needed to create them. Nobody has ever questioned the veracity of my blog. People tend to believe what you tell them.

I was just finishing up when I heard a car crunching along the gravel driveway. It was Spin's Jeep. I looked out the window and saw him and Laurel climb out of the car. Then I heard their steps on the porch.

My attic room is above the porch. The porch roof blocked them from view, but I could hear their conversation as clearly as if we were in the same room. Spin did his customary three little knocks on the door and then I heard Laurel say, "You knock when you come here?"

"Yeah, usually. Why?" Spin asked.

"I don't know, isn't it your house?" Laurel asked.

"Yeah, well, now that my dad's gone, I just, you know, sometimes knock," Spin said. "I don't always knock."

And then I heard their footsteps in the house.

"Hello?" Spin called. "Anybody here?"

I stood in the center of the hot attic room, my shadow pinned to the wall. Sometimes I'm stricken with dread. Panic attacks, Dr. Alter calls them.

"Hello?" said Spin.

"Yeah, hi, Spin. I'll be down in a minute," I called back finally. I tiptoed downstairs to the bathroom. I was wearing shorts and a tank top. I have wavy brownish hair that turns slightly blond in the summer. But it wasn't quite summer yet; I wasn't tan. My hair was a mess. I didn't get a lot of exercise over the winter. Some of my clothes were a little snug. I changed into baggy jeans and a light T-shirt. I took a pill that Dr. Alter prescribes for my dread. I was just about to go downstairs when I heard, with great relief, Sally's old Subaru pull up. She was honking the horn, clearly thrilled to see Spin's Jeep. I heard the commotion of her running into the house, Riley barking, Spin laughing and making introductions. When I could tell they were all in the kitchen, I walked downstairs.

At the bottom of our stairs is the front hall. There's a table there, and even though it's a valuable antique—a Whitman supposedly brought it here from Paris over two hundred years ago—it's really a living monument to clutter. On the table, and scattered on the floor around it, is always a jumble of newspapers, dog toys, tennis balls, dog leashes, and that day, the empty pie plate from the night before, which had been pushed underneath it by Riley. I grabbed the plate and walked into the kitchen.

Spin and Laurel were standing in the middle of our kitchen, holding hands, while Sally filled the coffeemaker.

"When did you get in, Laurel?" Sally asked, darting around the kitchen. "When did you get into New York—you flew into JFK, right? Where the hell does Joanie keep the coffee filters? Was it last night, or what?"

I was a little concerned about Sally's energy. She was wearing the same clothes she had worn out the night before. She looked like she hadn't slept.

"I got to New York the night before last," Laurel replied. "Spin picked me up at the airport and we stayed at Perry and Catherine's. What a beautiful house they have."

"We've never seen it, have we, Charlotte?" said Sally. I was standing in the doorway, and I smiled awkwardly when Laurel and Spin turned and noticed me. "Laurel, that's Charlotte. Charlotte, stop trying to be invisible, for God's sake. . . ."

"Lottie," Spin said. He grabbed me, like he always does, and planted a kiss on my cheek. "This is Laurel."

"I know," I said, blushing wildly. "We met last night."

"You did?" Sally asked. "You guys were here already?"

"I stopped by, just for a few minutes," Laurel said, moving in between Spin and me. "I actually had a dream about you last night, Charlotte," she said in a sort of flirty voice.

"Oh yeah?" I said. *What the fuck?*

"Don't worry, you had all your clothes on." She laughed, nudging me playfully with her shoulder. "What a cute kitchen, so quaint."

I moved closer to Sally, reeling from Laurel's comment.

"This place must seem kind of shabby after staying at Perry's," Sally said. "Jesus, Lottie, stop shoving me."

Laurel said, "I love old houses."

Now Sally caught my eye. We knew what Laurel was thinking. From the outside, our house still looks quite grand, with its porches and gables and porticos, but the inside, well, it's a little past its prime. We have the same refrigerator and dishwasher that were here before Joan and Whit married. They were once white, but the decades have mellowed them to the color of putty. The dishwasher leaks. The refrigerator hums a few bars, rattles, hums, and then rattles again. It's been playing this sad tune for years, but it still keeps things cold, so Joan sees no need to replace it. The cabinets were painted bright yellow sometime in the 1970s, but now the paint has chipped and they're dotted here and there with old grease stains. The kitchen floors are worn-out linoleum. The old butcher-block countertop is so scarred by decades of chopping and slicing, so stained from spilled red wine and the blood of countless rib eyes, that you could scrub it all day and it would still look like a body had been dismembered on it.

"You need to sand the counters down, the way they do in butcher shops," Sally tells Joan whenever she visits, especially when she brings friends with her. This is when Sally and I most acutely see all the afflictions of the aged house, all the clutter and disrepair—when we have company. We really only notice it when we look at it from the perspective of others.

"I'll sand it down for you before I go back to the city," Sally always promises. "I'll get Everett to help me. And let's get rid of some of this clutter." But she never does, because after a day or two at Lakeside, it all looks normal to her again, too.

I saw Laurel staring up at the space above the old sink. Joan was drying a batch of plastic bags. I hadn't noticed, or I would have taken them down the night before. Joan washes out old plastic bags and hangs them to dry above the kitchen sink. She fastens them to a long piece of twine with clothespins. Joan has used the plastic bags countless times, and plans to reuse them until they dissolve. She and Whit were into recycling long before it became common practice, when it was just considered being thrifty. You could call them cheap (most people do), given Whit's millions. They just can't bear to get rid of anything. Or they couldn't. (I often do that—refer to Whit in the present tense, even though he's gone.) Joan and Whit's mutual abhorrence of the ephemeral, their need to hang on to things, their love of coupon cutting, tag sales, dollar stores, their borderline hoarding tendencies—these were the very things that had originally attracted them to each other.

Sally and I were assessing our kitchen through the eyes of this stranger and we shared a sense of indignant pride: Our house is a great house, a Vandemeer house. How dare she judge it?

"Well, I like old places," Laurel said.

Sally gave me a look. How dare she patronize us so?

Laurel kissed Spin. He pulled her closer and then they were really kissing. It wasn't a terribly prolonged thing, but it was a little longer than I'd kiss somebody in front of others. In the kitchen. Before breakfast. I moved over next to the sink and pulled the Baggies from the line.

I was relieved when Spin and Laurel stopped kissing, but then she started *sucking on his ear.* I turned my gaze to the floor and started across the kitchen, where I managed to crash into Sally, who also appeared to be staring at the floor. "Oh, oops," I said, laughter hissing from my nose. We clutched each other. We were trying so hard not to laugh openly. Then Joan trotted into the kitchen, wearing a little tennis dress.

"Well, hello! You must be the famous Laurel. I'm Joan," she said, pushing her damp bangs away from her forehead with her wrist.

Laurel was no longer latched onto Spin's earlobe, but I was certain that she was going to hug my mother. I was dying to see her do this, actually, but she seemed to pick up on Joan's taut vibe and just extended her hand.

"So great to finally meet you. I'm sorry, I'm all sweaty," Joan said, shaking Laurel's hand.

"Hi, Joanie," Spin said. He gave my mom a little hug, as he always does, and she pushed him away playfully. "No, Spin, really, I'm absolutely drenched."

She smiled at Laurel. "I so wish I had been here last night when you stopped in, Laurel."

"No, no problem," Laurel said. "I didn't call first."

"Sorry, I'm such a sweaty mess. I know you're an athlete yourself, Laurel, so you understand. Sit, sit down! Charlotte will make us all some breakfast. I would have brought home some muffins if I had known you were coming. I had tennis this morning and then went for a run. I run every day."

Sally grinned at me and then at Spin, and we all tried not to laugh, thinking, Here we go, the five-mile brag. And sure enough, as Laurel and Spin sat at the table and Joanie guzzled a Gatorade, she began what Sally and I like to call her "Joan-a-logue." I knew that this would be the extended version. Our mother was slightly in awe of Laurel.

"I run five miles, every day," she began, wiping her forehead with a dish towel. "I'm sixty, but I still run every day."

This is actually a setup, and sure enough, Laurel replied, "No, you can't be sixty."

"I'll be sixty-one in August," Joan declared. She acknowledged that this must be hard for Laurel to believe, but she's never lied about her age. She thinks it's exercise that keeps her so young. She runs every day, even if she also plays tennis, as she had that morning. Yes, five miles every day, unless the temperature is over ninety or below twenty degrees. Her resting heart rate is fifty-five. She ran the Boston Marathon several times, but that was long ago. She should have been a bi-athlete. She loves to swim as well. Her great-great-grandmother was one of the first female lifeguards in Massachusetts; that's where her family is from. They're an old Boston family. She was a Garrison. The Garrisons came to this continent on the *Mayflower,* which is probably why she and her family have always been so healthy and live so long. She comes from hearty stock—not many people survived that first winter in Plymouth. Joan believes in exercise, and she asked Laurel if she knew that exercise is what keeps your brain sharp. Before Laurel could reply, Joan informed her that indeed it is. It only makes sense, she explained. You need to keep pumping oxygen into your brain, or it will atrophy like any other organ. All Joan's friends complain of declining memories, but Joan never forgets a detail. She asked Spin if it isn't a fact that everyone knows her to be the one among their friends with the keenest memory, and Spin sort of shrugged, winked at me, and nodded. Yes, Joan assured us all, she's as sharp as a tack. Well, her bridge games help, too, and her volunteer work. She likes to keep busy, and she's competitive. She's not ashamed of admitting that. It seems that being competitive is out of vogue these days, but why? Isn't that, after all, what a capitalist system is based upon—healthy competition? Her father, William Garrison, was the headmaster at Holden Academy for twenty-five years. When she was eight years old, she was playing sports with kids twice her age, and these were boys, not girls—the school hadn't become coed yet—

"Joan," Sally interrupted. "Laurel was training for the Olympics, so I think she knows about being competitive."

"Oh yes, yes," said Joan. "How exciting to be on the Olympic ski team."

"I wasn't on the actual team. I was short-listed. I tore up my knee during the trials," Laurel said. "Then, later the same year, I had my accident." Her voice trembled a little when she said the word *accident,* but she smiled bravely.

"Oh, that's right, dear. Spin told us about that," my mother said. "What a horrible thing."

"No, everything happens for a reason. I didn't realize it at the time, but if it hadn't been for the accident, I probably never would have gone to college, let alone graduate school. And I'm fine now. I can't ski as fast, of course, but I actually enjoy skiing in a way that I never did when I was competing."

"I'm so glad. I can see how skiing would become more enjoyable once it became a pastime rather than a profession," said Joan, who has only ever known pastimes, never a true profession.

"Yes, and I never would have met Spin if I hadn't turned into a recreational skier. So it was all for the best." Laurel turned to Spin, who looked at her lovingly.

I glanced at my mother. She was smiling. She was starting to like Laurel. I was, too. I couldn't help myself. She's pretty hard not to like.

"I'm gonna run over and say hi to Everett," Spin said.

"I'll make some breakfast if you want, Spin," I said. "Want some pancakes? Eggs?" But he didn't hear me. Everett's truck had started, and Spin ran out so that he could catch him before he left.

"I'll help you, Charlotte," Laurel said. "I'm starving."

"I never eat anything but toast for breakfast," Joan said, as if any of us had asked. "Toast and a banana."

"Is that right?" said Laurel.

"How about scrambled eggs?" I asked Laurel.

"Perfect," Laurel said.

Joan went upstairs to shower and Sally came and stood next to me. She was leaning against the counter, drinking her coffee and gazing at Laurel.

"So you stayed at Perry and Catherine's, huh?" Sally asked.

When I didn't hear a reply, I looked over my shoulder at Laurel. She was tapping something into her cell phone and frowning.

"We don't have cell service on this part of the lake," Sally said.

"Oh no," said Laurel. "I'm expecting an important e-mail. Do you have Wi-Fi?"

"Yeah, Charlotte, what's the password here, again?" Sally asked. She pushed her elbow into my side.

"*Banjoguy*, no caps, two three," I said.

Laurel tapped away at her phone. "It doesn't seem to be working."

I was breaking the last egg into the bowl. I repeated the password. She couldn't get it to work.

"Here, let me try," I said. "Let me wash my hands. Sally, hand me the phone."

I washed my hands and Sally launched into an account of her night. She had been with some old friends. The town of Harwich is boring. The Pale Horse Tavern is the only place to go at night. I dried my hands and reached for the phone that Sally was holding. She had taken so long with her story that Laurel's password screen was up.

"Laurel, I can't get in. You need to put in your code," I said. Most people will just tell you their password when this happens. Laurel asked for the phone back. I walked over to the fridge as she punched in a few numbers. Then she handed it to me.

I typed in our Wi-Fi password, and as I did, I said it out loud. "Banjoguy three three."

"Oh, I think you told me two three," said Laurel.

"No," I said, laughing. "I'm sorry, I said two threes. Three three."

We all had a little chuckle at the misunderstanding and Laurel sat back at the table to do her e-mailing. While I heated up some butter in a skillet, Sally casually wrote the numbers 7595 on a paper towel and handed it to me. It was Laurel's code. I stuffed it into my pocket. Sally and I have always done this. We love to spy on guests. We have since we were little girls. It was unlikely we would ever go into Laurel's phone. We just liked knowing that we could.

"We've never been to Perry's town house," Sally said when Laurel had finished her e-mailing and I was putting toast on the plates. "Well, we saw it in *Architectural Digest*, didn't we, Charlotte?"

"Yes," I said. "It looks really beautiful."

"It's nice," Laurel said, "but this house is much more comfortable. I was afraid to sit down on their upholstery, to tell you the truth. I can't believe they have those two adorable children and there's not a thing out of place in that house."

"The children each have their own servants, so I think it's easy," Sally said.

"They're nannies, Sal," I said.

"I've heard so much about this place and all of you that I couldn't wait to meet you."

"I wish Spin would get in here. These eggs are going to get cold. Should we just start without him?" I asked, putting the plates on the table.

Joan had come back into the kitchen, freshly showered, wearing shorts and a T-shirt—her gardening clothes.

"Just toast for me," she said. "I only ever have toast for breakfast. Sometimes a banana."

"What'd Spin tell you about us?" Sally asked, poking at her eggs with her fork.

"Well, not a whole lot. Not half as much as that old hunchback guy at the filling station I stopped at yesterday."

"Hunchback guy?" Sally asked, amused. Laurel was talking about old Anson Bergstrom. He did have a bit of a hunched-up posture; we just hadn't really thought about it before.

"That's old Anson. Yes, he's like a little old lady with all the town gossip," Sally said.

"I'm sure he's very nice. I just got a weird feeling. I tried to pump my gas, and he came running out and practically wrestled the hose out of my hand. 'This here's a full-service shop,' he said. 'If you wanna pump it yourself, you're gonna wanna go on up to Route 209. People who wanna get their gas a little cheaper go on up there, but yer gonna hafta pump it yerself.'"

She did an uncanny impersonation of Anson Bergstrom.

"And he kept trying to give me directions everywhere. I told him I have GPS, that I just wanted the name of a place to eat. 'Now, what yer gonna wanna do is turn right out the driveway and then go, oh, I don't know, maybe about half a mile, then you'll come to a stop sign. Then after, oh, I dunno, another quarter mile . . .' "

"Yeah, well, Anson's an old family friend. He was just trying to be nice," Sally said, sounding less amused. I shared Sally's defensiveness. Yes, Anson Bergstrom is a weird guy. But he's *our* weird guy. Laurel needed to shut it.

"I guess that's how he knew I was Spin's fiancée," Laurel said. "Oh, by the way, Spin owes you thirty-five dollars, Joan."

Joan had her back to us. She was standing at the counter, slathering her toast with jam. She paused for a moment when she heard what Laurel had said. When she turned and carried her plate to the table, I noticed there was a little hitch in her step, a slight limp, as if she had strained something.

"Thirty-five dollars?" she said, smiling at Laurel. "Whatever for?"

"My credit card was blocked. It happens all the time when I travel— security fraud protection or something. I have to remember to call the bank, tell them my card's not stolen. I didn't have any cash at the station, so the guy said that you have a house account and I should put Spin's gas on your account and then he can just pay you back."

"Oh," Joan said. She forced another little smile at Laurel. "That'll be fine."

"Spin doesn't have an account there," Laurel said. "I asked, but the guy said he always pays cash."

We heard Everett's truck drive off, and a moment later, Spin pushed open the screen door.

"Philip, toast with your eggs?" Laurel asked.

Joan, Sally, and I looked at one another. *Philip?*

Philip is Spin's real name. We had just never heard anybody use it. He was supposed to be named George, but his mom, Marissa, scrawled the name Philip on his birth certificate a few moments after he was born. She casually informed her errant husband of the name change when he held his son the following day. Whit always hated the name Philip. It had been the name of a very unattractive and awkward classmate from his boarding-school days. Marissa knew that, and he took her insistence upon the new name as a parting blow.

Now Spin was sitting at the table, devouring his breakfast. "I have dorm duty tonight and again on Thursday. We still have a few international students on campus."

"You couldn't get somebody to take your place? Laurel just got here," Sally said.

"No. I swapped with somebody the other night so I could go to the airport. I have to do tonight. All the kids'll be gone by the end of the week. Then I'm free."

Laurel said, "I had no idea that teaching at a boarding school is almost like going to one. So many rules, and so little time to yourself."

"You'll get used to it," Spin said. "Hey, did I tell you guys that Laurel applied for the job in the English Department that's opening up? I'm pretty sure you have it, Laurel-lee."

"Really?" Laurel said, excited by the news. "How do you know?"

"I've got a few friends in the dean's office," Spin said.

"It's such a beautiful campus," said Laurel. "I knew a few kids from Sun Valley who went to Holden, and of course I've read about it over the years. I always wanted to go to boarding school when I was a kid, but by the time I was old enough, I was on the ski team and training during the school year. I suppose you and Charlotte must have been day students, living here, so close," Laurel said to Sally.

"No," Sally said. "We went to public school. Harwich High."

"Have you had a chance to see the whole campus?" I asked Laurel. I didn't want Sally to get started, but she ignored me.

"Yup, Harwich High," Sally continued. "What a dump. When we went there, they couldn't even get certified by the state. Has that place finally been accredited, or what, Joan?"

"Sally, it most certainly was accredited. It was . . . well, I believe, there was something to do with the old gym. Anyway, Harwich is an excellent school," Joan said. "It was just listed as one of the top twenty public schools in the entire state, as a matter of fact."

I was clearing the plates and repeated my question to Laurel about whether she had seen the entire Holden campus.

"Not really. It was almost dark when we got there last night," she replied.

"I'll show you around now," Spin told Laurel. "You'll love it."

FIVE

It seems that Holden students and faculty either love it or hate it; there's really no middle ground. Spin loves it. He started spending summers there when he was very small, attending soccer and tennis camps, hanging out with the kids who lived on campus. He boarded there during his high school years, went off to college, and then moved back upon graduation. He teaches science. He's the varsity hockey coach, and he gives private music instruction: piano and guitar. Like most of the faculty, Spin lives in an apartment attached to one of the dorms.

By today's standards, Holden is a traditional prep school, but in its early years, it was a rather progressive institution. The school's founder, William Fenwick Holden, was an outspoken abolitionist, and the first two African-American boys ever to enroll at a private boarding school were admitted to Holden in the 1880s. W.F. paid their way himself. Holden Academy was a place where the freethinking sons and nephews of our country's great industrialists went to learn, and where a number of well-known writers, artists, designers, and architects went as young boys. Of course, some Holden students went on to become bankers and lawyers, but compared to, say, Exeter or Groton, Holden placed as strong an emphasis on the arts as it did on the more practical academic applications of science, history, and mathematics. Many of the boys went on to study painting at the Hudson School, for example, or sculpting in Paris. Like Whit, they were funded by enormous trusts set up by their fathers. And like Whit, they probably referred to their ancestors as "robber barons."

When we were teenagers, Sally and I liked to ride our bikes to Holden Academy at night. We felt a sort of entitlement to the place, based on our family connections. Whit and his brother Aaron had attended Holden, as did their father and grandfather before them. When they were old enough, Perry and Spin also boarded, but our grandfather had retired as headmaster when we were little. Joan couldn't afford the tuition, and Whit, while generous in spirit, didn't believe he should pay for the education of another man's children.

"I think you're lucky," he confided to Sally and me as we headed off to meet the school bus one day. I was just starting my freshman year of high school. Sally was a sophomore. "I always wanted to ride a bus and go to a public school."

"I know," Sally had said to Whit. "We are lucky."

Ten minutes later, when the bus stopped at the intersection in front of the Holden campus, we saw three girls leaving the school's dining hall. One of the girls said something to her friends, and we watched as they all collapsed into one another, suddenly sodden-legged and seizing, one of them apparently suffocating with mirth. We had met some of Perry's friends from Holden—sometimes he brought them to the lake for the weekend—and these girls were cut from the same cloth. They were "lame," according to Sally. I agreed. They all wore skirts and navy blazers. There was something ridiculously optimistic about the way their ponytails were set, something predictable about the athletic, slightly masculine cut of their thighs.

"Ugh," said Sally. "Look how stupid they all are. Wait a minute— who's this now?"

A tousle-haired, suntanned boy was jogging toward the girls, and

Sally practically sat on my lap to get a better look at him. We were both craning our heads for a last glimpse of the boy before the bus turned the corner.

"I hate preppies," Sally said.

"Me, too," I said.

"I think it would be fun to meet some of them, though," Sally added.

"Me, too."

It was that Friday night that we first pedaled over to the campus on our bikes.

Our mother and Whit didn't know what we were up to, but eventually they found out, and Whit always expressed a certain pride in our escapades.

"For over a hundred and fifty years," he'd announce to dinner guests, years later, "Holden students have found ways to sneak off campus to find mischief. Sally and Charlotte Maynard turned this tradition on its head by sneaking *onto* campus."

He didn't know all the details. He didn't know that Sally engaged in a series of affairs at Holden, not just with various members of the hockey and football teams but, one year, with a thirty-five-year-old history teacher named Ed Harriman. He didn't know that I snuck into the library at night and looked at the old yearbooks. Or that I'd go into the dean's office to read the students' transcripts and disciplinary reports. Sometimes I'd wander into the nurse's office to read the medical histories of the students. Some of these kids had serious issues: A girl I knew from grammar school was now anorexic; another was a cutter. One of the boys had been caught selling cocaine. For some reason, these reports gave me satisfaction.

It was Everett who discovered our nocturnal education at Holden. I was riding my bicycle up Town Hill Road one autumn evening and he was returning from the Pale Horse. It was late, probably close to midnight. That road is dark—there are no streetlights on any of the Harwich roads—and it's a long, steep climb. I saw Everett's pickup drive past. He had glanced out his window to see what kind of nut would be out riding at that time of night. I think he was pretty surprised to see that it was me.

Everett was at UConn and hadn't paid much attention to Sally and me in the past year or so. But he recognized me that night, even though I had my hood pulled up over my head. He pulled over and stopped his truck. I gave him a little smile.

"Hey, Everett," I said.

"What're you doing out so late?"

"I was with Sally. We were . . . visiting a friend."

"Where's Sally?"

"Why?"

"You said you were with her."

"She's still at our friend's."

"You're gonna get hit by a car. You need to put a reflector on the back of your bike. I almost didn't see you."

"Oh."

"I'll give you a ride."

"Okay, thanks," I said. He lifted my bike into the bed of the pickup and we started off.

"Does Joan know you're out?"

"I don't know," I said.

"What about Whit?"

"It's fine," I said. "They're asleep."

"Have you been drinking or something?"

I shook my head and tried not to smile. I was feeling shy suddenly, and embarrassed. I glanced at him a few times as he drove. When he turned onto East Shore Road, I realized I was sad that the ride was almost over.

"Where were you?" I blurted out.

"The tavern."

"I was at Holden," I said.

"Doing what?"

"Sally and I have a few friends there."

"I thought they locked up all the dorms after ten."

"They do, but the doors have keypads. Sally and I know all the codes."

"You know all the combinations to the dorms?"

"We know all the combinations to every building on campus."

"You do not."

"The science building. The dean's office. All the buildings. I can prove it. I just proved it to a kid who lives in the senior boys' dorm. I got him a copy of his transcript. He's giving me a hundred dollars to alter it before it goes out to colleges."

"Why would you want to stick your neck out like that? For some entitled Holden brat?"

"I don't know. It's fun."

"You know you could get arrested?"

"For what?"

"Trespassing, for one. Stealing."

"Who would catch us?"

"My uncle Russ, he's head of security. I'm tempted to tell him what you girls are up to. You're too young to be hanging around there."

"We're in high school. We're the same age as the kids who go there."

"But you don't go there."

"My mom grew up at Holden, you know."

"So?"

"The athletic building is named after Whit's grandfather."

"So?"

"So Sally and I like to go and swim in it sometimes. You know, with friends."

Actually, Sally was the only one who ever swam there.

"Boyfriends?"

I sank into my seat and shrugged. Sally was the only one with boy-friends.

"I just like it there," I said finally.

"You don't belong there. Be careful," he said, and then he pulled the truck over. We were still almost a quarter of a mile from Lakeside. My heart was racing.

"I thought you were driving me home." I wanted Everett to kiss me.

"You can get out here. I'm not gonna risk Whit seeing me drop you off."

"He wouldn't care." But Everett had already jumped out and was unloading my bike.

I got back on my bike and gave him a little wave as I rode past.

"I think he'd care," Everett called out. He drove slowly behind me until I turned into our driveway.

So it was our shared secret that united us at first. From then on, when Everett worked around the place with his dad, I noticed him. Sometimes I'd be sitting on the porch doing homework. Sometimes, if it was a weekend, I was out fishing on the dock, or rigging the sail-boat with Spin. I always called out to him now to say hello, and he'd mumble something in reply.

He caught me leaving Holden again, a few months later. This time, I had just pedaled out of the main gate when he drove past. He pulled over and I rode eagerly up to his window.

"Hey," I said, staring off down the road. It was cold that night and the words floated from my lips in little white puffs.

"Hey," he said. "Well, get in."

After I climbed inside the truck, he turned to me and said, "Do you know there are maniacs driving around the countryside looking for girls like you?"

I had been blowing on my hands to warm them. I didn't know what to say, so I just shrugged.

"I'm not kidding."

"Well, then, I'm glad you stopped. I don't want to be attacked by a maniac."

Everett started driving. "I should tell Whit. I should tell Whit what you're up to, before something bad happens."

We drove on in silence. His truck was old and had one of those bench seats in front. He turned on the radio, then dropped his hand onto the seat next to me. It was dark. I never would have had the courage if it wasn't so late and so dark, but I moved my hand over on the seat and touched his hand with my pinkie. I barely grazed it. I just wanted to touch him. He drove on. I moved my hand just a little bit closer, just so it rested against his.

Everett stomped on the brake and I was hurled against the dashboard.

"Would you put your fucking seat belt on?" he shouted. Then: "What are you, fifteen years old? Sixteen?"

I was crying. He had scared me. "I'm seventeen," I said.

"You're not seventeen."

I was sixteen, but I didn't say anything.

"What are you doing down there at Holden? Fooling around in the dorms with the guys? Huh?"

"No."

"Bullshit."

"Just let me out," I said.

"Put your seat belt on," he grumbled. "There's something really the matter with you," Everett said finally. "You and your sister both."

"We're just bored," I whispered.

"Are you crying?"

"No."

"Stop crying."

"I can't."

"I can make you laugh."

"No you can't," I said, recalling our childhood games. Everett, Sally, Spin, and I used to play a game where we'd sit and stare into the eyes of one of the others. The first person to smile lost. Sally always won.

I felt him looking at me. I glanced at him from the corner of my eye and then it was hard not to smile.

"I saw you smiling," he said.

"I wasn't," I said.

"I can make you," he said. "I can make you smile."

"Okay. Try," I said, scowling with all my might.

That night was our first together. I snuck over to his place when I saw his bedroom light go out. I tapped on his window. He let me in.

SIX

Spin and Laurel came to the lake every afternoon that first week.
Sally was in the city, but she e-mailed constantly, wanting to know
what I had found out about Laurel.

"She's stopped posting on Facebook," Sally said. "She stopped
blogging, too."

"I think she's respecting our privacy," I said. "Spin's privacy. You
know, she's not nearly as braggy as she seemed on her blog. She's interested in others. I have a feeling she's a good writer."

"Based on what?"

"She likes to observe people. They say that's what makes a writer
great, her curiosity about others."

"I've never heard anybody say that," Sally said.

"It's just a known fact," I said, annoyed. Sally thinks she knows
everything.

"Some people are just nosy," she said.

Whatever.

Spin was busy that week. It wasn't just his duties on campus
with the remaining students. He had his work for the Lake Marinac
Task Force—the group devoted to keeping our lake healthy and
clean.

Joan, Sally, and I are content to know as little as possible about the lake's task force. We're aware that Spin and a few others are constantly measuring and sampling the water. We just don't care to know all the details. Spin is a fascinating person with a great personality, except when he talks about the lake, or any environmental issues, really. Then he can be kind of a bore. On Laurel's second day here, while we all sat out on the porch enjoying the lake breeze, she asked Spin about the task force.

"Did you start the thing or what?" Laurel asked him.

"Oh no, it began long before I was even born," Spin said.

"It was in the early 1970s. Whit was one of the people who started it," Joan interjected. She thought it important for Laurel to know that she was on the Holden crew team then. She had been the captain of the first women's varsity team at Holden. "We practiced every morning on the lake," she explained. "You can't believe how cold it was some mornings, but we were out there every day."

"Yes," Spin said. Then, when Joan offered nothing to link her rowing to the task force, he proceeded to tell Laurel that a few decades ago our lake was in jeopardy. There was an overgrowth of invasive plants (algae, blah, blah, blah). Runoff from lawns and farms (phosphorus, blah). Fertilizers (nitrogen, whatever), resulting in algal blooms. The task force hired biologists to do a study, then came up with a plan to keep the lake alive.

"So the lake was actually dying?" Laurel asked.

"No," Joan said.

"Yes, it was dying," Spin said. "Lakes and ponds die all the time. They're living, breathing organisms, just like us." He shielded his eyes then and squinted out at the water as if he were trying to read its very pulse. Joan turned to me and rolled her eyes.

"Lakes need nutrients in the form of phosphorus and nitrogen," he continued. "But if they get too many nutrients, which can happen in the summer, the whole system is thrown out of whack. The water temperature rises. Too much algae blooms and it hogs up all the oxygen. And then you can have a real situation on your hands."

"One worries about summerkill, dear," said Joan to Laurel. "Now, who would like to go to the market with me?"

"Summerkill?" Laurel asked.

"Yes, summerkill is when large populations of fish die off suddenly," Spin said. "Lack of oxygen."

We haven't had a summerkill in years. Spin has been working on a study with a team of environmental scientists at Yale; it's a six-year study following the placement of giant aerators in the water. That's why he regularly tests the water quality at various points on the lake.

Now Spin was carrying on about invasive species.

"There are plants that aren't indigenous to the lake," Spin said, "but they arrive anyway, carried in on the feathers of ducks and geese, sometimes attached to the undersides of boats. So we have a team of volunteers, and they take turns monitoring the one boat ramp on the lake. We inspect each boat to make sure there's no vegetation. But we can't inspect every canoe or kayak that people launch."

"Spin," Joan said, unable to bear another minute, "I don't think your obsession with all this algae and whatnot is good for you, I really don't. You can't even enjoy the lake anymore."

"What do you mean?" Spin said, laughing. "Of course I enjoy the lake."

"He's like the lake's constant diagnostician, always looking for some kind of pathology," Joan said to Laurel. "He can't even enjoy a nice sail."

Spin told Laurel not to listen to Joan, but she continued. "This lake is one of the cleanest, healthiest lakes in America. But the sight of one little sprout of—what is it, Spin? Eurasian killjoy?"

"Eurasian milfoil," Spin said. "And I don't know that I'd call it one of the cleanest lakes in America."

"He sees anything green at the bottom of the lake and he's like a hypochondriac who finds a new mole," Joan told Laurel.

"Go ahead and laugh," Spin said, "but the reason this lake is so healthy is because we're so proactive. Anyway, this is boring to Laurel."

"Boring to Laurel?" I said. "It's boring to everyone, Spinny."

"I don't think it's boring," Laurel said. So Spin proceeded to enchant her with facts regarding acidity levels, nitrogen ratios, and all the wonderful microorganisms that he serves and protects in our Lake Marinac.

Everett pulled up, mercifully, in the middle of this speech. He parked in front of his house and then wandered over to our porch.

"Hey, Joanie, Spin. Hey, Lottie," Everett said. Then he grinned at Laurel and said, "I'm Everett, you know, from last night."

"Yes, hi, I know! I was able to recognize you even with your pants on," Laurel said. Everett stammered as he explained to Spin about her arrival.

"Oh," Spin said. "You and Lottie were out there all nakie? Wasn't it freezing?"

"Yes," I said.

"Well, I guess all your phosphorus or blue-green algae isn't doing its job, Philip," Laurel said.

Everett had just dropped the Australian shepherds back at their home and had picked up another young dog from Ridgefield.

"This new guy's huge," Everett said. "He's a Leonberger."

"A limburger?" Joan asked.

"A Le-on-ber-ger," Everett said, pronouncing each syllable.

"I've never heard of such a thing. Let's see him," she said.

"Okay, but let's put Riley inside. The people who own this guy are clueless. He's nine months old and they haven't neutered him. He seems pretty mellow, but I don't want to take any risks."

We put Riley in the house and then Everett opened the passenger door of the truck. Snacks leaped out, then turned to bark at the enormous dog, who sort of tumbled out behind him.

"Jesus, that is a big dog," Spin said.

"He's beautiful," I said. I wandered over to meet him. He was the size of a Saint Bernard but had the coloring of a German shepherd. Snacks was circling him in an assertive way, his legs stiff and straight, his tail rigid. Snacks is like a little drill sergeant whenever a new dog arrives, snarling and barking rules at the new recruit. He just needs them to know that this is his place—he demands respect. He's aware that he's the size of a football with stubby legs, so he always shows the newcomer his teeth. I think he wants new dogs to visualize their jugular betwixt them. They all seem to do that, as they become very cowed in his presence. Everett says that Snacks does the bulk of his job for him. Now the big Leonberger flopped over and rolled onto his back, his mouth grinning, his tongue lolling out to the side.

Snacks trotted over to a nearby shrub and lifted his leg, and that was that. The Leonberger got up and lumbered over to me.

"Oh my God, I'm in love," I said.

"You say that about every dog I bring here," Everett said. He gave me a little hug, but I wiggled out of his arms; I didn't want the others to see. Everett called out to Joanie that she could let Riley out. Within minutes, the three dogs had established a friendly rapport. Spin offered Everett a beer and he sat on the porch with us.

"Did you guys hear what happened over at Mildred's yesterday?" Everett asked. Mildred Swan is our closest neighbor. She's widowed now, but her husband had been one of Whit's oldest friends.

None of us had heard a thing.

"Oh," Everett said. He squinted at the label of his beer bottle, enjoying our suspense.

"Well? What happened? Is she okay?" we all asked at once.

Everett just sipped his beer. "Mr. Clean is back," he said finally.

"NO!" Joan cried out.

"Are you joking?" Spin said. "So he—he hit Mildred's place?"

"Yup!" Everett said. "She just got back yesterday from Nantucket. I guess she was visiting her grandkids for a few days." He took another swig of his beer.

"Oh no, poor Mildred," Joan said. "I saw a patrol car pulling out of her driveway this morning. I thought they were just checking on the place while she was away. Are they sure it's Mr. Clean?"

"Pretty sure," Everett said. "Everybody was talking about it at the

post office. I stopped in to check on her on my way home. He didn't take anything. Her niece is there with her now."

"Did he, you know—clean?" Joan asked, shuddering.

"Yup," Everett said. "Same old thing. Looks like he stayed a night or two. Washed the bed linens. Made the bed. Organized her fridge. And, get this—he changed her cat's litter box."

Joan and I screamed. Everett and Spin laughed.

"What's so funny? Who's this *Mr. Clean?*" Laurel asked.

We have very little crime in this town. Some of the homes surrounding the lake are vacant during the winter months, and very occasionally there are break-ins. Usually, it's kids from neighboring towns looking for drug money. But during the summer of 2014, the summer before Laurel arrived, there was a series of home invasions here on the lake. They all seemed to be committed by one individual. The police had found the same set of fingerprints at each home, but none of the prints was identifiable. The person had no criminal record. The thing that had everybody in a state of borderline hysteria was the fact that the intruder never took anything. He just hung out in the house, and he always tidied up in some way before he left.

The whole town was horrified by what he did, by what investigators called his "pattern of criminal behavior." He never stole anything except for small amounts of food, but he always left the place cleaner than he had found it. There was usually a clean set of sheets on one of the beds, leading investigators to conclude that he'd slept there. He seemed to know who came up on weekends, and he'd break into their homes during the week. He'd watch TV, read, or at least look at books—the owners could tell because he'd usually reorganize their bookshelves. At one house last summer, he used a treadmill and logged in over ten miles. At another, he played with the children's Play-Station. Dishes in the sink? He'd wash them. Laundry in the dryer? He'd fold it. At one home, he scrubbed the bathtub grout. At another, he managed to remove an old red wine stain from the carpet.

There was a lot of commentary in the *Harwich Times* about the intruder last year. They allow anonymous comments on the newspaper's

Web site, so people say stuff they wouldn't say in person. For example, this, from last summer, when he first got his nickname:

JRD: I'd like to see him try breaking into my house, he'll be polishing the business end of my Ruger with his tonsils

LEXIE: Is that my Ruger in your mouth, or are you just glad to see me, Mr. Clean?

JRD: LOL! Mr. Clean!!!!!!!

WINSOME: Glad I live in Westfield, not Harwich

JAMESP: There's like zero crime in Harwich, I grew up there

BILLFEN: JAMESP, what the hell are you talking about, we have crimes here. This newspaper won't report most of them

KELLYQ: Mr. Clean!

FT: They report crimes in this paper.

BILLFEN: Rarely. Look who buys the ads. Real estate brokers. They don't want it to look like anything bad happens in this town.

JAMESP: Um, BILLFEN, try getting out of your little town and seeing the rest of the world. There is really very little crime in Harwich.

BILLFEN: Um, JAMESP, try coming back to this town you freak and I'll serve you up a crime you'll never forget you smug hipster

JAMESP: WTF? Is there a moderator on this board? I just got threatened.

KATHYK: I live near the lake and have noticed that the police are patrolling quite a bit, which is reassuring

LOLA: I just saw a happy bald guy with meaty arms walking down the street with a mop

KELLYQ: No . . . not . . . Mr. Clean!

JAMESP: Dear Harwich Police, I have a tip. Start investigating a psychopath who calls himself BILLFEN on the Web

BILLFEN: Hahahaha. JAMESP, I know who you are

JAMESP: Moderator?

"I'm sorry." Laurel laughed once we had briefed her. "This is the funniest crime I've ever heard. Mr. Clean!"

"I don't think it's funny," Joan said, pulling her sweater tightly around her shoulders. "I'm going to start locking the doors at night."

"Joanie, you should lock them anyway," Spin said.

"I've always felt safe before this," said Joan. "You know what? I wish I had a gun."

"Joan, no!" I said. The last thing our mother needs is a gun; she's very impulsive.

Everett laughed and said, "You'd have to learn to shoot the thing. Besides, this person seems harmless. He probably has a mental illness."

"I'm an excellent shot!" Joan said. Of course she's an excellent shot.

"Whit and I used to skeet-shoot with Bowdoin Auchincloss. Bow-die belongs to a field club in Millbrook, and we went all the time. I would need a shotgun, though, not a pistol or a rifle. A shotgun's just the thing; you don't have to have great aim, just point it in the general direction of the intruder and then spray him with bird shot or buckshot or whatever. Where would I get one, Spin?"

"Don't you have one, Ev?" Spin asked.

"NO," I said before Everett could reply. "He's not going to come here. None of the houses he's entered have dogs."

"As if Riley would do anything," Joan scoffed.

"Wait," Laurel said. "You know what hikers are starting to use out west? Hornet spray."

We all looked at her.

"The kind that shoots fifty or sixty feet," she said. "It's like high-powered Mace. People use it in case they come across a bear. I used to keep a can next to my bed when I was living in L.A. We'd had some break-ins in the area."

"Hornet spray! What an excellent idea," said Joan. She got up and rummaged around in the kitchen, returning a few minutes later with a rusty old can of hornet spray.

"Lottie, read that, will you? I don't have my glasses," she said, wiping grime from the label as she handed it to me.

" 'Kills wasps, hornets, and other flying insects from as far as forty feet.' It doesn't say anything about janitors, Joan," I said.

"He's not a janitor; he's a lunatic!" she replied. "Well, the idea is to blind them, right, Laurel? To immobilize them."

"Exactly," said Laurel. Then she turned to me and said, "Spin tells me you're a writer, Charlotte."

"No," I said, my face burning. "Not really; I just write things for the Internet."

"You mean, like, for *The Huffington Post*?"

"No—they don't pay. It's not really what you would consider writing, though, what I do. It's just for money."

"What do you mean?"

"Mostly, I write, well, listicles," I said, but I sort of mumbled it.

"You write with *testicles*?" Laurel laughed. "Is that what you just said?"

"Listicles," I said.

"Now, *I* was always into writing poetry," said Joan. "When I was at Princeton, I thought I might become a poet. Of course, the motivating factor there was my handsome poetry professor, who had a thing for me. He ended up becoming the poet laureate—"

"What are listicles?" Laurel asked, already trained, like the rest of us, to distract my mom when she's about to launch into an autobiographical soliloquy.

"You see them all the time on the Internet," I said. "You know, they're articles that are lists. Like 'Fourteen Ways to Overcome Social Awkwardness' or 'The Top Ten Reasons Men Cheat.'"

"How do you come up with them? Do you just make them up or what?" Laurel asked.

"Certain themes attract readers. Once you get to know what they are, you basically come up with new lists that are related to popular themes. 'Reasons Men Cheat' and 'Reasons Women Cheat' are the highest-trending ones, always. I just search for articles from Web sites like *Psychology Today*, places like that, and make up lists. You have to cite studies. You can't just make things up out of thin air. You write things like 'A study in Amsterdam revealed that saying a person's name when you meet them and when you say good-bye instills a sense of trust in the person.' That would be for a listicle numbering ways to make a great impression on a job interview."

"I actually find myself reading these lists quite often," said Spin.

"Most people do," I said. "And when you're reading one list, you'll see a column of similarly enticing or completely sensational lists on the side, and you're likely to click on at least one of those. It's all just content created to lure people to advertisements on the sites."

Laurel said, "I had no idea there was a name for that. Listicle! Perfect. So what listicles have you written, Charlotte?"

"I couldn't name them all. I write them every day; I've written hundreds, probably."

"Did you write any today?" she asked.

"Yes," I said.

"Well, what were they?"

"Today I wrote 'Fourteen Ways to Overcome Social Awkwardness.' I'm working on one called 'Twenty-three Great Household Hacks,' and your wasp spray as a home-protection device is a great one. Would you mind if I use it?"

"Of course not. I didn't invent it. Like I said, people use it a lot for that reason. Oh, I love those 'life hacks' lists. I know a few."

"You can sell them," I said. "I can give you the name of the editor I send them to. They don't pay much, but if you do enough of them, it's worth it."

"I don't have time, but I can give you some general life hacks. Here's one," Laurel said. "As long as you're dressed reasonably well, you can check your luggage or shopping bags in any hotel and retrieve them later. Give the porter a few bucks. Free storage."

"That's a good one," Everett said.

"There's a lot you can do in hotels," she went on. "The high-end hotels. Take an elevator up to any floor in the early morning, grab a newspaper off one of the doors—they're usually in a little bag with the name of the hotel on it. Then you own the place. Tuck it under your arm and go to the pool. Visit the club floor, where they have buffets, help yourself. Go to the gym."

"I love these," I said.

Spin was laughing. "You sound like you have a little experience with this," he said.

"Of course I do," said Laurel. "I couldn't afford a gym membership when I was in college."

"These are great," I said. "I'm gonna use them if you don't want to."

"Go ahead. Let's see, what else? Oh, you can only do this once, so make it worthwhile. When you're going on a trip, have a trusted friend give you her credit card. Use it for all the hotels, restaurants—anything but plane tickets. When the trip is over, have the friend report it stolen. The friend has proof that she never left the area, so the credit card company reimburses her. You just got a free trip. Make sure you buy the friend who loaned you the card an expensive gift, though."

There was a moment of silence. Everett glanced at me and then at Spin.

Laurel laughed. "Of course, I would never do that, but I have more. I'm always thinking of them. There's a bunch you can do with gift cards. You can buy a Costco gift card online and then buy anything you want there without having to pay a membership fee. Most people don't know that. You can do it at any of the wholesale clubs."

"Huh," I said. "I had no idea."

"There's no crime in it," she said. "You're still buying the stuff. Also—you should be writing these down, Charlotte—if you're going on a trip, buy a new camera at any major electronics store. When you get back, download all the photos and videos to your computer, remove the memory card, and return the camera."

"That's why I love her," Spin said. He wrapped his arms around Laurel and was beaming with pride. "She's an evil genius."

"Oh," she continued, "when you get a parking ticket—I've done this many times; in fact, I've never paid for parking anyplace where they have those meter tickets. Just park anywhere you want. When you get a parking ticket, take a photo of a nearby car that does have the paid meter ticket on the dashboard. You have to get a close-up shot of the dashboard so that you get the date and time. Just mail it in with the ticket."

"Um, wow. Great ideas," I said. "But I think they have to be legal for the sites I write for."

"Oh, that's no fun," Laurel said. "So I guess the hack to remove all traces of blood so that no forensics team will be able to find them— no good, huh?"

I couldn't help myself. "There isn't a way to remove blood . . . is there?"

"Quite a few ways, actually, but never use bleach. That's where people go wrong. Soap, water, and meat tenderizer is probably your best bet."

We were all silent. Laurel laughed. "It's research for my novel! I read articles about this stuff every day."

SEVEN

I was pretty obsessed with Mr. Clean. I even went so far as to make a chart listing the homes he had stayed in, identifying the similarities. Some of the houses had alarm systems, but none was turned on. None of the houses had dogs. When he entered the houses, nobody was home. The first few break-ins were weekend places, but the last two before Mildred's were occupied full-time. There was a couple, Sarah and Jim Cooper, and a family with three kids. The Higginses were hit, too. They live on Tinker Hill Road, so not technically on the lake, but nearby. Mr. Clean didn't stay the night in these houses; he went in during the day, while everybody was out. He did the usual tidying up and moving things around, but no damage was done. No physical damage anyway.

According to the Web, our Mr. Clean isn't the only one who's into this type of thing. It's a form of voyeurism. Sometimes the intruders break into homes at night when the occupants are there. These people delight in their night-ops stealth. They're very creepy. They don't steal; they just like the thrill of being in the house while people are sleeping. The thrill of getting away with it, I guess. I get it. When I was a little girl, I used to love sneaking around this house and spying on Perry, my mother, and Whit. I especially loved to spy on our guests.

And now I enjoy the fact that I have this alter blog persona that nobody in my life knows about. I have a secret. I am somebody important. I have the paychecks to prove it. The fact that nobody knows about it makes me feel even more important.

Last summer, when Mr. Clean began his rampage, I did some scouring of online forums. It's amazing how many are devoted to strange hobbies and obsessions. That's how I found my friend Matt—on a Reddit forum. Matt's from Australia and a bit like Mr. Clean. He likes to break into people's homes when they aren't there. He's done it since he was a teenager; he's middle-aged now. For Matt, the fun is "casing the joint." (He loves old movies.) When he chooses a house, he watches it for days. He studies the behavior of the occupants, figuring out the best time to enter and the safest exit strategy, should somebody arrive home early.

Matt called himself "Ghostify" on the forum. It was one of those AMA (ask me anything) forums. People post stuff like "I just had a face-lift. Ask me anything." Or "I'm a gay man married to a woman. Ask me anything."

Ghostify posted: "I like to enter people's homes when they're not there, but I don't steal. Ask me anything." He was very popular. Hundreds of people asked him about his methods and motives. Some people were very unkind, while others seemed to admire him.

I privately messaged him last fall and we became friends. I learned a little about him. (Like his real name is Matt.) He related to a lot of what I told him about Mr. Clean. Matt was concerned about the cleaning part, though. He thought it indicated that our guy might be dangerous.

Matt won't tell me what he does for work, but he's always at his computer, and he responded right away when I e-mailed about the return of Mr. Clean. He wanted details. He repeated his concerns about Mr. Clean's behavior. He said the cleaning was meant to disturb people. It was a form of vandalism. It wasn't enough just to go in and look around: Mr. Clean wanted people to feel afraid.

"Don't you want people to feel that way when you break into their homes?" I asked Matt.

"Nobody ever knows I've broken in," Matt said.

"What's the thrill, then, for you?" I asked.

"I'm not sure I'd call it a thrill," Matt replied. "But part of it is not leaving a trace. Being invisible. I feel good when I'm in a place where I don't belong, but the most gratification comes from the fact that nobody will ever know I was there. Your cleaning bloke doesn't like being under the radar. He wants people to feel violated. The fact that it's a prosocial violation is even more disturbing. He's a sick fuck."

"Jesus," I replied. "I hadn't thought of it that way."

He wanted to know how long Mildred had been gone. He told me he never breaks into homes of the elderly and never the homes of people who are single. Too risky. Singles are too unpredictable. Seniors are often home, even if their cars are gone. Matt told me he always knocks on the front door to make sure that nobody's home. If there's no answer, he goes around and enters through the back. Most people have a door or window that is either unlocked or easy to unlock in the back.

I told Matt that I didn't think his knocking strategy is very smart. "I never answer the door if somebody knocks and I'm here alone," I said.

"Even in the day?" Matt asked me.

"Yes," I replied.

"Why?" Matt asked.

It took me a minute or two. I found it a hard question to answer, but finally I just typed: "I'm shy."

He then told me that he hadn't taken into account the possibility of there being "social-phobics" in the homes he was scouting. He thanked me for the insight and asked me if I had ever tried coun-seling.

Are you fucking kidding me? I wanted to type. I'm not a social-*phobic*. Counseling? This twisted pervert who breaks into people's homes to sit on their sofas and probably shit in their toilets thinks I need coun-seling? I don't have social-phobia. I lived in New York City for almost two years and attended crowded lectures every day at Columbia University. When I was only fourteen, I traveled around to bluegrass festivals all up and down the East Coast with Whit, Sally, and Spin—I've played banjo solos in front of thousands. But I didn't respond. I still wanted to be able to consult with Matt about Mr. Clean. I could see how he could jump to conclusions—he knew almost nothing about me. He had probably never been in a relationship; I'd been involved with Everett for over ten years.

Social-phobic? What the fuck?

I wanted to type that, but I didn't. I just logged off and went downstairs to get ready for bed.

I work, as I've said, in a little room in the attic. In the winter, I sleep up there, too, because it's the warmest room in the house. But it's too hot to sleep there in the summer. In the summer, I sleep in Aunt Nan's old room on the second floor.

Nan was Whit's older sister. She and her husband, Bill, lived outside Philadelphia, but they would visit Lakeside every June, until they became too old to make the trip. Because Nan became so familiar with Sally and me, and because they saw the Whitman kids so rarely (they were often in Nantucket with their mother and stepfather), Nan would get confused in her later years and think that Sally and I were Whit's children. At a certain point, everybody stopped trying to correct her.

Uncle Bill could be a little grumpy, but Sally and I always loved Aunt Nan. We would peek into her bedroom and look at the voluminous cotton nightgowns that she would wash by hand in the bathroom sink and hang to dry by the window. She was on the large side, with pale, squishy thighs and a huge pillowy bosom. She wore necklaces made out of coral and sometimes jade. As the only female in Whit's generation, Nan was in possession of most of the Whitman jewels—diamond necklaces, chokers, and bracelets that Whit referred to as "baubles." But when she came to Lakeside, she'd bring her casual trinkets. Sally and I loved the coral necklaces, and one summer, Nan gave one to each of us as a gift.

"I bought these for you girls in the Bahamas," she said. "A nice lady sold them on the beach."

"Did they come from a reef? Did the lady swim down in the ocean and cut them from a reef?" I asked her.

"Perhaps. I'm not exactly sure where she got the coral," Nan said, but I was already imagining myself diving for coral in the Bahamas. That was one of the places where I would live when I grew up. When I was little, I always imagined that I would travel the world and live in exotic places as an adult, and one of those places would be the Bahamas. I would go into the coral business. Every day I would put a knife between my teeth and swim down to a brilliantly colored reef. There I'd dig at the reef with my knife, cutting loose bright pieces of coral, which I would later string together into necklaces and bracelets. I would sell them on the beach, where Sally and Spin and I would live, with pirates and fishermen as our neighbors, and seals so tame that they'd come flopping onto our porch and peer into our window. I remember trying to smell the ocean on my necklace, but it smelled like Aunt Nan's suitcase and a perfume she wore called Joy.

Aunt Nan loved to knit. She took up knitting years ago to help her quit smoking, and kept a basket of brightly colored yarn next to her bed. When she wasn't in her room, Aunt Nan carried her knitting around with her, working the needles constantly. Sally and I loved to watch as sweaters, socks, mittens, and scarves took shape on her broad lap. After breakfast each morning, we would sit with her out on the porch and she would ask us what we did for fun, her needles clacking against each other.

"What do you two have planned for tonight?" she would ask. Nan had no children and was wonderfully clueless about what kids did.

"I don't know. I guess just hang out," we'd say.

When we were young teenagers, she'd ask us, "No dates? Why not go out dancing?"

"Where?"

"Oh, we used to have wonderful dances at the club. Don't you ever go and dance at the club?"

"That's just for old people."

"We used to have dances at the club all summer long," Nan liked to recall, peering up at us over her eyeglasses as she spoke. She always sat on one of the rockers while Sally and I sat wedged together on the old porch swing. Sally was taller and pushed against the floor with her bare foot to make the swing move. Aunt Nan was the eldest in Whit's family; she was at least sixty by the time Whit and Joan married. Her hair was white and cut into a sensible bob. Caked talcum powder was usually visible in the folds of her armpits. Her fingernails were short and neatly manicured and her thick index fingers were remarkably nimble as they tipped the tiny loops of yarn in and around the needle, in and around, then in and around again.

"Didn't you also dance at the Harwich Inn?" Sally would prompt, her elbow digging into my side.

"Oh yes, we'd have great fun dancing at the inn."

The old Harwich Inn had burned down in the early 1970s, but it was once a very popular nightspot on the lake. There had been a restaurant and a dance hall at the inn once, and Sally and I loved to hear stories about it.

"What kind of music did you listen to?" I would ask, biting my lip to keep from laughing.

"Oh, we had wonderful music. A band would come up from New York every summer. The bandleader's name was Winslow Hobbs. Did you ever hear of him? Winslow was his first name. Isn't that a wonderful name? It was the Winslow Hobbs Quartet."

Sally would start choking with suppressed giggles at this point, but she managed to squeak, "No, Auntie Nan, I don't think I've ever heard you talk about him."

"No? Oh, he was very popular. He was a—well, you know, he was a—black man."

"Oh?"

"Yes, the Winslow Hobbs Quartet, they were very popular. I'm sure

Whit remembers Mr. Hobbs—he ended up moving to this area after he retired. But when I was a girl, they were only here in the summer. The Conways put them up in the rooms behind the inn for the entire summer. Winslow Hobbs was quite a good-looking man . . . a very handsome fellow. He was a black fellow, you know, but he had been educated at a conservatory in Louisiana, believe it or not, so he knew classical tunes in addition to the popular songs they played here at night. He was a very talented man, Mr. Hobbs."

"And you say he was a dark-skinned man?" Sally would ask, ignoring my hysterical breathing.

"Yes, dear, but I never notice that kind of thing. I don't notice a person's race. You could be red, white, green, or striped and I wouldn't notice. I see what's *inside* a person."

"I think Whit told me he learned the banjo from one of the guys in the band?" Sally or I would say, encouraging her to go on.

"Yes, yes, he did. We would go over to the inn sometimes, in the afternoon when the men in the band would be relaxing out next to the lake. One of the gentlemen, the bass player, also played the banjo, and he's the one who taught Whit. I would go there with Whit sometimes, though, of course, we never told Father."

"Why not?"

"Oh, *you* know," Nan would confide. Her white cheeks would turn pink and she would lower her voice, then glance around to see if anybody was in earshot, as if her father, long dead, might be lingering. "It was a very different time. It would have been very scandalous for a young lady to be seen chatting with members of a *band*."

Sally and I spent hours fantasizing about Aunt Nan and Winslow Hobbs, the one black man she had apparently ever known. And we suspected that she had known him a lot better than she let on. We had seen photographs of Nan when she was a teen and we knew she hadn't always been plump and short of breath. Her hair hadn't always been white. She was once a raven-haired beauty. Aunt Nan was entirely different in the photos, almost the exact opposite of what she was now, so we imagined that her personality might also have been in stark contrast to the one she now possessed. In our minds, young Auntie Nan had once been a voluptuous, sex-crazed nymphomaniac.

Around the time we were in middle school, Sally and I discovered a treasure. It was a cardboard box filled with dirty paperback books—a thrilling collection of trashy, pornographic stories that we found in the woods behind old Mr. Finch's house. He was creepy, old Mr. Finch, from then on. We read the books over and over again, and for quite some time we imagined that all the grown-ups in our world, especially the women who appeared to be the most polite and wholesome, were constantly throwing themselves, lusty-eyed, shuddering, and heaving of bosom, at their Peeping Tom neighbors, traveling salesmen, or, in the case of Aunt Nan, bandleaders. We loved devising stories about young Auntie Nan sneaking out, late at night, when old Mr. and Mrs. Whitman were fast asleep. We imagined her running barefoot along the lakeshore in a sheer nightdress, her long hair streaming behind her, her eyes darting this way and that.

"He would be waiting for her," Sally would say.

"And her panties would be moist," I would chime in, giggling.

"GROSS," Sally would say. Then: "His cock was so hard that it ached. He would tear off her nightgown, even though she begged him not to."

"What? Why would she beg him not to?" I'd ask. I always got bogged down in the logistics, which annoyed Sally.

"The woman always begs the man to stop whatever he's doing, stupid. It's in all the books."

"I guess it would have been hard to explain all the shredded nighties to her parents. Okay, she begged him not to, but he ripped it off her body anyway."

"With his teeth. Then he'd turn her over so he could see her ripe buttocks," Sally would offer, and we'd both carry on, constantly interrupting each other, crying with laughter as we spoke.

"He would *enter* her, he would *ram* her," Sally said.

"From *behind*, he entered her from behind, and that's when Aunt Nan started bucking like a wild bronco—"

"She was screaming with pleasure and he had to put his hand over her mouth so the people at the inn couldn't hear them."

"So she bit him, and then he gave her pert ass a spanking."

"NO! Aunt Nan's breasts were pert. Her ass wasn't pert, it was—" Sally could barely say the words, she was breathless with laughter.

"It was ripe," I would say.

You can see how it was impossible, some days, for us to look at Auntie Nan without collapsing in helpless giggles. But we adored her. Sally cried so hard at her funeral that our mother felt her forehead to see if she was coming down with a fever.

"Good Lord, dear," Joan had whispered to her in the church pew. "People can hear you."

Sally had wiped away her tears and took a few deep breaths to control her sobbing.

In the car, on the way home, Joan said, "Sally, you're so sensitive. Nan was old. She had a good life."

Sally and I remained silent in the backseat.

"She's so emotional," Joan said to Whit, who was driving. "I really worry about her."

EIGHT

Riley's barking woke me up from a very deep sleep. He was racing around the hall, broadcasting a sound that was somewhere between a canine bark and a human scream—*a woof, woof WOOOOOOOOOOOOOOOOOF, woof woof WOOOOOOOOOF.* I had never heard him go off like that. My heart was racing. I jumped from my bed and peered out into the hall.

Joan came running from her room and grabbed my arm.

"There's somebody outside," she whispered.

"No, it's probably just a raccoon or something."

"I'm telling you, there's somebody out there! I heard a car on the driveway. Wait. Shhhh. Listen. Somebody's on the porch." She was squeezing my arm hard.

"I can't hear anything above the dog."

"If it were a raccoon, Riley would be outside. Listen to the way he's barking; he's terrified."

Joan was right. The dog often took off at night when he heard animals outside, but now he was racing from the door to the front windows and back to the door again, not daring to go out. His barking was shrill and hysterical.

"Should we call nine one one?" I asked, my heart pounding.

"Wait, wait right there," Joan said. She tiptoed back into her room and then, when she returned, she clutched me by the wrist and said, "Stay behind me. I have the hornet spray."

"WHAT?"

"SHHHHHH! Just do what I say. When we get downstairs, run into the kitchen and get the phone. I'll guard the door."

But I was behind Joan, clutching her nightgown. "Joan, no, no, come with me," I said. "Come in the kitchen with me."

Together we descended the stairs until we stood at the very bottom, in the foyer. The dog was whining and circling our feet. I was clutching Joan's wrist.

"Riley is such a coward," Joan whispered. "Why won't he go out and attack?"

"He's stupid," I said. "Come on, let's go in the kitchen."

"Wait, I don't hear anything now," Joan said.

We both stopped breathing.

"It was nothing," Joan whispered after a moment. "A raccoon, nothing."

We started toward the kitchen, when suddenly the dog resumed his maniacal barking. The front door remained closed, but a cold gust of air burst from it. The dog door! Whatever it was had just pushed open the flap of the dog door.

"Stop!" Joan cried. "Stop, or my dog will attack!"

We heard the *thwap* of the dog door and then a thud as somebody tumbled onto the floor. Joan wrenched her arm from my grip. Then she stood, legs planted square like a navy SEAL, turned her face to the side and, yelling, "CLOSE YOUR EYES, LOTTIE!" sent a long jet stream of hornet spray in the general direction of the intruder.

After a brief silence came the scream.

"I've called the police!" Joan said. "Get out! Get out!" And she sprayed again, this time holding the nozzle down until she heard the words "MOM! MOMMY."

It was Sally. It was my sister, Sally.

There followed then a minor hysteria. I switched on the hall light and we saw Sally kneeling, with both hands over her face. She was coughing and crying. "WHY? Why?" she cried. "Why the fuck did you do this to me, Joan?"

"Oh, honey, oh my God, sweetie, I thought you were a killer. I thought you were breaking in."

"I can't breathe. I can't breathe!" Sally was rolling around on the floor now. She wore a black skirt and a white blouse—she must have come straight from a concert—and she was tugging the blouse from where it was tucked into the waistband of her skirt. She rubbed frantically at her eyes with the hem of her blouse.

"Oh God, oh, sweetie, I'm so sorry. I'm calling the ambulance," said Joan.

"NO!" Sally appeared to be hyperventilating. She was panting. "I can't breathe." I was kneeling next to her, trying to pull her hair back from her face, but she pushed me away.

"Honey, I think you're breathing too much," Joan said.

"WHAT? You want me . . . to stop . . . breathing?" Sally barked. She was coughing between words.

"No, you just need to slow down your breathing. You're going to hyperventilate."

"She's suffocating, Joan, not hyperventilating." I was crying now, too. "She can't breathe!"

"I'm calling an ambulance," Joan said, starting for the kitchen.

"JOAN! NO!" Sally staggered to her feet.

"Honey, what if you suffocate?"

"No, Joan, I'm not going to the hospital. Don't call."

"Sweetie—"

Sally took a few shaky steps. She was holding my hand. "I just need water."

"Let me call Everett," Joan said.

"What? No! I just need to rinse out my eyes. OH, THEY'RE BURNING," Sally cried.

"Okay, okay," Joan said, "let's go rinse out your eyes."

I led Sally to the kitchen sink. I tried to help her splash water on her eyes, but she pushed me away and stuck her entire face under the running water.

Joan was tapping out a number on the phone.

"Sally," I said, but she wasn't listening.

"Sorry to wake you. Can you come over?" Joan was saying.

Sally pulled her face from under the water. "JOAN! Who is that? I told you not to call the hospital!"

"No, sweetie, it's Everett," Joan said. Then into the phone: "Sally's having trouble breathing."

"Fuck," Sally said, and put her face back under the cool water.

"I know, but she doesn't want me to call the ambulance."

"Because I'm fine," Sally barked into the sink.

When Everett arrived a few minutes later, Joan and Sally and I were engaged in a sort of shoving match over the sink.

"Get AWAY!" Sally said.

"Let me just see your eyes," said Joan.

"Let go of her, Joan. Just let her go," I said.

"I just want to see if her eyes are red!"

"Hey, hey. What's going on?" Everett asked. We stopped what we were doing and stared up at him. I saw him wince when he looked at Sally, so I looked at her, too. My sister's eyes were swollen; her cheeks were striped with mascara. She was gasping and sobbing.

"What happened?" he asked.

Sally turned back to the sink and splashed more water on her face.

"I sprayed her with hornet spray," Joan said.

"What? Why?" Everett asked, then added, "Did you call the ambulance?"

"No, no, no," Sally said, turning to him now, wiping her face with her sleeve. "Don't call them."

"Shhhh, Sally, let me see," Everett said. He put her face between his hands and gently tilted it up. I could see that the skin around her eyes was scarlet, making the irises—what little we could see of them—seem even more vividly blue than they usually were.

She clutched the front of Everett's T-shirt and said, sobbing, "I'm fine. My eyes are just—burning a little. I can't go to the hospital. I won't go. If you call the ambulance, I'll send them away." She coughed, and then said, "I'm fine. It was hard to breathe at first. I don't need to go. Everett, listen to me, now. Nobody can make me go to the hospital without my consent."

"Okay, okay, Sal," Everett said. "Just take it easy."

Sally pushed her face into his chest. She was a little hysterical. Joan gave me a look, the old *there goes crazy Sally* look. I glared at her.

"Did you get any of the spray in your mouth, Sal?" Everett asked. "Because if your nose and throat are inflamed, you could have trouble breathing."

"No, no, no," Sally said into his chest. "It's just my eyes. They already feel better."

"But sweetie, you could have permanent damage," Joan said.

"Well, maybe you should have thought of that before you blinded me," Sally shot back.

"I thought she was an intruder," Joan explained to Everett.

"I *am* an intruder. It's what you think of me. You *knew* it was me. You *knew* it was me. She wants me to go to the hospital, Everett. It's what she wants. She wants me gone."

I stood behind Sally and put my arms around her. "We know, Sally. We know you're fine. It was all a big misunderstanding. Right, Joan?"

"Yes, yes, sweetie. I thought you were the cleaning man. I thought you were a criminal."

"Sally, I'll go with you to the hospital," Everett interjected. "They'll just look at your eyes and your throat. You're right, they can't make you stay. I'll bring you back here after, but you really should go. If you got any spray in your throat, you can swell up. You could have trouble breathing."

"I don't think it's in my throat," she whispered.

"Your voice doesn't sound so good, Sal," I said.

"No," Sally said. "I know what you're thinking, all of you. I'm fine. Everett, I'll sleep with Lottie. If I have trouble breathing, she can call you. I'm just going to stay here with Lottie. If it gets hard for me to breathe, she'll call you and you can take me to the hospital. It's . . . I'm already fine."

Joan said, "It was so stupid of me. I feel awful."

"I know, Joan," said Sally, forcing a little smile at our mother. "I know you didn't do it on purpose." She clutched Everett's hand. "I'm fine. I know she didn't try to hurt me. I know what happened. It wasn't on purpose. Just—it was all an accident. I know what's going on. I know it was an accident."

Sally slept with me in Aunt Nan's room. Joan gave her some cold cream to wipe the streaks of mascara off her face, and when she came into the bedroom, she did look much better, though her eyes were still swollen. She stood in front of the dresser, examining them in the mirror.

"My face is going to be covered in blisters," she said.

I sat up in my bed so I could see her face. "I don't know," I said, "I think it's going to peel a little, but I don't think you'll have blisters."

"I hope not."

"Do you have to go back on Monday?" I asked. "I think it'll be cleared up by Monday."

Sally wandered over to the other bed and pulled back the covers.

"I'm not really sure if I'm going back," she said. "Do you have any weed?"

"No," I said. "I almost never smoke anymore, but when I do, it's with Everett. He might still be up." I leaned over to look out the window.

"No," Sally said. "Don't let him see you looking over there."

"Honey, he can't see me. He wouldn't be looking up here, anyway."

"He might be. I wish Joan hadn't called him," Sally said.

"It's fine," I said. "Don't worry. If you want, I could run over there and see if he has a joint or something. Have you been having trouble sleeping?"

"Yeah, a little. I took a sleeping pill, but they never work anymore. I just thought smoking would help take the edge off. I haven't been sleeping well at all, actually."

"Sally, let me just run over to Everett's."

"No."

When Sally got sick the first time, when she was at Juilliard, it started with her not being able to sleep. She didn't sleep for days and then everything became distorted in her mind. It happened again a couple years later, and she ended up in the hospital for over a month.

"No, I'm fine," she repeated. "Tell me some funny stories. Tell me what Joan's been up to lately."

She was lying on her side, facing me. She kept touching her eyes with her hands.

"I don't think you should keep touching your face, Sal," I said.

"I can't help it," she said, and I saw that her eyes kept filling with tears and that she was trying to wipe them away.

"Are your eyes tearing because they hurt, or are you sad?"

"I don't know. Just tell me some stories."

So I told her about poor Mildred and Mr. Clean. She smiled when I told her about Laurel's crazy life-hack ideas. She wiped away streams of tears with her palms.

"What's wrong, Sal?"

"I don't know."

"I thought you were doing better."

"I was. I just feel like I'm about to have a sad turn again. And, well, I actually was just replaced as first violinist. I'm not working. I came up here to stay for a while."

"That's great. I mean, I wish I could pretend that I'm sad, about your job and everything, but I'm happy you're staying. You've been wanting to do your own composing, anyway. Now you'll have time. It's the summer; we'll have a great summer."

Sally put her arm over her eyes. She didn't want me to see her tears.

"Let's try to go to sleep," I said.

"Okay."

I switched off the light and we just lay there for a few minutes in the dark.

"Lottie, I still have that thing where I'm afraid of being the only one awake," Sally said.

"Do you really? Still?"

"Yes. Not if I'm alone. If I'm in my apartment alone, I'm fine. It's just when I'm with somebody else, I get anxious if they go to sleep first. Will you stay awake until I'm asleep?"

"I'll try."

"Remember how Whit used to make us read *Robinson Crusoe*? Remember how he made us memorize parts whenever we said we were bored or couldn't sleep?" Sally asked. The sleeping pill was starting to work. Her voice sounded far away.

"Yeah," I whispered.

"I miss Whit," Sally said.

"I know. Me, too," I said.

"'I learned,'" Sally whispered, "'to look more upon the bright side of my condition, and less upon the dark side . . .' What was the rest of it? Something about 'secret comforts'?"

"I don't remember," I said.

"'All our discontents'—that's it, Lottie, remember? 'All our discontents about what we WANT . . .' Remember the way he always shouted the word *want*?"

I smiled in the dark.

Sally continued: "'All our discontents about what we WANT . . .'"

I said the rest of the words with her, and, like her, I imitated Whit by lowering my voice and emphasizing the last word: "'appeared to me to spring from the want of thankfulness for what we HAVE.'"

"Why *Robinson Crusoe*?" I said. "Why didn't he make us memorize poems or Shakespeare or something useful?"

"You know, when I was in the hospital, I had a therapist I saw every day," Sally said. Her voice was fading.

"Yeah?" I said.

"She wanted to talk to me about Whit all the time. I mean, *all* the time. She asked me why I didn't like to talk about him, and I said, 'Whit's not my father.' I don't know why she kept wanting me to focus on that."

"I guess maybe it was because it wasn't long after he died that you started feeling so bad again," I said. "I guess she thought there was some sort of connection."

"She used to say, 'You're allowed to miss him, Sally. You're allowed to mourn him.'"

"Shhhh," I said. "Let's go to sleep."

"But the weird thing was, she also said, 'You're allowed to be angry at him. . . . You're allowed to hate him.'"

"Why?" I asked. "Why would she say a thing like that?"

"I don't know," Sally said. "Whit was great to us. He was great to everybody. Everybody loved him, I told her that. And he fucking cared about us, unlike our own father."

(Our father is still alive. He's a former actor, former addict. Now, apparently, he's a "sober coach." We haven't seen him in years. He's never sent our mother a dime.)

"I always told her how great Whit was," Sally said. "I think she kept forgetting. She kept forgetting how much we cared about him."

"Let's go to sleep," I whispered.

"She didn't get how much we loved him. I can say that now. I don't know why I couldn't while he was alive. I don't know why it's so embarrassing. I loved him like a father."

"Me, too," I said.

"Why would I be angry? Why would I hate him?"

"I don't know."

"Don't go to sleep before me."

"I won't," I said.

NINE

I never look at a clock when I wake up in Aunt Nan's room because of the precise way the sun inches across my quilt and later creeps up the wall with each passing hour. You absorb time, over time, if you stay in the same place long enough. I've slept in this bed for over twenty-five years—outlasting the darkness of childhood nights (is there anything darker?). Then, later, drifting through the long dream of adolescence with its strange new flesh, warm odors, and tingling awkwardness. So I knew it was close to 10:15 when I awoke the next morning because of where the sun's pallid stripe was draped across the lower corner of my bed. Sally's bed was empty. I figured she had gone out for a walk, but when I sat down at my computer, I saw the e-mail.

    FROM: SMaynard@qmail.com
    TO: Charly90@qmail.com
    SUBJECT: I'm at Everett's. Come have breakfast with us!!!

That was it. No message, just a few words in the subject line and all those exclamation points. I ran down the back stairs, then out the laundry room door so that Joan wouldn't see me. I pushed open

Everett's door and went inside. I could hear Sally talking at a rapid clip. I didn't like the tempo of her voice, not at all.

Everett was sitting on his bed. Sally was on the floor beside him, kneeling next to a pile of books. She was dressed in the skirt and blouse from the night before. She was yanking books from the bookshelf and examining their covers as she ranted.

"I know you must have it, because I went through all the books Joan donated to the library and it wasn't in them and Joan said Whit gave you a lot of old books."

"What are you looking for, Sal?" I asked.

She just kept tossing books around. Everett turned and gave me a sad look. He was tired. How long had Sally been here?

"Sal?" I said. "What's the book about?"

"It's a book about Plato. I was trying to explain to Ev about 'The Allegory of the Cave.' Tell him how obsessed Whit was with it, Charlotte. The man was fucking obsessed. Where the hell is that book?"

"Sally," said Everett. "Let's get something to eat, then maybe you'll feel like sleeping."

"Absolutely obsessed with it," Sally continued. "I think you learn about it in college philosophy classes. It's Plato. He could've learned about it at Holden, I don't know. How are we supposed to know? We went to public school. We didn't study Plato. But it's basically this. Ev, listen—there are these people. They live in a cave. They're shackled in such a way that they always face one wall of the cave. I guess they're kneeling there on the ground or something, you know, all chained together. And they're Greek, like Plato; this whole thing happened in Greece."

Sally carried on with how the cave people spent their lives staring at images moving across the wall in front of them.

"The thing is," Sally said, "these cave people? They think the things they see are real. They'll see a rabbit bouncing by and they'll go, 'Hey, there's that rabbit again.' Then an urn goes gliding in front of them and somebody's like, 'Look, there's the urn. I bet the frog comes next.' Then, if the frog is next, they think that guy who predicted it is some kind of fucking genius. They don't say, 'Maybe that's just a picture of a rabbit.' Or 'There's the shadow of an urn.' They think this stuff they're seeing is real. Do you see what I'm saying, Everett?"

Everett yawned and nodded.

There was more. "One of the cave guys is able to leave the cave. I don't know why he can leave when all the others can't leave. It's not important. Well, on his way out, this guy notices that behind the place where they've all been kneeling, shackled, their whole lives, there's a fire, and in front of the fire, there's a wall, and between the fire and the wall—"

Everett put his head in his hands.

"I know," Sally said, "it's confusing. Just try to envision it."

Between the fire and the wall, she explained, people are crouching and they're holding these stick puppets above them, moving them along the wall, and it's *the shadows* of these puppets that the people of the cave have been watching all their lives.

"They're not real. See, Everett?"

"Yup, not real," Everett said. Sally was standing on her tiptoes, pulling books off the top shelves. Everett nudged me and mouthed, "All night long."

"Sal?" I said.

"So the guy who's leaving the cave, he's like, 'Okay, what the fuck is that?' But he just walks past the whole puppet show setup, climbs out of the cave, and then he's almost blinded by the sun. I mean, imagine you're in a dark cave all your life, then one day you walk outside and—BAM! The sun. Right in your fucking eyes. You'd be fucking blind. So he can't see at first, and he actually wants to go back to the cave because the light outside is so harsh, but slowly his eyes adjust and he sees that there's a sun and stars and a moon and that he's standing on real ground and there are real things all around him. Real trees, rabbits, frogs—"

"Okay, Sal. I get it. Can we—"

"And he notices that when the sun hits him a certain way, he makes this outline. This outline looks like him, but it's not him. It's a shadow. It's all an illusion. That's when the guy realizes that he's spent his whole life looking at shadows!"

"Jesus," said Everett. "When is this gonna end?"

"I know, right? The poor fucking guy," Sally said. "So then he goes back to the cave. And now he can't see when he's *inside* the cave, but eventually his eyes get used to the cave again, and he sees all his friends and his family there, and he's like, 'Wake the fuck up, people.' He realizes those aren't real animals on that wall, they're just—"

"Great story," I said. "Let's have breakfast. Everett? Hungry?"

"Okay, here's my point," Sally said. "Whit thought he was the guy who left the cave. I see that now. He thought the cave was that whole prep school, Upper East Side, corporate, Wall Street, socially conforming place that his family came from. He thought when he moved up here to Connecticut, he was finally seeing things as they really are, and Joan, you guys—all of us—we were real. Everything else was fake. When Perry and Spin came to visit, he tried to get them to feel as if they had left the cave, too. But you know, now I think *we* were the ones living in the cave. I think Lakeside is the cave. I think Whit made all these shadows. Not on purpose, but I think we were the ones living in the cave all along."

She turned away from the books and smiled at Everett and me. "Isn't it funny how everything can suddenly be so clear?"

"Let's all go back to sleep," Everett said, stretching out next to me. "You should sleep, Sal."

"Oh hey, by the way, Everett, you got an e-mail from Russ Wheldon and another from somebody named Lisa," Sally said. I felt Everett freeze up.

"What the hell? How do you know that, Sally?"

"I used your computer to send Charlotte an e-mail."

"But how did you get into my computer? I have that thing password-protected," he said.

"Please," Sally said.

"What?"

"It took me three guesses. TheChiefs. The name of your old band. Switch it to something random, like just some word with a hashtag and a number. And by the way, does my mom know you're using her Wi-Fi?"

"Let's eat," I said. "Maybe if you have something to eat, Sally, you'll be able to have a little rest."

I was checking out the cereal collection in his kitchen when I saw a car pull into our driveway.

"Hey, who do we know with a silver car?" I called out.

Sally and Everett were behind me almost instantly. Now a man was getting out of the car. Sally and I followed Everett out the door.

"Looks like a trooper," Everett said.

He wasn't a tall man, nor was he terribly short. He might have been in his early thirties. I thought he was handsome.

He watched us approach from Joan's front porch.

"Hey," Sally said as she reached the steps. We were right behind her. I was still in my nightgown. Everett was pulling a T-shirt over his head as we walked.

"Can I help you with something?" Sally demanded, but before the man could reply, Joan had opened the door and greeted him with a smile.

"Hello, I'm Joan Whitman. Come in, come in."

"Wait, Joan, just wait. I don't know this guy. Who are you?" Sally asked, pressing herself into the doorway, inserting herself between the man and our mother.

"I'm Washington Fuentes, local state trooper. We're looking into the series of home invasions."

"Yes, yes," said Joan. "Do come in."

"Just wait, Joan," Sally said. "What is it you want to ask my mother about?"

"Sally, honey, please. This man just wants to ask us if we saw anything, I'm sure."

"Are you mother and daughter?" Fuentes asked Sally. He tilted his head a little as he looked at her. He might have been trying to see what was going on with her eyes. They were still quite red.

"Sorry, we don't answer questions," Sally said.

"Oh, for heaven's sake, Sally," said Joan.

Fuentes smiled and said to Sally, "You won't answer a question about whether you're mother and daughter?"

"That's right."

"Are you an attorney?"

"No," my mother said, answering for Sally. "She's a musician, the first violin in the New York Symphony Orchestra."

"What do you want?" Sally demanded.

"I just have a few questions for your mother."

"Are you detaining her as a witness?"

"As I was starting to say, we're asking people who live in the neighborhood—"

"So are you detaining her as a witness?"

"No."

"Okay, then can you step back a little so we can close the door? Then will you please remove your vehicle from this property?"

"Okay, now that's just enough," said Joan. She pulled Sally into the house and glared at her. "Sally, this officer is investigating the break-ins, and I want to help him. It's my obligation as a citizen to help," Joan said.

"No, it's not," said Sally. "It's not your obligation."

The man turned to Everett and smiled. I had a feeling that Everett wasn't smiling.

"You must be the caretaker of the property?" Fuentes looked at his notebook, then said, "Mr. Hastings?"

Everett was silent. He just stood there with his arms crossed.

"Wait," Fuentes said, "Everett Hastings? I know you. You were a year behind me at Harwich High. We played baseball together."

I felt Everett relax. He took a step closer, paused, and then laughed in disbelief. "HOLY SHIT! Washington? Washington Fuentes!"

They actually gave each other a hug. "You guys remember Washington, right? From high school? Washington, these are the Maynard girls—Charlotte and Sally."

"Aren't you Ramón Hernández's son?" I asked. Now I did remember him. Ramón has a very lucrative landscaping business and knows everybody in this and all the surrounding towns.

"His nephew. My mom shipped me here for the last two years of high school," said Washington. "She thought it would be good for me to live up here with my uncle, instead of down in the Bronx."

"I don't remember you," Sally said.

"I remember you," Fuentes said.

"What kind of name is Washington Fuentes?" Sally demanded.

"What kind of name is Fuentes?"

"No, what kind of name is Washington? Is it a family name?"

"No . . . my dad just liked the name. You know, it's American."

"So is it George Washington Fuentes?"

He smiled. "Nope, just Washington. Washington Fuentes. Like it says right there." He pointed to his badge. "Can I ask a few quick questions and get it over with? I have to do the entire area, I have to talk to all your neighbors."

Sally answered him with a short, disparaging laugh. Then she turned to our mother and said, "Joan, if you allow him in, you're consenting to a search without a warrant."

"I'm a *Law and Order* fan, too!" Washington said to Sally.

"What? I don't even know what that is," Sally said. (Not true—she actually spent a summer binge-watching the show and now she thinks she's a legal expert.)

"Oh, for goodness sake, Sally. I have nothing to hide. Come in," Joan said.

"Thank you, ma'am. I won't take up much of your time," Fuentes said.

"Come in, come in. *Mi casa es su casa!*" Joan said.

"*Muchas gracias, señora!*" said Washington, following our mother into the house.

"Coffee, Mr. Volentes?"

"Yes please to the coffee. Oh, and it's Fuentes, ma'am."

"Oh, I am sorry. And I'm usually so good with names. I have a splendid memory."

"Nice kitchen," Fuentes said once we were inside. "I like old places. It's very quaint."

"That's what everybody says about this kitchen," said Sally.

"Rustic, too," I offered. "Sometimes people call it rustic."

"Looks like you got something in your eyes, Sally."

"Yes, unfortunately, Sally did get something in her eyes, Officer," replied Joan. "And if there's anybody who needs questioning about a crime, it's me, for almost blinding my poor daughter last night."

"Joan," Sally said. "It was an accident."

"Nonetheless . . . you see, Officer, last night—oh, this is actually related to your investigation, because I have never felt unsafe in this town until yesterday and I've lived here almost all my life. Half the time, I don't even lock the door, but last night, after what we heard about poor Mildred—"

"So did you notice any unusual cars in the neighborhood yesterday?" Fuentes asked.

"No, and I ran by there early in the morning. I run five miles a day, rain or shine—"

The five-mile brag had begun.

When Joan was finished with all the details about her heart rate and her many activities that provide the oxygen that fuels her enormous brain, she managed to answer the few questions Fuentes had. And she was absolutely no help.

"I guess that's all I have for now," said Fuentes. He thanked Joan for her information and the coffee and then Sally led him to the front door. I followed.

"Well, I hope you find your cleaner, Washington Fuentes," Sally said. "Do you still live in town?"

"Actually, I've just moved back. I was assigned to Bridgeport when I first joined the state police. I've been living there for a few years. Heard that a spot opened up here in Litchfield County and thought I'd try for it. Just got stationed here last month. I'm staying at my uncle's until I find my own place. It's nice to be back here, away from the city. Pretty quiet except for these B and E's. Anyway, it's been great seeing you. You really haven't changed, Sally."

"You must have changed a lot, because I still have no recollection of you whatsoever, Officer Fuentes."

"Hey, you know, please don't call me Fuentes. My friends call me Washington."

"Well, I'm not your friend," said Sally.

TEN

A very unbalanced troll who calls herself Tricksortreats had returned to my blog and was cluttering up my comments section with her nastiness. My readers are loyal and they can't wait to take down anyone who flames me, but I don't moderate comments. It's another gimmick that has gotten me attention in the blog community. I don't block—I actually like to engage—but there are a handful of readers who want the blog to be a "safe place" and they see Tricksortreats as "hostile" and "threatening to the community." Some of my readers told me they worry that I have enough on my plate as it is, given that Wyatt needs to see a specialist about his abnormal bone growth. I've tried to ignore it (I guess I was in denial), but he's developing a sort of hunch in his back. Curvature of the spine isn't terribly uncommon for children with his disorder. He might need some painful and possibly dangerous surgery and, at the very least, a lot of physical therapy. Otherwise, he'll be a hunchback when he's an adult.

So far, about fifty comments had been posted in response to Tricks's nastiness. I posted that I was inclined to ignore her, that she obviously has some serious psychiatric problems and if we ignore her, she'll likely return to Trollville and leave us all alone. Then I drew a stick-figure drawing of Topher and me in our bedroom. I'm wrapped up like a mummy in the sheets and he's humping the curtains like a dog because I'm too exhausted for sex. The "too exhausted for sex" theme is one of the most popular. I'm always guaranteed three hundred comments at least after a post like that.

I heard Sally playing her violin when I started work that morning, but when I finished a couple of hours later, the house was quiet. I wandered downstairs to her room. The door was ajar and I was pleased to see that she was asleep on her bed. She really can get out of control when she doesn't sleep for a while.

I went outside to join Joan in the front garden.

"Sally's asleep," I said.

"I know," said Joan. She was hosing a tangle of weeds.

"I was worried, but if she was able to just go off to sleep like that, I'm sure she's fine."

"I put something in her coffee," Joan said. "Sweetie, move back now. I need to get the irises; they're starting to come in there near the steps. I don't want to get you all wet."

"What do you mean, you put something in her coffee?"

"Oh, what's it called. Chompsapan? Clomazapan? Something like that. I called Jim Alter and he told me to check what meds she had packed. I found them. He told me to give her the clompsapan. Said she could take a double dose."

"Clonazepam? He told you to give her clonazepam without her knowing?"

"Well, I didn't ask him, but I'm sure he would have agreed."

"Agreed with drugging Sally against her will? Joan, that's so unbelievably sick. Sally's paranoid enough. She has delusions that people do stuff like this to her. What if she found out you really did that? What if she had gotten in her car and started driving?"

"I have her keys, Charlotte. I did the right thing. She wouldn't have taken the medication. She loves it when she's all high-strung. I just can't take it. Not now. I mean, think of Spin. Laurel's just arrived; we don't want to overwhelm her, especially now that they're going to be staying here."

"Staying here?" This was news.

"Just for a couple of weeks. They're having all the dorms and faculty housing painted at Holden. Everybody has to leave campus for the rest of the month."

"When did you find this out? When were you going to tell me?"

"I just found out this morning. Spin called and told me, and I invited them to stay here. They're moving in tomorrow."

"Why don't they go to Perry's?" I asked. My heart was racing.

"They're going to Perry's in two weeks, once the little ones are out of school. Perry and Catherine are going to their place in the Hamptons."

"Does Sally know?" I asked.

"I'll tell her later, when she wakes up."

Joan was stooped over in the flower bed now, plucking at weeds. Gardening is one of Joan's hobbies. This is a family joke, as our gardens are a disaster. She toils out there all spring and summer, yanking at weeds, moving rocks around, digging, mulching, sweating, swatting at mosquitoes, and the beds always look the same—a tangle of old overgrown perennials and masses of weeds.

"What a mess this place is," she said, glancing over at Everett's house. "Why doesn't Everett do more? He could really do more. I can't do it all myself. Everett could help."

I sat on the porch swing and gazed at Everett's house. "I can help with the garden," I said, but I kept swaying on the swing.

"Well, I can do it, too, but that's not the point."

"What's the point?"

"The point is that if he were paying rent, he'd be paying two thousand a month, probably more."

I was feeling defensive about Everett. My mother hates it when people help her in the garden. Every time Everett tries, she accuses him of removing the heirloom perennials that she transplanted from her aunt's garden, or some other nonsense. I didn't feel like getting into a big thing about it, though.

Joan grabbed one last weed and thrust it onto the little pile she had created.

"Can you toss those into the compost heap after dinner?" she asked me. I nodded.

"Well, I think I'll go upstairs and die now," Joan said. It was the old family joke; we never tired of it.

Sally slept for almost twenty-four hours. I wouldn't give my sister any drug without her knowing it, but I was glad that my mother had. Sometimes, it's just sleep Sally needs, and then she's fine. She was wearing a little summer dress and unpacking her giant duffel bag when I peeked into her room. Her phone was attached to a portable speaker. Music was playing.

"Hey, Sal," I said.

"Hey," she said, smiling. "Man, I really slept."

She was back to her old self. What a relief. As she put away her things, I lay on her bed, listening to the music. It was violin and piano. A clear, simple, fluid melody.

"Is that you playing?" I asked.

"Yeah. With a guy I do session work with sometimes."

"What is it?"

"It's this thing I'm working on. I'm trying to write music for this film."

"Sally, this is really pretty. What's the film about?"

"It's about . . . well, it's an historical thing, set in the West in the 1800s, but not a Western. Sort of a sweet, sad film. I have to watch it again."

"I like it," I said.

"Can you help me with it?" Sally asked. "I want to add something with the violin. Can you play the piano on this section? I don't have the music, but I can write it up for you, if you need me to."

I listened for a few minutes. "No, I have it," I said.

Sally and I had been playing music together since we were children. It was Whit who taught us how to play the piano, then the ukulele, and eventually the banjo. He did this soon after we had moved to Lakeside. He had tried, with limited success, to teach Perry these instruments, but Perry practiced only when he was here, so he never really learned how to play anything. I liked playing the banjo the most, I guess, because I wanted Whit's approval. I got to be a fast little picker, and Sally and I became competitive about who was faster. One day, Sally heard the song "Orange Blossom Special," a bluegrass standard, one of Whit's favorites, and it was then that she became determined to learn the fiddle. "Orange Blossom Special" is written for the fiddle. The tune is meant to sound like the engine of a train getting faster and faster. Whit bought Sally a violin and she became obsessed with it. She made me play along on the banjo while she was practicing. There used to be a video of us from when I was probably no more than six and Sally was seven. Years later, Whit posted the video on his banjo page on YouTube.

Because I was so small, I used to play sitting on the old sofa in the music room, so that I could rest the weight of the banjo on my crossed legs. Sally stood facing me. She could really "play the hell" out of any tune, as Whit would say. We had over 200,000 views on our "Orange Blossom Special" video, but we had to take it down when Sally started playing professionally, because she was getting creepy, stalkerish comments. Anyway, I played the songs that Whit taught us—mostly bluegrass music, Appalachian music, some folk songs—but Sally played everything—classical music, jazz, Celtic music, old spirituals. She even taught herself how to play pop and hip-hop songs on her violin. (It's really only called a fiddle when you're playing bluegrass.)

One Christmas Eve, when I was around eight, Sally and I played "Ode to Joy" on the banjo and violin for Whit and Joan. It was planned as a surprise; we'd been practicing for weeks. We gave it a lovely Baroque sound, the way Sally had arranged it. Whit wiped away a tear when we were finished. The next day, when Perry and Spin arrived to celebrate Christmas with us, Whit insisted that Sally and I play the melody for them. And we did play it, or at least we tried, but this time, soon after we began, Sally glanced gleefully up at our stepbrothers. I followed her gaze, and we saw Perry's hate for the first time. Sally messed up her chords. Spin, who was just a little boy, sitting on Joan's lap, clapped, but I saw Perry give a little smirk. We stopped and then started playing again, together, but then Sally fumbled once more, and, bursting into tears, she thrust the violin at me and refused to finish the song.

We spent the rest of the morning in the music room, trying to sort out Sally's composition. I really hadn't been playing much since Whit died, so I was glad when Joan called us for lunch.

"Look how nice this is," Joan said. She was standing over the sink, husking a few ears of corn. "It's from the farm stand. Can you believe they have corn this early?"

"It is early," said Sally. "It must have come from Florida or something."

"No, it's from the farm stand."

"You may have bought it at the farm stand, but sometimes they sell produce that they don't grow themselves. They never have corn until the very end of July," Sally said, forcing a smile in Joan's direction.

"Sometimes the corn comes in early if it's been a warm spring," Joan insisted. "It's been very warm this spring."

Why? I thought. Why must they engage each other like this?

Sally started sorting through a pile of papers on the counter. She turned to me and held up a Christmas catalog, then pointed at the stacks of paper and mouthed, "What the fuck."

Sally was right. The clutter had really gotten out of control these past few months. I wandered into the mudroom and grabbed the recycling bin. I tried to be casual when I placed it next to Sally, but Joan saw us.

"Please do NOT throw away my mail; I haven't gone through it yet," she snapped. And then: "It said 'local corn' on the sign, Sally. I don't think the Hansens would lie about what they sell."

Sally dropped the papers on the counter and said, carefully, through gritted teeth, "But they didn't say it was theirs. *Local* could mean New Jersey. Pennsylvania even. They'd have corn there by now."

Joan placed both hands on the countertop and took a deep, dramatic breath. "I'm sure you're right," she said, surrendering.

Sally had gone over to look out the window. Joan turned to give me her imploring look, as if to say, *Are you listening to this?* Then she said, "Now, what's going on with the orchestra? Will you be touring this summer, Sal?"

"They will. I was actually hoping that maybe I could spend a little time out here."

"That would be nice," Joan said. She had moved on from the corn and was washing lettuce. "The lettuce is from the farm stand, too," she said cheerfully, "but now you have me thinking that they had it flown in from New Zealand."

She placed the lettuce on a plate and started dabbing the leaves with what appeared to be part of an old bath towel.

"I'm not going on tour with the orchestra; I'm taking a leave," Sally said. She was now checking expiration dates on the many vitamin and mineral supplements that Joanie likes to keep on our windowsills.

Joan said, "Is that right. Starting when?"

"Well, pretty soon," said Sally. "Actually, now. Jesus Christ, this vitamin E is from 2004. This has to go, Joan. I keep telling you, this stuff goes bad if you leave it in the hot sun."

"Might as well have a little holiday while the weather's nice, huh?" Joan said. "And don't you dare throw any of those away, Sally. I mean it now. How's your roommate? Ellie?"

"Ella. It was Ella. I'm not really living there anymore."

Joan turned and looked at her. "Where have you been living?"

"I've been living there, in the Chelsea apartment, with Ella. Until now. Now I'm living, well, here."

"Oh, Sally."

"Just for now."

Joan exhaled slowly. Her back was turned to me, but I could imagine her rolling her eyes. She reminded Sally that she'd spent every moment of her teen years griping about Harwich and how she couldn't wait to leave it "for the real world." "And now you've spent most of your adult life returning. Again and again." She turned her attention to me. "And Charlotte, honey, now that we're on the subject, the same goes for you, too. It's time you got your own place. I mean, I know you love Harwich, you could get a place here in town. It would just be . . . healthier for you to be on your own."

"I don't love Harwich," I said. How could she even have thought that?

"No one's forcing either of you to stay."

"I'm not here to stay," Sally said. "I'm just visiting. Jesus Christ, I'll leave today if you want. And why shouldn't Charlotte stay here? This house has eight bedrooms. I can't even imagine what Whit would think if he heard you say that."

"I hate this town," I repeated. "And Joan, I've told you before, I'll pay you rent. I make plenty of money."

"No, no," Joan said. "I don't want your money. Let's just drop this."

She placed tuna sandwiches on the table, and I grabbed one and started eating.

"Sally, eat," I said. "Sit down and eat."

The not eating is also part of it. She'll stop eating if she's getting sick.

"Sally," Joan said, "Perry and Catherine are staying at the Lockwoods' this weekend. They're stopping for a drink on their way back to the city."

"Okay, when?" asked Sally.

"I think around three-thirty or four. Also, did Charlotte mention that Spin and Laurel will be staying here for a couple of weeks?"

"No," Sally said.

Joan explained about Laurel and Spin. Unlike me, Sally appeared to be delighted with this news. "I want to get to know her better," she said.

"Good," said Joan. "But listen, can you girls swap out the storm windows for the screens? I have to run to the store to get the burgers and everything. It's been getting warmer at night. Everett said he'd do it yesterday, but he ended up working on somebody's stone wall."

"Joan, *all* the upstairs windows? That'll take us all day," I said. "I put the screens in the attic windows last week; it took hours. The storm windows are so old. They weigh a ton."

"Just do the ones in Spin's room, Sal's room, and mine. We'll all be sweltering tonight if we can't open the windows."

We started on the windows in Joan's room and then moved on to Spin's, which is just at the corner where the two oversized wings of the house intersect. The first level of Lakeside is clad in fieldstone, but the second and third stories are covered with scallop-shaped wood shingles that have, remarkably, survived a century of driving lake rains and snowstorms. Sally and I admired once again the craftsmanship that had gone into the design and placement of the shingles. When we were young, we used to climb out there on the porch roof, right at the corner where we now stood, and pretend that we were on the bow of a glorious schooner and that the lake below was a sea filled with sharks, pirates, and treasures. One afternoon, Whit wandered out of his workshop and saw us up there.

"HEY!" he had shouted, and Sally and I started pushing each other to be the first to climb back in through the windows. "Girls, it's okay. Quit shoving," he had said. "My sister and I played up there when we were kids, too. Just watch out for loose shingles. I've got a guy coming out to re-shingle the whole roof. He's a roofer from New Hampshire and he wants one of my banjos."

People used to joke that Whit Whitman stopped paying for things the minute he came into his money. Everybody likes to barter, but Whit thrilled at any opportunity to swap services for goods, or vice versa. He seemed to experience physical pain when he had to reach into his deep pockets for the things that could only be acquired with cash—things like heating oil, electricity, and food. He and Joan scrimped on these luxuries as much as possible, but they had to accommodate us kids to a certain extent—we insisted on using electrical lighting rather than flashlights when moving around the house at night, for example. Whenever he could, though, Whit bartered. He traded music lessons for auto repairs, garden vegetables for old tools, old banjos for new tools. He occasionally traded his expensive custom banjos for major equipment or household renovations. He had never paid Everett or his father, Bud, a penny for their work as caretakers. He never needed to, as they lived in a lovely lakeside cottage and the work they did around the estate was in exchange for their rent.

Whit did pay us kids for chores. He paid Sally, mostly, because she always outbid the rest of us. Yes, that's right: Whit had us bid for household jobs, as if we were contractors. He wanted to teach us about how a free economy works. When we were kids, Sally's desire to win at everything, her hypercompetitive drive, made her the hardest worker in the house—and the most poorly compensated. On a typical summer morning, Whit would announce at breakfast that the vegetable garden needed weeding. He'd ask if anybody wanted to make a little cash.

Perry would usually start out by saying, "I'll do it for, I guess, ten bucks."

I would underbid just a hair. "Nine-fifty," I'd say.

"Five dollars!" Sally would call out defiantly.

Perry and I always laughed at her. "You're doing it again, Sally," I'd tell her. "Remember when you got paid two dollars for cleaning out the entire attic?"

"Yeah, well, you guys got nothing," she countered.

"Now, that's what I call a good work ethic," Whit said, winking at Sally. His praise buoyed her through the beginning of the weeding.

It wasn't until the second or third hour of toiling in the heat and mosquitoes, while Perry and I sailed back and forth in front of the beach, taunting her from the boat, that she saw her mistake. Next time, she would let one of us be the "winner."

Now Sally said, placing a storm window carefully on the roof, "The last time I did this, Whit paid me a dollar a window."

"Did he help you? I remember that he'd help with heavy stuff like this if he was home," I said.

"Whit was always home, Charlotte." She laughed.

It was true. Whit was always home. He was always busy. And he made a lot of noise. I can't remember a quiet afternoon, ever, when Whit was alive. He would listen to bluegrass while working in his shed, and the breeze usually carried the frenetic sound of the fiddles and banjos up to the house and out across the lake. The neighbors would often comment on how extraordinary it was that the music carried so far, and he took their comments at face value, rather than wonder why they were delivered in such terse tones.

"Yes," he would say, "the hills around the lake create a giant amphitheater effect. Wonderful what it does acoustically!"

It wasn't just that Whit created a racket in the shed. He was a large man and a stomper. The sound of his work boots on the old wooden stairs could be heard throughout the house as he came and went. He liked to sing. He sang to the dog, he sang to Joanie, he sang to himself in the mirror. And then there was the incessant banter—on the phone, in the driveway, down by the lake. People loved to stop to chat with Whit. There were men hanging around the shed year-round, "shooting the shit," as Joan liked to say. The guys on the town's road crew would always stop for coffee if they drove by and saw Norm Hungerford's car. (Norm was Whit's childhood friend, and his car in the driveway always meant coffee in the pot.) Sailors and rowers in the summer, skaters and cross-country skiers in the winter—everybody who traveled across the lake stopped to catch up with Whit.

"You know, it was the silence that caught me so off guard those first few times I came home after Whit died," Sally said to me. "You were here all the time, so maybe you didn't notice it, but the atmosphere felt completely different here after that."

"I noticed it," I said. I would walk outside and listen for a song from Whit's shed, and when it didn't come, I'd suddenly have to hold on to a wall to steady myself. It would be hard to breathe sometimes.

I tried to talk to Joan about it once.

"Sometimes I find myself having actual conversations with him," I said to her not long after the funeral. Sally had gone back to the city, but I had decided to stay here at Lakeside with Joan. "When I walked in the house today, I almost called out to him."

"Did you, dear?" Joan asked, glancing at her watch. It was a Saturday. She had a tennis tournament.

"I guess it's because it's so quiet. If he hadn't been so noisy before, the quiet wouldn't be so . . . strange. How can you stand the quiet?"

"I keep busy. I don't really notice," Joan said.

"Have you been able to go into his shed yet?" I asked her one day.

I hadn't been able to bring myself to open the door to Whit's shed since the funeral. When he was alive, I had rarely opened the door without finding Whit on the other side, covered in sawdust, humming or singing along with the music on the old boom box there. He always gave me a big grin. Sometimes, he'd give me a new instrument to try out. I imagined it would be too much for our mother to go inside the shed as well, but Joan had replied, "Oh yes, I was in there this morning looking for a broom and dustpan, and sure enough, there they were. He was always taking things from the house and leaving them in that damn shed."

ELEVEN

We had just removed the last of the storm windows from Spin's room when the cars pulled up. I grabbed Sally by the wrist and peered around the front edge of the house and down at the driveway. Spin's Jeep was in front; Perry had pulled up behind him in his shiny black Range Rover. I squatted down low on the porch roof and pulled Sally down next to me.

"Don't let them see us," I said.

"Why not?" Sally asked.

"I don't want to see anybody yet."

Perry's voice came from below. "Joan's car isn't here."

I heard the voices of his children, Emma and Jake. Jake was saying, "Where's Nana Joan?"

"Maybe nobody's home," Perry said. "Jesus, look at this place. Still a total mess."

"It's like *Grey Gardens*," we heard Catherine say.

Sally clutched my wrist too tight. "What the fuck?" she hissed.

"Was it more . . . kept up when your dad was alive?" That was Laurel.

"Um, no," said Perry. "But for some reason I thought that was Bud Hastings's fault. I thought Everett would start fixing things up once his dad retired. He's supposed to be the groundskeeper now, but things are as bad as ever."

"The *groundskeeper*," Sally whispered. "As if we live on *grounds*. As if Everett were a servant. Everett, who's known Perry since they were kids."

"Shhhh," I said.

Now we heard them walking along the porch, just below us.

"I think we should wait outside until Joan gets home," said Spin. "Let's take the kids down to see the lake."

"Why?" Laurel asked. "Why don't we just go in?"

"Well, at least let's knock, give them a little heads-up."

"Really, Spin? You knock now?" Perry asked.

"Yeah, ever since Dad died. I knock, and then go in."

"That's weird," said Perry.

"I thought it was weird, too," said Laurel.

"I know, I just feel that it's the right thing. I don't think she's here, anyway."

We stayed perched on the roof of the porch. I saw that the rain gutter was filled with leaves from last fall. Nobody had cleaned the gutters in who knows how long. They were dark with mildew and had started to decompose. No wonder there was rain rot all along the edge of the porch floor.

"She's not there, so just go in," Perry said.

"Wait, I do want to see the rest of the property," said Laurel. "I haven't seen the whole place, just the house and the dock."

We heard them walking down the porch steps. We heard Catherine say, "Is there some way to get this cleaning maniac to break into this house?" We heard them all laugh, even Spin. Sally had her hand on my wrist and she squeezed it tight.

A moment later, they were down on the lawn, facing the lake. Little Jake had found a stick and was chasing Emma around in circles. Riley, our dog, was trying to get the stick from Jake, and Catherine cried out, "Spin, grab that dog. He's trying to bite."

"He doesn't bite," Spin laughed. "C'mere, Riley."

"We can't stay up here all day," Sally whispered.

"I know. Let's just wait until Joan comes," I replied. We sat back against the house. The lake was calm and a slight breeze moved the clouds across the sky, creating panels of shadow that shifted across the water's surface. Near our shore, two geese glided along behind a family of ducks, who complained loudly about this pair of oversized tagalongs. Out beyond our float, old Ethel Garner was sailing her Sunfish. She sailed past the float once, then tacked and sailed past it again, this time waving to Spin and the others.

"Hi, Mrs. Garner!" Spin called out to her.

"Hi, dear. OH, HI, SALLY! HI, CHARLOTTE!" Mrs. Garner shouted, and Sally and I watched in horror as the group on the lawn turned around and gazed up to where Ethel had been waving. Sally stood and pretended she was moving one of the storm windows. I smiled and gave them all a feeble wave.

"Sally! Charlotte!" Spin cried out happily. "There you are! Didn't you hear us knocking?"

"No," Sally replied. "No, we didn't."

They were shielding their eyes with their hands so they could see us better.

"What the hell are you two doing up there?" Perry asked.

"We're trying to swap out the storm windows. What does it look like we're doing?" said Sally. "We're taking care of this old house of yours."

"The shingles are loose; you'd better be careful," said Spin. "Here, let me come up and help you."

"Where's Everett?" Perry called to us. "Isn't he supposed to do this stuff? Isn't that his job?"

Spin had been correct about the loose shingles; the one beneath my foot was almost completely dislodged, and I enjoyed the fleeting image of it leaving my hand like a boomerang, slicing Perry's prematurely balding scalp from his tanned forehead, and then returning to me.

"No, don't come up, we'll come down," Sally said, but we could hear that they were already in the house.

"You should have let me do that," Spin said as he helped us with the last window.

"Well, you can do the others. You two are staying here, right?" Sally asked.

"We were planning to, but if it's a problem, we can always stay at Perry's," Spin said.

"Of course it's not a problem. This is your house, too," Sally said, and I caught Laurel shoot a quick glance at Spin. I knew Sally saw it, too. Her cheeks had turned pink. She and I both sensed that they had misunderstood; that they thought Sally felt some kind of ownership, which, of course, was ridiculous. It was our mom's house. Hers, Perry's, and Spin's.

Laurel said, "Let's get our stuff, Phil, and then maybe Sally and Charlotte can show us around. I've never walked around the property, or even seen the entire house."

Again, we were momentarily confused. Yes. Phil. It was his real name. She liked calling him that. Never mind that nobody called him that—not his friends, not his colleagues, not even his own mother, who had given him the name. It seemed that Laurel wanted her own name to call him. I wasn't sure why this irked me, but it did.

We met up with Perry and Catherine downstairs. After Spin's car was unloaded, we all went on a little tour of Lakeside.

Sally loves showing off the property; she's done it many times. She was always fascinated with the history of Lake Marinac and all the Vandemeer cottages. She devoted many hours one childhood summer to reading about them at the Harwich library. When our family used to participate in the annual garden tour of the Vandemeer homes, Sally was always the tour guide. She started right in now, telling Laurel about how the house came to be situated there on the point. It was because of Holden Academy, she explained. In the early

years of the school, in the mid-1800s, Holden boys used to hike the
four miles from the school's campus to a campsite on Lake Marinac.
The campsite was on the point of land where we now stood.

"This used to be called Point Bliss," Perry interjected. "My
great-grandfather had the name changed to Whitman's Point."

"Well, technically, according to town records and maps, it still is
Point Bliss," Sally corrected him. "But everyone in the area has called
it Whitman's Point for generations."

"They call it Whitman's Point because it *is* Whitman's Point,"
Perry laughed. "It was legally changed by my great-grandfather."

"That's not actually true," Sally said, "but who cares? Anyway, it
was 1904 when your and Spin's great-great-grandfather George
Perry Whitman decided to have his classmate Karl Vandemeer build
Lakeside Cottage. He had loved Holden Academy, and his fondest
memories involved the days and nights camping on Point Bliss. The
school abandoned the tradition of camping on the lake sometime
around the turn of the century, after one of the kids drowned in a
canoe accident. So George bought the whole point from the school
and had the trail along the lake—really not much more than a cow
path at the time—improved up to right about there, where the
driveway begins. Later the state widened the carriage road for auto-
mobiles all the way around the lake."

"My grandfather paid for the original road, so he had it curve inland just before the point," Perry said. "When it eventually was extended, it curved back alongside the lake about a quarter mile past our
property. That's why Lakeside is one of the only houses that has any
considerable amount of acreage right on the lake. The other cabins and
houses were all built across the street from the lake. Now you can't
build anything on the lake. The few areas that haven't been developed
are protected by the wetlands commission or are part of the state
forest."

"Yep," Sally said. "The Whitman estate once consisted of thirty
acres, most of Point Bliss, or if you prefer, Whitman's Point, and the

land leading up to it. Over the years, as property taxes rose, the property was pared down to just over eight acres, just the point itself. The rest was deeded over to the town's land trust."

"That's the old carriage house, Laurel," Spin said, moving on. He explained that Everett's parents had moved into it during the 1960s, that they retired to Florida a few years ago. "Everett stayed on here. It doesn't look like he's home now. We grew up with him; he's like the third brother."

"I wouldn't go that far," said Perry. "We hung out with him when we were kids because there was nobody else to hang out with."

"He's the closest friend I have," said Spin. His loyalty to Everett made me want to tackle him to the ground and smother him with kisses and tickles, just like we used to do to him when he was little.

Sally explained to Laurel that there had once been a stable attached to the carriage house and that was why it was a little distance from the main house and situated so much closer to the road. She then led the way down the sloping lawn behind the main house to the boathouse.

"Downstairs is mostly water. You can motor or paddle a boat right into the place and tie it up in the little bay down there," Sally said.

"We used to have a great old motorboat—a Chris Craft—but the boat died sometime in the eighties," Perry said. "It was a real classic, that boat. All wood."

The boat was before our time. Sally and I smiled politely.

"It was named *Marissa*," Perry explained. "After our mother."

Perry and Catherine didn't stay long; they had plans that night in the Hamptons, so they just sat down for a quick iced tea and a chat on the porch once Joan arrived home. Spin and I played with Jake and Emma. Though we don't see them often, I always pay a lot of attention to Perry's kids. Jake was almost three at the time and Emma

was six. My blog kids are about the same age, and I like to observe
Jake's and Emma's behavior so that I can write more accurately about
children that age. But also, I love children, and for all that we
like to carry on about their fancy house and their hired help, Perry
and Catherine must be good parents, because their kids are so smart
and sweet.

Spin was helping Emma stand up on a paddleboard in the lake and
I was chasing Jake around on the lawn next to the porch when I heard
the conversation turn to the wedding plans.

"Have you and Spin set a date yet, dear?" Joan asked Laurel.

"Yes, August twenty-second. We're going to Paris for our honey-
moon, and that way we'll have a couple of weeks before the school
year starts," said Laurel.

"We have friends who run a very boutique-y holiday villa and flat
rental business in Europe and we've arranged for them to stay in the
most charming apartment right in Montmartre," said Catherine.

"I'm so excited," said Laurel.

"Have you been to Paris before?" Joan asked.

"No, never. I've been to France, but I was in the Alps, skiing. I've
always wanted to go. I can't wait."

Perry was anxious to get on the road; the kids get cranky when
they're stuck in traffic. We saw them off, and after Spin and Laurel
unpacked their stuff in Spin's room, they came downstairs and joined
Sally and me in the music room. Sally was working on her piece. I
was listening to it and thinking about little Jake and Emma and
things they had said that I could use in my blog.

"Oh good, Spin, I need your help," Sally said when they walked
in. "This is what I was telling you about, this is where I need you."

"Okay. What is it?" he asked. "Let's hear what you have."

Sally tucked her violin under her chin and played the basic melody. It really was such a pretty song, sort of haunting and sad, though.
Spin was intrigued. He sat at the piano and played a few chords.

"Wait," Sally said. "Go back, go back. What was that minor
chord? That was it."

Spin played the chord again. Sally wove a new line through the chord, and then Spin followed with another clever chord change. Now they were in it, playing the phrase over and over. Suddenly, Spin pulled his hands away from the keys and said, "This isn't fair to Laurel. It's so boring. We can do this later."

"No, babe," Laurel said. "You guys play. I want to check things out. I still feel like I could get lost in this place. Charlotte, can you show me around the house?"

"Sure," I said. I followed her out of the room.

"I think you've seen most of the house—that was the music room we were just in. It used to be called the sunroom when Whit was little. His sister and cousins used to call it the conservatory. It was more of a greenhouse then, with lots more plants. Whit's grandmother was really into flowers."

"I love all the windows, but it must get awfully hot in there in the summer."

"Oh, it does," I said. "We rarely go in during the summer—at least not in the daytime. But it's really beautiful in the winter. You'll see. Spin spends Christmas Eve here with us. He always has, so I hope you'll both keep doing that. We put the Christmas tree in the music room, and it's beautiful with all the windows. You can see the snow falling all around you. It feels like you're outside, but you're nice and warm. And the frozen lake, well, you'll see, it's nice. This is the living room; we don't spend a lot of time in here."

We paused for a moment and she looked at the enormous fireplace and all the old overstuffed upholstered furniture. I motioned for her to follow me.

"So here, we're back in the main hallway."

We walked through the wide hall and into the family room on the other side.

"The TV's in here," I said, pointing to the small TV that sat on an old wooden trunk. "We only have basic cable; I hope you're not into any regular series on HBO or anything like that. Joan will only pay for basic. I watch everything on my computer."

"I do, too. I don't really watch much TV," said Laurel.

She wandered over to the bookshelves that run from floor to ceiling on the long interior wall. The shelves hold hundreds of books, many of which are rare first-edition volumes of great classics. Joan's uncle Hunt, Hunter Garrison, once owned one of the largest collections of rare books in the United States. Joan had been his favorite among his nieces and nephews. He was gay, childless, and had left her a large part of his collection in his will. The rest are at the Smithsonian Institution. The books should be in a climate-controlled vault someplace, but instead, they sit on our shelves, and each year the humid summers and dry, heated winters take their toll.

"These are Joan's books. I'm not sure if Spin's mentioned them," I said to Laurel, giving her the quick history of the collection, but she was looking at the framed photographs that sat on a table next to the shelves.

"Is this Spin and Perry?" she asked. She had picked up a photo of Spin, Perry, and Everett when they were all boys. Everett and Perry were teenagers, and Spin was about six or seven. They all were in a midair leap from the dock. It's a great shot. Freckles, grins, messy boy hair, and everywhere, long, exuberant arms and legs. Whit always loved taking photos of us jumping from the rope swing or the dock. "Who's the third kid?"

"That's Everett," I said.

She moved on to another photo, a beautiful black-and-white picture of my mother. Joan was wearing a sleeveless summer dress. She was out on the lawn and she was bent over, helping baby Spin try to walk. He was wearing nothing but a diaper and he was between her bare legs, holding onto her fingers for support. They were both barefoot in the long grass, both laughing up at the camera.

"Oh, look how pretty your mom was. Is that when you were a baby?" Laurel asked.

"No, that's Spin."

"It must have been strange for your mom to have a stepson who was born, well, so close to when she married his dad," Laurel mused.

"I guess it was, I don't really remember. They used to come up here with a nanny, I do remember that. Marissa wanted the nanny to take care of Spin when he was here with us. I guess she didn't really trust my mom and Whit to take care of him. But my mom loved Spin like her own baby. She just doted on him."

"Why does everybody call him Spin?" Laurel asked.

"Perry says he was the one who first called him that. Sally says it was me and her. We were small. It's hard to remember."

Laurel was really studying the picture. She turned it a little, as if she were trying to catch my mother's expression from another angle. I saw the corners of her lips turn up ever so slightly. It was almost as if she were looking in a mirror, trying to match my mother's smile.

"Apparently, everybody just called him 'the baby' for almost his entire first year. The name Philip was a touchy subject between his parents," I said.

I found a framed photo of Spin as an infant, smiling toothlessly at the camera. "He was so cute. . . . Sally and I treated him like a little doll. Like a pet, really. When he started walking, he loved us to spin him around and then we'd crack up when he staggered away from us like a little drunk. He'd always want to do it again. 'Spin,' he'd say. 'Spin.' So we started calling him that—at least that's how we remember it."

"That's sweet," said Laurel, but she was still staring at the photograph of my mom and Spin. I got the feeling that she hadn't been listening that closely.

"I think Spin was the son my mom always wanted," I said, removing a pile of old newspapers that had been stacked next to the fireplace last winter. The pages were yellow now. "Joan grew up with boys. She had two brothers and she lived on the Holden campus, which was all boys at the time. I think she really didn't know how to deal with Sally and me. She would have been more comfortable with sons."

"Well, I think she did okay," said Laurel, and just when I was about to thank her for the compliment, she said, "I mean, it's not like you and Sally are the girliest girls, anyway. Is this Spin's dad? I've only seen pictures of him when he was older."

She was holding my favorite photo of Whit. Sally took it with a Polaroid sometime in the early nineties, so it's not a very large print, but my mom set it into a larger frame. He's standing in the door of his banjo shed, a coffee cup in hand. He's winking into the camera, winking at Sally with that great smile.

"Here's another one of Spin," I said. I wanted her to put down the photo of Whit. I didn't like her touching it. "This is great, Laurel; my mom was teaching Spin how to do a back dive off the dock."

She was still staring at the picture of Whit.

"It's really hard to do a back dive without a diving board," I continued, moving the picture closer to Laurel, "but Joan taught Spin to do it. You have to really spring off your feet, see? Sally and I always landed flat on our backs."

Laurel placed Whit's photo back on the shelf, but she kept staring at it. Finally, she turned her attention to the diving photo. It was such a lucky shot. Whit had managed to catch Joan and Spin at just the right moment, when they were both in mid-arc, my mom in her Speedo one-piece, her sleek athlete's torso just a few inches higher than Spin's. Their arms were stretched over their heads, their fingertips about to hit the lake. My mom still looked like a girl in that shot. Spin was just starting to show the muscles of a man. I handed the photo to Laurel and she glanced at it, smiled, and then turned her attention back to the small photo of Whit.

"Through here is a little pantry and then we're back in the kitchen," I said. I walked out of the room and she followed behind me.

In the kitchen, Joan was bustling about, making dinner preparations. She had made a bunch of hamburger patties, which were piled onto a plate on the counter.

"Lottie, I went out to start the grill and couldn't find it. Laurel, we grill here almost every night in the summer, but we haven't used that grill once this year. I have no idea where Everett put it last fall. Lottie, go ask him where it is."

"He's not home," I replied.

"Well, it has to be someplace. Look behind Whit's shed," she said.

I was happy to leave Laurel. I'm not used to small talk, not used to having to entertain others. It's exhausting. I was walking across the lawn to look in Whit's shed when Everett pulled up in front of his house. He gave a little honk, but I didn't wave, I just went into the shed. A moment later, Everett followed me inside.

"How's Sally?" he asked.

"She's better. Joan drugged her and she slept from yesterday morning until today, almost straight through."

"Joan drugged her? What do you mean?"

"She shot her with a tranquilizer gun. What do you think?" I said. I started to walk away, but Everett grabbed my arm.

"What're you so pissy about?"

"Nothing," I said.

Everett had left the night before and stayed out all night. I kept waking up, listening for Sally, so I noticed that his truck wasn't in the driveway. I don't mention stuff like this anymore. Everett once talked about moving somewhere else because he wants to be able to have a life without my knowing everything he does. I don't want him to move. But last night I heard him drive off. I knew he was at the Pale Horse, and I thought I'd wander over when he got home.

"Laurel and Spin are staying here for two weeks," I said. "Joan invited them without telling us, so I'm, you know, not that pleased."

"Oh," Everett said.

"Yeah, I have to go inside. Can you get the grill?" I tried to push past him, but he grabbed my hand.

"Babe, what's wrong?" he said. "Look at me. What's the matter?"

I was tearing up. I had turned my face away, but he wouldn't let go.

"What is it?" he asked again.

"I'm just not used to having company in the house. I don't know Laurel. And I'm worried about Sally. . . ."

Everett pulled me close and gave me a hug. I pressed my face against his chest and put my arms around him for a moment, held him so tight, just for a moment, then I pulled away and walked out of the shed and toward the house.

Everett always thought Whit never knew about what went on between the two of us. He imagined that Whit would have been enraged, that he would have fired him and thrown him out of his house if he knew. But Whit did know. One morning, the summer after we first started hooking up, Whit had woken up early and saw a young woman leaving Everett's house. He had chuckled to himself, he later told me. He couldn't see who it was through the lake mist, in that silvery predawn light, but it wasn't the first time he'd seen one of Everett's girlfriends coming or going. He was, therefore, very surprised a moment later when I tumbled in through the dog door and landed at his feet.

"Charlotte!" he said after a moment. "Where the hell are you coming from?"

"Um—"

"Did I just see you leave Everett's?"

"No," I said. "Well, it's not what you think. I was just out walking. I just stopped at his house to say hi."

Whit looked puzzled. I replayed the moment obsessively in my mind all morning, wondering if he was angry or disappointed in me. Ultimately, I realized that he had just seemed to be surprised. He had looked at me, then he'd ducked to look through the window at Everett's. Finally, he'd shrugged.

"I need a coffee," he had said. That was it.

That afternoon, I was walking down to the beach for a swim when he called me over to the shed. He was holding a banjo.

"Here, I want to see how it sounds. I'm sending it to a guy up in Northern California."

I took the banjo from him and sat on the bench outside the shed. I plucked at a few strings, listening carefully.

"It's in tune. Just play something," Whit said. So I played one of his favorite songs. It was an old folk song he had taught me when I was little, and I embellished it with some crazy licks during the chorus. He sang along. It was impossible for Whit not to sing to a tune.

Wake up, wake up darling Corey
What makes you sleep so sound
The revenue officers are coming
They're gonna tear your still house down

Whit was belting it out by the final verse, and I ended with a few good fast strums.

"Sounds pretty sweet," I said. I turned the banjo over and saw the inlaid mahogany that surrounded the drum and the graceful curve of the neck. "It's beautiful, Whit."

Whit smiled when I handed it to him. He looked it over with pride.

"I think it's the best I've ever made," he said. "It's the closest I'll ever come to making art, this banjo."

"That's what you say about every banjo you make."

"This is it, though, this one's the best."

From Everett's house came the sound of his truck starting. We watched as he backed out of his driveway and then drove off. Everett gave us a little honk as he passed, and I waved.

"The thing you haven't considered," Whit said, gently tightening one of the strings, "is what'll happen when it's over between you two. Nothing can ever come of this thing. You're never going to stay here in Harwich, and he's not likely to leave."

"Yeah, well, so what? We're just having fun," I said.

"You're setting yourself up for some awkward times ahead, once one of you starts dating somebody else. That's all. It's just too close to home. It puts Everett in a compromising situation. I'd hate to think that he'd have to move from here because of any fallout from this."

I remember thinking the words I wished he had said. I remember thinking, And you're just a kid. And I care about what happens to you. I want what's best for you. Those were the things a father would say. But Whit wasn't my father. Whit was worried about Everett.

"You're like your mom. You're a free spirit, you'll never stay here," Whit said dreamily. "This town was always too small for her."

"Funny how she still lives here," I said.

Joan was absent from Harwich for almost a decade after she graduated from Holden, and in Whit's mind, this departure was just another shining example of her joyous devil-may-care attitude, which he so admired.

The summer after her second year at Princeton, Joan took a job as a nanny with a family in New York City. She didn't return to Princeton in the fall, nor did she return to Harwich. She told her parents that she had asked for a leave of absence from school, then sort of disappeared into the East Village, where she was spotted, very infrequently, by some of her old Holden friends, who would report back to her anxious parents. She was fine, they told my grandparents; she was planning to call. The year passed and Joanie didn't go back to school. She never went back. She did come out to Harwich from time to time, and her mother worried about how thin she had become. She was jittery. She was a chain smoker. Often, the reason she came home was to ask for money. She was modeling those first couple of years. She told her parents that she might start acting. She was seeing this guy. He was studying at the Actors Studio. A few years later, she returned to Harwich with a haircut like Debbie Harry's. She was so thin and pale. She didn't tell her parents much about her life in the city or the husband that she never brought home (our father, the actor), but she would entertain some of her old friends with stories of her previous exploits. She had been a regular at Studio 54; she had partied with Mick and Bianca. She had slept with Warren Beatty. Now she had Sally on her hip and was pregnant with me. Within a year, her hair had grown out, her deviated septum had almost fully healed, and she was sprinting across the tennis court in her old Holden whites. It's hard now for anyone to imagine she ever left Harwich at all.

TWELVE

Ever since we were children, whether we dined outside or in, each of us has always sat at the same place at the table. Joan had her end; Whit had his spot at the other end of the table, which now is occupied only when we have guests. I used to sit next to Whit. Spin sat next to Joan. Everett, who ate many meals with us while growing up, also had "his" chair, which was across from mine. I'm only telling this now because on Laurel and Spin's first night here, there was an awkward moment when we all sat down to eat at the porch table.

Spin held Joan's chair out for her and then Laurel moved to the seat on the other side of Spin. This was Sally's seat. I know—Sally and I are no longer children. We should have been able to cope with this, and, of course, we did after a few moments of watching Sally walk around the table, muttering about having no place to sit. There were several empty chairs, of course, but Sally had that jaded, faraway look she gets when she's been working on music too intensely for too long. It's hard for her to snap out of her work sometimes.

"Sal," Everett said during her second lap around us. "Sit here, next to me." Sally plopped into the chair he had pushed out with his foot and she stared sullenly at Laurel.

Joan launched into her plans for the Fourth of July barbecue. We have it every year. The town puts on a great fireworks display here on the lake, and we invite the same crowd that would come when Whit was alive: friends from the club, some of our old friends from school, various Holden classmates of Spin's and Perry's. The fireworks are set off right here on the end of Whitman's Point, so the town's volunteer firefighters and their families join us as well.

"This year, it'll also be an engagement party," Joan said. "Everybody's dying to meet you, Laurel."

"And I'm dying to meet everybody," Laurel said. "You'll have to let me help with the preparations."

"It's totally casual. A kind of a potluck thing. People really come for the fireworks. And the music. All the picking and fiddling crowd will be here—you'll love it," Spin said.

"So you guys are getting married at the end of August?" I asked. I wanted Sally to know that they'd set a date.

"Joan, Perry thinks that the house and the 'grounds,' as he calls them, could look a lot better," said Sally, ignoring me. "Maybe you should think about getting the place fixed up a little before the Fourth. Look, there are leaves all over the place from last year and the weeds are getting so high down near the beach. The place looks like a dump."

"A dump," Joan laughed. "Don't be silly. Do you have any idea what those landscaping guys charge? Anyway, it's fine. It looks the way it always has. We'll rake the leaves; I hadn't even noticed them."

"Didn't you tell me there is a trust or something that covers those types of expenses, Philip?" Laurel asked. "Would that come out of your own trust fund or what, babe?"

She took a bite from her burger and looked first at Spin and then around the table as we all silently grappled with our alarm and confusion.

"Could you pass the butter, please, Spin dear," my mother said finally.

While we were growing up, we never heard Whit or Joan talk about money, unless it was about how not to spend it. The topic was as mysterious as sex to us when we were children. We knew that people liked it, that they craved it. But we also knew you weren't supposed to talk about it, that doing so was indecent somehow. The grown-ups in our house really didn't seem to want to touch it with their hands. Of course, now we were able to joke about it with one another—me, Sally, and Spin; we could laugh at our parents' bizarre relationship to money. But Laurel's question had to do with whose money belonged to whom, and I can't speak for the others, but I was dreadfully ashamed. I knew nothing about the various trusts that Whit had left behind. I just knew that Joan was living off the interest of some of it.

"Here you are, Joan," said Spin finally, with a forced laugh. He shoved the butter plate at my mother.

"Mmm, these hamburgers are great," Everett said, and we all dove into our food, mumbling about how delicious the salad was, how tender the corn, how perfectly cooked the burgers! Laurel glanced from one of us to the next, chewing her food slowly, and I thought I caught a little smile, a little show of delight. Joan appeared to be choking on something; her face was very red and she grabbed her water and sipped at it between little coughs.

"We don't need to have anybody come here," Spin said. "The place looks fine. It's got character, as Dad always said. Perry and Catherine are more used to the Hamptons. They like things a little more formal, that's all."

"But this place is looking a little shabby," Sally said. Clearly, she wanted to help Spin. Also, though she had been highly offended by Catherine's *Grey Gardens* remark, she had long wished that Lakeside looked nicer. Why couldn't it better resemble the grand house in the old Whitman photos, with the formal gardens and lovely, uncluttered rooms?

"You don't notice it, Joan," Sally continued, "because you're here all the time. Why not let somebody come and fix the landscaping, for example? You could get a few guys to come in twice a week and mow. Tend to the gardens. Maybe pull out some of those weeds growing up near the beach. If we let them get too long, the wetlands commission won't let us remove them."

Joan looked at Spin and then at Sally. "I don't think we need that. Everett and I can pull those weeds down by the beach. I just hadn't thought about it, but you're right about wetlands. I'm going to pull them out tonight, when it's dark, just to prevent any commotion from the wetlands nuts. I'll pull the weeds."

"No, I'll do it," said Everett. "Hey, Lottie, will you pass the corn? Which weeds are we talking about, now?"

"But the rest of it," Sally said. "How about getting one of the crews that work on some of the neighboring properties? And, well, I think it would be a good idea to have a cleaning person come in once a week. Maybe that woman who works for Ethel. Just to help you with the heavy stuff, you know, washing the floors and the bathrooms."

"No, I don't want any strange person in the house," I said. "I'm happy to do the floors, it's good exercise. The bathrooms, too. And we don't need a landscaping crew. Everett does a lot around here. It might not be that obvious, but he's always mowing and fixing things. There's just a lot to do. I think you're being ungrateful to Everett, Sally."

I passed Everett the corn and he mouthed, "Thanks, babe," and gave me the little dopey smile that he knows I love.

I kicked at Sally under the table, and when she looked up, I shook my head and scowled. What was the matter with her? Strangers coming in to clean. It was bad enough having Laurel here.

"I don't want people wandering all around the place," Joan said definitively.

When I saw Sally catch Spin's eye and shrug sympathetically, I realized that she had told him she would speak to Joan about the condition of the place.

"You two haven't left yourselves much time for all the wedding preparations," Joan said cheerfully, changing the subject. "Will it be in Ketchum? I've never been to Idaho."

"We're not planning on having a very big wedding," Laurel said.

"Mostly family and close friends," Spin added.

"Right," Laurel said. She was twisting her engagement ring around her finger and biting her lip.

"That sounds lovely," Joan said. There was another awkward silence as Laurel gave Spin a pained look.

They don't know how to tell us we're not invited, I thought. Marissa doesn't want us at the wedding.

"Joan . . . Spin and I were wondering—of course we'll understand completely if this is something you don't want, but—we were wondering if we could have the wedding here. At Lakefront," Laurel said.

"Lakeside," Sally said. "It's called Lakeside."

"Oh, sorry," Laurel said. "Lakeside."

Joan smiled, but her eyes revealed a mounting panic. "A wedding? Here?" she said. "What a lovely idea! But you're right, the place isn't in shape at all. I mean, I don't know how we could possibly get the house in order in such a short time."

"We want to do it all outside, under a tent," Spin said enthusiastically. "A laid-back country wedding. Nobody would even need to go in the house. We'd be down in front of the lake."

"But Laurel, what about your folks? Don't they want to have the wedding there, where you have family?"

Laurel's eyes filled with tears. She looked down at the table.

"Um, well, my family's had some problems. After my sister died, my parents split up. . . ."

Spin reached over and placed his hand on hers.

"Oh no, I'm so sorry, Laurel," Joan said. "I know that's not terribly uncommon after a tragedy like that."

"It's a lot more involved—I won't bore you all with it. I've had to detach from my family in recent years. I had to do this for my own strength and . . ."

I was tearing up at that point, fully ashamed of my own selfishness in not wanting Laurel here. She'd been through so much at such a young age.

"We don't have to talk about this now," Spin said.

"No," Joan said in a thin, strained voice. She's not good with emotions—she doesn't cry, and she gets very confused when others do. She just wants it to stop. "I'd love it if you two had the wedding here. What a lovely idea, Spin, really, but is Marissa okay with this? She hasn't been up here since before you were born. I just would've thought she'd want it in the city someplace, you know, where she has more friends."

"Actually, she's fine with it," Spin said. "I mean, she'd love to help arrange the caterers and everything. The house would be like, you know, just a venue."

"A *venue*?" Joan said.

"No, obviously, it's more than that. I want to do it here because it's my family's home. It's *our* home. But my mom is looking at it like it's just a space—a very scenic space. That's the only way she can be comfortable with it."

"Well, now I see why you're so keen on having the place fixed up," Sally said to Spin. "I actually thought you were trying to help Joan."

"But Sal," Spin said, "I was."

He paused, as if trying to find the right words. "You know, Joan, we do need to maintain Lakeside . . . a little better. We can't let it fall apart."

"It's hardly falling apart, dear," our mother protested.

"I'm going to go down and look at those weeds," said Everett. "I can pull them up now."

"Wait now, Everett. I have my irises coming up there, I don't want you to pull those," Joan said. "Those are transplants from my aunt Sis, so don't start pulling everything out of the ground."

That was the whole problem. Joan really can't stand having anybody change anything; that was why the place looked the way it did.

"I know which are weeds and which are irises," Everett replied, grinning at the rest of us. He grabbed his beer and then started down the slope of the lawn toward the lake. Joan jumped up and followed him.

"Now, Everett, just wait. I'll help you."

We watched Everett break into a little run, and then Joan started to chase him.

"She runs five miles a day, Everett!" Sally called out.

"I have to go out and do some water temps this evening," Spin said. "Why don't you come along, Laurel?"

"That sounds like . . . hell," Laurel said, laughing. "Don't get me wrong. I love looking for algae as much as the next guy, but I have some work to do."

She was a good sport. I liked her more and more. We're uptight. How was she supposed to know that we don't run around hugging people or asking about who pays for what? It must have been hard for her to feel at home with us. People are much more easygoing out west, everybody knows that.

"There'll be a beautiful sunset tonight, Laurel," I said, smiling at her.

"Maybe another night. I have too much writing to catch up on."

"Yes, tell us about your book, Laurel," Sally said. I hoped Laurel hadn't picked up on her sarcastic tone.

"It's a novel," Laurel said.

"What's it about?" Sally asked.

"Oh, it's too boring. Really, if I started describing it, you'd all fall asleep. Charlotte, did I hear you made a pie?"

Joan and Everett couldn't have picked many weeds; they were back before we'd finished clearing the table, and we all enjoyed the pie. It was the peaches that made it so delicious. Joanie had bought them at the farm stand.

When we finished dessert, Everett stood, stretched, yawned dramatically, and then announced that he was tired.

Fuck him.

I wasn't going to go over later; he didn't need to hint that I shouldn't. Out all night the night before. I wasn't going over to his house. Everybody said good night to him, but I couldn't, I was carrying all the dessert dishes back into the kitchen.

THIRTEEN

S he's not at all like I thought she was going to be," said Joan the next morning. She and Sally and I were having coffee on the porch. Laurel had gone out sailing with Spin. "I think she's very sweet."

"She's nosy," said Sally. "She wants to know everything about us, but I ask her one thing about her book, and it's like it's classified information. Nobody's allowed to know. Her life is top secret."

"I didn't get that from her," I said. "It's boring to describe your writing to others; she just didn't want to bore us."

"I hate when people talk about anything they write," Joan said. "It's like when people tell others about dreams they've had. There's nothing more boring. I consider it a sign of very good breeding not to talk about yourself all the time."

Sally and I just stared at each other, grinning.

"You did *not* just say that, Joan," I said.

"I wish there was coffee in my mouth so I could spit it out," Sally cried.

"What?" Joan asked. "I don't know what you girls find so funny. When I was at Princeton, I took a creative writing class. My professor told me that I had great promise, but I was so bored having to read everybody else's stuff. . . . What? What on earth is so funny?"

Laurel and Spin returned around lunchtime; Laurel stayed at the house, while Spin headed out with Harry Noyes to inspect the lake further. Sally announced during lunch that she was going into the city for the night. Her roommate had found someone to rent her room, so Sally needed to get the stuff she'd left behind or it would go out with the trash. She said that she was glad to go: It would help her to think about her work while she drove. She was planning to return the next day and promised not to come in through the dog door if she arrived during the night.

"Just wear a gas mask if you do," I said.

"What're you guys talking about?" Laurel asked.

"Oh, the other night—wait, I forgot, Laurel, you're part of this story. You're the one who told us to use hornet spray for protection," said Joan.

"Laurel told you to do that?" Sally asked, and she got that dark look. Sometimes you can almost see the circuits in her brain get crossed, you can almost hear the chaos of sparks and little pop-rock explosions in her temporal lobes or wherever it is that your moods form. "It was Laurel's idea to have you almost blind me?"

"Not you, of course, Sally, don't be absurd," said Joan.

"We were all worked up about Mr. Clean," I said. "Listen, Sal, it's really hot in your room—I was in there earlier looking for a towel. Do you want to move to Perry's old room for the summer? I think you should."

This changing of the subject seemed to work. Sally and I went upstairs to sort out her stuff, and by the time she drove off an hour later, her mood had improved.

I went up to the attic to work on my blog. I heard Joan drive off a few hours later (golf), and I wandered downstairs to the porch. Laurel was there, sitting cross-legged on the floor, her laptop open in front of her.

"Hey," she said.

"Hi. I hope I'm not interrupting your writing."

"No, not at all."

It was a perfect afternoon, no humidity. I thought I might go for a swim later, when it got darker.

"Is Sally moving back in here for good?" Laurel asked.

"She does this occasionally—takes a break from the symphony schedule," I said. "She'll probably just stay for a few weeks, maybe a month."

"Watching you and Sally makes me miss my sister. I can tell how close you two are."

"Oh," I said. "Yes, I know about your accident. I'm so sorry."

"Thanks," Laurel said. "I was closer to her than anybody. We were Irish twins—eleven months apart."

"Oh, that's really close. Sally and I are fourteen months apart. Who was older, you or your sister?"

"I'm the younger one," said Laurel. "Marcie was the superstar of our family. She was the golden child."

"Really? *She* was the golden child? Was she actually in the Olympics, or was she a Rhodes Scholar, or what?" I said, but then immediately added, "Oh, I hope that didn't sound insensitive."

"No, not at all. You're hilarious, Lottie. Sally's the golden child in this family, but I can tell that you're actually the smartest."

I said, laughing, "No, Sally's not the golden child, that would be Spin."

"I think he'd argue that it's Sally. Or maybe that was when he was growing up. Maybe when his dad was alive."

"I don't know," I said. "I think I'll go back inside—let you get back to your work."

"Philip told me that his dad adored Sally. And you, too, of course, but especially Sally."

"He did."

"She was the favorite, according to Philip—I mean Spin," Laurel said.

I had stood up, intending to go back inside, but now I sat back down and turned to face her.

"Whit didn't have favorites." I was trying to hide my sudden anger in his defense. "He wasn't like that. I think he just felt less responsible for how Sally and I turned out."

"Oh," said Laurel.

"I think he was able to let us be who we were. He put more pressure on Perry and Spin."

"Oh, okay," Laurel said, but she said it in a doubting tone. What the fuck had Spin told her?

"I mean, he was really fond of Sally," I admitted. "I never knew Spin picked up on that. Because we all loved Spin the most. He was just the best kid. Always everybody's favorite. I think Whit had a little bit of guilt when it came to him. I can't believe I'm talking about this. I've never really discussed this with anybody."

"Well, let's change the subject," Laurel said. "What's the story with you and Everett?"

Now I was speechless. I leaned over and examined a frayed piece of my sandal, so she couldn't see how red my face was.

"There's not really a story."

Laurel laughed. "Oh, there's a story. Why is it such a big secret that you two are involved?"

"We're not really—involved. Not anymore. It's just sort of an old thing. We used to be together."

"But you've known him all your life, right? That's so romantic," Laurel said.

"It is?"

"Totally. Yes. Have either of you dated other people?"

"Yes, of course. Well, Everett has. Actually, he still does. We're not really in a relationship anymore, not an exclusive relationship. We were. He lived with Sally and me in the city when we were going to school there."

"I knew Sally went to Juilliard, but I didn't know you also went to school in the city. Where'd you go?"

"Columbia. But I didn't really enroll. I just took some courses there."

"You must have done well in high school to have been accepted."

I wasn't sure if she was toying with me here. It seemed likely that Spin would have told her that I barely graduated from high school, since I skipped so often, especially my senior year, when Sally first moved to New York.

"No," I said. "When I say I *took* courses at Columbia, I mean I literally took them."

Laurel was intrigued.

It's no big secret. Spin, Whit, my mom—everybody knew I did it. Actually, they all sort of got a kick out of it. I missed Sally when she went to Juilliard and I was always taking the train down to see her. After my last day of high school, I went to the city and just stayed. Sally had received a full scholarship to Juilliard, but, as I said, I didn't get the best grades. I wanted to be with Sally. So I used some of the hacking skills I'd learned at Holden, and then later on some online forums.

"You'd be surprised how incredibly lax the IT security is at most schools." It was nice to have someone to tell this to, again. Someone to impress. And Laurel was lapping it all up. "In my experience, the most prestigious, most heavily endowed schools are the sloppiest. MIT? The easiest to hack into, from what I've been told. You'd think it'd be the hardest, with all the techies there, but it's not. I have a few online friends who are serious hackers; I'm just a lightweight. I was able to print out college IDs for both Columbia and Barnard, get student registration numbers, the whole deal. I never officially enrolled, of course. The IDs just got me building access and I only took courses that were in large lecture halls, so it's not like I took a seat that somebody else had paid for. These lectures always have empty seats. I know I'm not the only one who did this. You can use the ID to take online courses, too. You can't get credit, though. You have to pay to actually get your grades and a diploma, but you can take all the courses and get the same education."

"That is the coolest thing I've ever heard," said Laurel. "I love a good scam, and that school is so heavily endowed. You must have felt great when you walked through those halls, knowing you hadn't paid a cent, while all those other chumps had taken out loans."

Actually, I used to feel a little guilty, certainly not great, when I thought of the sacrifices others made to attend college. I explained to her again my rationale about the lectures—all the empty seats.

"But you had a student ID. You must have been able to get your-self on a food plan, use the cafeterias."

Now I knew Spin had told her.

"They throw away tons of uneaten food every month at Colum-bia. There was a piece in the *Columbia Spectator* that revealed how much food they waste," I said. "Actually, I wrote it."

Laurel laughed and said, "I love it! You were on the school news-paper?"

"Yeah, I was studying journalism. The piece I wrote about the food wastage was well researched and fact-checked and—stop laughing at me—it was true. So it wasn't really stealing. It was just using food that would have been thrown away."

I was laughing, too, at this point. It's a weak argument, I know.

"You said Everett moved in with you and Sally?"

"Yeah, so we had been together as a couple most of the time that I was in high school, and—"

"He's older than you. Right?"

"A couple of years," I said. I wasn't sure what she was getting at. "He did a semester at UConn and then . . . well, he had to take some time off and he never went back. He was working for a contractor, learning masonry, and he'd come down to the city on weekends. Eventually, he ended up staying there, too. So it was Everett, me, and Sally."

"Did he 'take' courses, too?"

"No, Everett worked as a dog walker. He'd make twenty dollars a dog and he'd often walk five dogs at a time. He got kind of a big cli-entele right away."

"I'll bet he did," Laurel said.

"Yeah, he's great with dogs, and a lot of people have dogs on the Upper West Side, where we were living. Morningside Heights. Upper East Side, too. Those were sort of his territories."

"That's not what I meant," Laurel said. "He's so good-looking and he's got that super-flirty, laid-back thing going for him. That's hot as hell. I bet all the housewives went nuts over him."

"I have to get back to work," I said, standing again. Her words had struck a nerve and I had a feeling that she had meant them to, but she jumped to her feet and reached for my hand.

"Charlotte, I'm sorry. It seems like everything I say is wrong. I meant that as a compliment to you—this is just the way my girlfriends and I talk."

"Okay," I said, pulling my hand from hers to push my hair away from my face.

Laurel continued, "I've known we were going to be friends, you and me, from the minute we met. I mean, I love Sally and your mom and everyone, but I feel we would be friends if we just met at some random party or something, you know? Like, if I never met Spin. Don't you feel that way?"

"Oh," I said. "Yeah."

Truthfully, I hadn't felt that way in the slightest until she said those words. But now that she had suggested that we had a bond that went beyond the obligatory familial one, I felt it, too. I was flattered that she thought of me as a friend. I spent too much time alone, I suddenly realized, and it was nice having a woman besides my mother and Sally to chat with, somebody who saw me and my situation with Everett from a fresh perspective. I felt a little guilty that I hadn't been more pleasant and sociable with her since her arrival. Circumstances had forced her to be plunged into our family with no time to acclimate herself to us. In normal circumstances, someone like Laurel would meet her fiancé's family before moving in with them. She would receive them in small doses—a dinner here, cocktails there. When Aunt Nan used to swim in the lake, she always started by standing,

ankle deep, on the shore for a few moments. She would bend her thick
white knees and splash water onto her thighs and shoulders. Then
she would take a few more steps, stop, and repeat the splashing of
her body before she finally spread her arms wide and let the lake lift
her into her slow, languorous breaststroke.

"I need to get used to the water," she'd explain when we asked her
about this splashing ritual. "It's a shock to the system the way you
girls go running in. You shouldn't let your body experience such a
rapid temperature change."

I realized now that Spin had submerged poor Laurel into our
family without giving her time to get used to us. We can be a little icy.

"I think you're lucky to have each other, you and Everett," Laurel
said.

"Thanks, Laurel," I said. I had to blink to keep the tears back now.

"What's the matter? Sit down," Laurel said. "I'm sorry. Tell me what
the problem is."

"There's no problem. It's, you know, what do they call it? A 'friends
with benefits' situation, that's all," I said.

"Is he in a relationship with anybody else?" Laurel asked.

"No," I said. "Just random hookups. He likes to party, he's pretty
popular."

"It's interesting that he hasn't committed himself to anybody else,
though," said Laurel. "Maybe that's because of his feelings for you?
Or is it because he lives here and it would be too awkward?"

"No," I said, "that's not it." Laurel was my friend; I wanted to open
up to her, so I told her the truth. "Everett is actually in another relationship. It's with a married woman. He doesn't know that I know
about it."

"See! I thought so. Do you know who she is?"

"Yeah," I said, and now I looked off at the lake to see if Spin and
Harry were still in sight. "She's married to a big New York attorney.
They built a weekend house on the other side of the lake. She comes
up during the week sometimes. I guess she's an artist or something.
That's when he sees her. When the husband is in the city."

There they were. Spin and Harry were motoring around the point on the far side of the lake. You could barely see the two of them; the little skiff looked like a toy.

"How did you find out?"

"I'd rather not say."

"Hacked into his phone?"

I didn't say anything,

"Charlotte, you need to change. Everett's not going to change. You need to change."

"I know, I've heard it from everybody. I need to set boundaries. I need to tell him I'm not going to have sex with him anymore unless he's monogamous. I've tried that, and he just ended up getting all sneaky. He hated it. He said he felt like he was married, and he doesn't want to be married, he's too young. This was last summer, actually, and he said he wanted to move out. He didn't like the fact that I could see when he didn't come home at night. So, you know, I stopped making an issue out of it. If he moved, I'd never see him."

"So how do things stand now?"

"Like I said, he pretends that he's just casually dating. But . . . I know he's involved with this woman." It was hard not to tear up when I said this. I was pretty sure Everett was in love with her.

"What's her name?"

"I'd rather not say. Her husband's kind of a big deal."

Laurel stretched out on the porch floor until she was flat on her back and then pulled her knees up to her chest. Then she straightened her legs, pointing her toes up to the ceiling. I wondered if she was going to do a whole yoga routine, but she didn't. She hugged her thighs, then lowered them to the floor and sat back up, her legs crossed in the yoga sitting position. I don't know what it's called, the yoga serenity position or something.

"You can make him yours, you can make him commit to you," Laurel said.

"Indian-style" is what Whit called the position she was sitting in. He used to tell me to sit Indian-style on the floor when he first taught me how to hold a banjo. I always thought Indian-style meant Native American Indians. I assumed that's how Native Americans sat around their campfires. Now I wondered if Indian-style was actually a reference to Indians from India and Hinduism and yoga.

"You're being too passive," Laurel said. She was looking out at the lake. Each foot rested on top of the opposite knee, and her hands were relaxed, palms up, on top of them. I was very impressed with how straight her back was.

"You have such great posture," I said. "I could never sit like that, and I've never had a back injury."

"I didn't sit like this before I broke my neck," Laurel said. "Practicing yoga, learning to straighten my spine, is what helped me recover. You can't just wait to get better after a trauma. You have to work at it. You have to go beyond your comfort zone every day."

I hoped she wasn't going to try to teach me yoga positions, but she just sat staring at the lake as I rocked in the old swing. It was late afternoon, the time of day when the sun angles in under the porch roof and there's no escaping it unless you go inside. We're on the eastern side of the lake, so we get the sunsets, but also the intense late-afternoon rays. There was a nice breeze off the water that afternoon, though, so I just closed my eyes and saw brilliant orbs of gold and white spinning against my eyelids. I heard a motorboat speed by and then the rapid splashing of its wake against our dock.

"Change, go outside your comfort zone," Laurel said quietly.

I heard the dull drone of a bee. I heard the leaves of the dogwood tree rustling in the breeze. Whit planted the sapling when he was a Boy Scout. Now it towers over the porch. When there's a storm, it claws at my window. It produces white flowers in June, every other year. It had burst into full bloom just days before Laurel arrived, and now its branches were laden with white blossoms. When I opened my eyes, the petals were drifting in the air all around us, white as snow.

"It makes me anxious, the idea of his leaving," I said quietly.

"That's a feeling. It's not real. I hate when people let feelings control them. I don't understand it. On the other hand, people seem to enjoy fear; sometimes I wish I had that."

"Haven't you ever had anxiety? Fear?"

Laurel thought for a moment. "I guess when my sister and I had the accident. I was afraid then. I thought I might die. But I don't understand why people fear random things."

"I guess that's what made you such a good skier. Learning not to be afraid of getting hurt."

"I never learned it, I was just never afraid of getting hurt. I don't pay attention to feelings. I don't really believe in them. To me, feelings are like ghosts. Nobody's ever been killed by a ghost. Nobody's ever photographed one. But people fear them. I think people like to be afraid. In fact, I know they do. Isn't that funny?"

I felt the blood pulsing against my eardrums.

"He's not going to change, Lottie. He needs to be scared, that's all. You just need to scare him a little. Like I said, most people enjoy danger. It's a turn-on. You can use that."

Laurel's hands still rested on her knees. She sat straight, tall, and perfectly at ease.

FOURTEEN

Joan was having dinner at the club. Spin and Laurel were heading off to the Pale Horse Tavern.

"Why don't you come along, Charlotte?" Laurel asked.

"No," I said. "I'm pretty tired."

"Lottie doesn't go out much," Spin said. "When's the last time you went out for a meal? Huh, Lottie? Two thousand and ten?"

"*No,* it wasn't that long ago," I said.

"Well, come with us," he said, and he crouched down and grinned at me. I knew what was coming and screamed with laughter. I turned to run, but he tackled me the way he used to when he was in high school, driving his shoulder into me like a linebacker. Laurel gave us an indulgent smile as he lifted me onto his shoulders and pretended he was carrying me out of the house.

"Jesus Christ, Spin," I cried out. "Put me down." I was weak with laughter. Finally, Spin put my feet back on the floor and I swatted him playfully around his head. Then I followed them out to the porch and waved them off.

It was after six on a Monday and Everett wasn't home. I wondered if Lisa Cranshaw had stayed at the lake for the week.

I was supposed to write a listicle for BuzzFeed. They wanted a few for the twelve-to-sixteen-year-old female consumer, so I took my laptop down to the kitchen and wrote "23 Beauty Hacks for Hot Summer Days." I just rehashed stuff I had written multiple times. ("Use waterproof mascara on the tip of an eye pencil for waterproof eyeliner! Get 'beachy' hair by mixing table salt with water and spraying the solution on your hair while still wet!")

Then I cruised the Web for images of kittens and puppies and came up with "These 12 Kitties Are Having a Really, Really Bad Day." The kittens all looked adorably forlorn. There seems to be a breed with very small ears and sad faces. They're great click bait, very appealing to the female teen. Well, everybody, actually. I had just sent those off when somebody knocked on the screen door. The door is right next to the table, but I had my back to it and I jumped out of my chair. Really, people don't just stop by very often.

It was the trooper.

"Oh," I said. "Sorry, I wasn't expecting anybody."

"No, no, I'm sorry if I startled you," he said. He just stood there on the other side of the screen, smiling.

"It's Washington, right?" I asked.

"That's right. Good memory," he said.

I opened the door and stepped out onto the porch. "Easy name to remember, because, you know . . . I remembered that it was Washington."

"I'm actually looking for Everett," he said. "He wasn't home."

"Yeah, I don't know where he is. Do you want to leave him a note?"

"Oh, I just have a situation over at my uncle's."

"Yeah, right. You're staying at Ramón's," I said.

"He took my aunt and cousins to a wedding yesterday in New Jersey. They're staying down there for a few days. It's right there on the shore, really nice. Anyway, last night . . . It's okay. I can come back later, when Everett's here."

"No, please. Go on." I was curious.

"Well, last night a bat came in the house and tried to attack me."

"It tried to attack you?" We have brown bats in this area. They eat a lot of mosquitoes, but they don't typically attack anyone.

"I have this thing. I'm fine with anything. You know, throw anything my way and I can deal with it. Except bats. They . . . I'm . . . I don't like them."

I was trying not to laugh. "Are you afraid of bats?"

"No, not generally, no. I mean, I don't mind if they're flying around outside, but this one came in the house. It came after me, I swear. That's why I look a little rough. I slept in my car last night."

"Can't you call one of your trooper friends?" I asked.

"I don't have any friends up here. These guys aren't thrilled that they sent me up here from Bridgeport—kind of an old boys' setup here."

"Do you have a tennis racket?" I asked.

"No, I don't play. I've always wanted to take it up, though. Why? Are you looking for somebody to play tennis with?"

Now I laughed. "I can't believe you grew up here and don't know the first thing about bats."

"I didn't grow up here, I just lived here during high school. My mom sent me to her brother's because the schools are better up here."

"Come in," I said. "You need a tennis racket."

I grabbed one of Joan's tennis rackets from the front closet and handed it to him.

"Yeah, okay, so what do I do? I swing at it? Do I serve? Is it like what Serena Williams does or what?"

"That does it," I said. "I'm coming with you. I'm afraid you're going to kill the poor bat."

And then I did this remarkable thing. I followed him right out to the car and climbed into the passenger seat, as if I get in cars with people I don't know every day. Washington Fuentes got in and started up the car, and off we went, right down the driveway, right past the massive stone pillars where the iron gates used to be.

I've thought about this a lot. This is what I think happened that night.

Everett trains some dogs at their homes, but the real problem dogs spend a few weeks with him here. Everett says living with the dogs helps him sort out what's really wrong with them. A couple of years ago, he took in a slightly neurotic Great Dane. I was at his house when the owner of the dog came to pick him up. This woman was a sort of nervous soccer-mom type. When she stood on Everett's front steps, the dogs all barked with excitement.

Everett told the dogs to shush and they all piped down. Then he invited the woman inside.

"Blue, come," Everett said, and the giant Great Dane trotted across the kitchen floor.

"Oh my GOD! BLUE!" The woman shrieked and the dog jumped up on her and would have knocked her over with his massive paws if Everett hadn't blocked the dog and made him sit.

"It's important to know how to curb the dog's enthusiasm," Everett explained. "You need to lower your energy level, and he'll lower his."

"I'm just so shocked at his transformation!" said the woman.

"I haven't even shown you what he's learned," Everett said.

"But the floor. The tiles! He would never walk across a tile floor before, or any hard, shiny surface. He was petrified. He always was phobic about hard floors."

"Oh." Everett shrugged. "Didn't know that."

"But how did you get him over his fear?"

"I didn't know he was afraid, so I guess I didn't reinforce anything and he just forgot he was afraid. You must have been reinforcing his anxiety."

"I don't think I was."

"You wouldn't notice, but your dog did. I expect dogs not to be afraid of floors. I've actually never known a dog to be afraid of floors, so I guess he picked that up from me."

I think that's what happened that evening when I drove off with

Washington Fuentes. I really don't leave the property very often. Joan, Sally, Spin, and Everett are all aware of this, and though we've never discussed it, they're very careful with me when there is talk of going anyplace. "If you're up to it," they'll say. "There'll hardly be anybody there." Maybe they were reinforcing my fears? I've had anxiety attacks that they've all been witness to. I sometimes need to get home in a hurry, and in the past year or so, I've found it easier just to stay home.

So maybe it was the fact that Washington didn't know any of this. Maybe it was the conversation with Laurel. Feelings aren't real. They're like ghosts. I reminded myself of this when our house was no longer in sight. When Fuentes drove up East Shore Drive, cheerfully commenting on how scenic it was, I found myself agreeing with him. I pointed out landmarks—the inlet where Chief Marinac had once lived; Mine Hill Road, which leads up to the old iron mines; the old inn on the left, which is now a house.

Soon we were on Railroad Street. The old Connecticut Valley Railroad track runs alongside this road, and we followed it into Harwich Center, which used to be a train depot. The railroad stopped service to this area in the early 1950s, and the old train station is now an antiques shop. The railroad bed is used by hikers and equestrians. You can follow it for miles, all the way up into the Berkshires. Right after the depot, the railroad bed curves away from the road. If you follow the trail into the woods a short distance, you'll come to a tunnel that was blasted into the hill over a hundred years ago. Go through the tunnel and you'll come out just behind the Holden campus. It's a shortcut Sally and I often took when we snuck onto campus in our teens.

"So I have no idea how it got in," Fuentes said.

"Are any of the windows missing screens?" I asked. My heart was racing but I tried to keep my voice calm. I was thinking about Sally and the tunnel.

The way to the tunnel is dark at night. You have to take an abandoned service road to get there. You have to park on the road and walk a short path to get up to the tunnel. I've only gone there once at night in a car. It was in Everett's truck. He had left the headlights on to light our way, but the path swerved out of their glare, and I held on to Everett's belt as we scampered up the little incline to the railroad bed. We were both out of breath as we ran, stumbling, up over the frozen bank, over the slippery rocks. Long, stiff, winter-dead weeds stabbed at my hands when I tripped and fell. Everett helped me back up.

"No, and all the doors were closed," Fuentes said.

The old railroad bed is lined with stone dust. We really started running when we got there, Everett and me. Our eyes were adjusting to the dark, but we ran toward a towering black hole that cut into the night sky. I remember the way the air changed when we stepped inside the tunnel. There was a sudden stillness. Everett called Sally's name and the echo of his voice gave us comfort. The tunnel was empty; there was nothing but hard ledge bouncing Everett's voice from one end to the other. When it stopped, I heard the slow drip of water on stone. Then the moaning.

"Hey," Fuentes said. "I know I look a little rough, but do you wanna grab something to eat or something?"

I liked that Fuentes assumed that I did stuff like that—going to restaurants.

"Thanks, I already ate," I said.

We drove past a woman pushing one of those jogging strollers. We passed old Norm Hungerford's house—Whit's old friend Norm—and I saw him out on his lawn, filling a bird feeder with birdseed. My breathing eased up a little.

"I don't understand. You slept in your car because of a bat? I mean, you're not supposed to kill them, but I guess you could have if you were so scared."

"I would have if it wasn't dive-bombing my head. I would have shot it if it had landed someplace, but it was flying all over the place. Scary as hell."

"Shot it?" I laughed.

"I know. There's no way. All I have is a pistol, and I'm not the best shot. But I would have shot *at* it, you know, just to let it know I meant business. Just to scare it away."

"They're not like bears—you don't scare them away with gunshots. You need a tennis racket, that's all. You just have to sort of guide it out. Or you can throw a towel over it if it lands on a wall, then carry it out. I can't believe that scared you. You're a member of the Major Crime Unit?"

"I'm not afraid of people. But . . ." He shuddered. "Bats. I just have a thing, okay? I have a thing with bats. I don't mind mice or rats. But bats? No."

"What is it specifically, though?" I said. I couldn't help teasing him. I loved that this very macho trooper was afraid of a little bat. "Is it just because they're like rodents that fly? Little beady-eyed rodents. That fly?"

"Okay, okay," he said. "Stop."

"And they have little faces that are sort of half pig, half human?"

"Stop it," he said.

"They're ugly but harmless. They eat mosquitoes," I said. "I actually love them."

"Let's see how much you love them when one bites you in the neck and starts sucking your blood."

"Are you in a *Twilight* fan club or something? You just need a tennis racket."

"Then, the next day, you wake up, and you have fangs," he continued. "You're a vampire. Let's see how much you like 'em then."

He was so funny, I was almost sorry when we pulled up to Ramón's house.

"So what if they eat mosquitoes? Why are bats better than mosquitoes?" he asked me as he parked the car.

"They will give you rabies, some bats," I conceded. "That's the only danger. Fear is just a feeling, feelings aren't facts. They're like ghosts. Nobody's ever been killed by one. Have you ever seen a photograph of one?"

I grabbed my mother's tennis racket. Then I taught Trooper Fuentes how to remove a bat.

FIFTEEN

I'm trying to understand," Sally said. She had climbed into my bed very early the following morning. I was annoyed. I turned away and she drove her knees into the backs of mine as she whispered into my ear, "You went to Ramón Hernández's house with that trooper guy? That is the craziest thing I've ever heard. I can't get you to go to the Housatonic Diner with me, but you'll go to the house of somebody you don't even know?"

"I know Ramón Hernández."

"But you said Ramón wasn't there. You were with George Washington Fernandez. You don't know him. What if he'd started interrogating you?"

"Fuentes, not Fernandez. What time is it?"

"Interrogation time!" Sally started tickling me, and I screamed at her to get out of my bed. I'm superticklish.

"Get out, get . . . OUT," I said.

"What if he probed you? What if he . . ." Sally suddenly froze. I took the opportunity to drive my elbow into her boob.

"Ow, fuck. Shhhh, somebody's walking in the hallway."

"It's probably Spin. He has to go back out this morning with the task force. Poor Laurel."

"Poor Laurel," Sally scolded. "Why would you feel sorry for her?"

"I like her, Sally. It's just bad timing that Spin's so busy this week."

"Please," Sally said, rolling over onto her back and staring at the ceiling. "I wish everybody would get up. I figured something out for that score, but I need the piano, and I know Joan'll get upset if I start playing too early."

"What time is it?"

"It's got to be almost seven. I left the city around four, I think. It was still dark."

"Did you sleep, Sally?"

"I'm not tired, and I also don't want you to keep asking me about my sleeping habits, I'm not a—"

She stopped abruptly. I turned and saw that my bedroom door was open a little. Laurel was peering into the room.

"Morning!" Laurel said.

"Hey, Laurel," I said. "I hope we didn't wake you up."

"No, not at all, I get up early to write. That's when I do my best writing. I heard you two in here. Can I come in?"

"Sure," I said.

"Yeah, come on in," Sally said.

There are two beds in my room and a chair at the desk, but Laurel came over and sat on my bed with Sally and me.

"Oh, okay, why don't you sit on the bed with us?" Sally mumbled. "Because there's no place else to sit. . . ."

"I heard you went out on a little date last night, Lottie," Laurel said.

"What?" I said.

"A date?" Sally said. "Who told you that? She wasn't on a date. What the hell?"

"We saw Everett when we got home last night," Laurel said, ignoring Sally and squeezing in closer to me.

"You did?"

"Yeah, he came over and had a beer with Spin and me on the beach. He seemed a little . . . unsettled. He wasn't okay with you taking off with that guy, that's for sure."

"I was gone for an hour. I caught a bat for him and he drove me home."

"Everett seemed to think there was more to it. He couldn't understand how you would go off with some guy you don't know."

"I know him now. Anyway, Everett said he played baseball with him. I don't know what everyone is making such a big deal about."

"He was jealous, Charlotte."

"No," I scoffed.

"He said he was a little freaked when he got home and Joan's car was gone and you were gone, too. He said you could have left him a note."

"He expects you to leave him a note?" Sally said. "Does he leave you notes? What the fuck?"

I was annoyed, too. And maybe a little pleased.

"Spin said he was glad that you had gone out and were fine with everything," Laurel said.

I couldn't help but bristle at this. "What do you mean?"

"Oh, Spin told me about your agoraphobia. I had an aunt who had that and she went to a therapist and did cognitive behavioral therapy. It really helped."

Sally had been lying back against a pillow, but now she sat up and glared at Laurel. "What are you even talking about? Who has agoraphobia?"

"I don't have that," I said. "Did Spin say I did?"

Now Laurel looked like she was going to die of embarrassment. She covered her face with her hands and said, "Shit, I did it again."

"Why the hell did he say that? My sister doesn't have anything like that," Sally said.

"Guys," Laurel said. Her voice was trembling. "I'm really sorry. I think I keep coming across as rude. . . ."

Now she was crying, her face still in her hands.

"Wait, no, Laurel, don't cry," Sally said. She gave me a look; I could tell that she felt as bad as I did. Spin did once send me a link to an article about agoraphobia. He was concerned that I might end up like that, I guess. He probably told Laurel that he was concerned. She was going to be his wife; of course they told each other everything.

"Laurel," I said, "it's fine. I am a homebody. Spin probably thinks it's something more than that."

"I keep trying to fit in and everybody thinks I'm horrible."

"*No,*" I said. "Nobody thinks that. Laurel? I have had anxiety about leaving the property recently. But something you said yesterday really helped me."

"Really?" She sniffed.

"Yeah, the thing you said about feelings being like ghosts."

Sally had moved away from Laurel when she first sat down, but now she moved in closer.

"Come on, stop crying," Sally said. "What's all this about ghosts?"

"And I . . . just being with you two . . ." She was sobbing now.

"Oh, Laurel," I said, putting my arms around her.

Sally pushed in closer and said, "Sister sandwich." And Laurel giggled through her tears as we hugged her.

We all spent the next few days absorbed with our various projects.

Laurel liked to write on the porch. She had found a little folding TV table in one of the closets and set it up facing the lake. She worked there during the mornings. I worked, as usual, up in the attic, though I had to move downstairs after lunch because it gets so hot up there.

I had run into a little bit of a dilemma on the blog. LoneStarLiza, a longtime follower, wanted to raise money for Wyatt's upcoming spinal surgery. She wanted to set up an online auction of sorts, and a bunch of my readers got all excited and started making plans about how to set the thing up. These conversations were taking place in the comments section of my posts. They kind of took over the blog. I would write a funny post about a hyperactive tiger mom at the playground, and instead of commenting about that, they'd all carry on with their ideas about how people could donate items to the auction, how people would be able to pay for the items. It was getting out of hand.

I couldn't let them have the auction, of course. What I was doing with my blog was entertainment. I was providing entertaining content for bored moms; it was almost like a TV show—a show about a quirky family that everybody could relate to. And, like a TV show, I was getting paid by sponsors. I wasn't breaking any laws, as far as I knew. But accepting donations for a sick child? A child who's not real? That would be fraud. I never took any law classes at Columbia, but I was pretty sure that would have been illegal. And it was wrong. A lot of my followers have families with struggles of their own. I couldn't let them continue trying to figure out ways to help my family.

At first, I thanked them all for caring, and explained that we didn't need help with medical costs. Our insurance was paying for everything.

But my kind readers persisted. There must be other expenses, they said. What about all the therapies?

I replied that, amazingly, our insurance covered most of that. Then I wrote an entry explaining that their loyalty to the blog was helping out more than anything else they could do. The blog's popularity had been what attracted the sponsors, and the income from that helped with our living expenses. Truthfully, I had a six-figure contract with the diaper company. I didn't reveal that the blog earned that much, of course. I made it sound like it was just a little extra income to defray some of our living expenses.

Sally spent many hours a day in the music room, working on the film score. One afternoon, when I ran into Laurel in the kitchen, she commented on Sally's music.

"She's really persistent," Laurel said. "She keeps playing the same thing over and over."

"Oh?" I said. "I'm so used to hearing music. Whit and Sally always played instruments in the house. Spin, too, when he was here. You'll get used to it. I don't even hear her, to tell you the truth. Is it disturbing your writing?"

"No, not really," Laurel said.

"It'll be much quieter at Perry and Catherine's," I said. Laurel and Spin had one more week with us, then they would be joining Perry's family in the Hamptons. The following weekend was the engagement party.

Now that Joan had committed to having the wedding here, she had lost her enthusiasm for the party.

"It's too much," she said one afternoon when Laurel and Spin had gone sailing. We had convinced her to let Ramón and his crew help spruce up the grounds, and Joan had been harassing them all week. They were overpruning the hedges. They were trampling her fresh mint.

"I think they just want to move some of the mint away from the footpaths. It's gotten a little out of the gardens," I said. We had mint everywhere.

"Everybody'll be sorry when there's no fresh mint for the iced tea," Joan said. We were sitting on the porch, drinking iced tea at the time.

"There's still plenty," I assured her.

"I wish I hadn't let them railroad me into having the wedding here," she griped. "Why wouldn't they have it at Holden? The chapel is so beautiful."

Joan had a point. A lot of people have weddings there. "I think that if you're a member of the faculty, you can have the reception right there on the green," I said. "They can put up a tent there."

"Oh, look, they almost went over."

We could see the sailboat out in the middle of the lake. A gust seemed to have caught them off guard when Spin pulled in the mainsail, and now we could hear their laughter as they scrambled from one side of the boat to the other.

"I guess Laurel wouldn't have sailed, growing up in Idaho."

"No, I guess not," I said.

"I can't imagine what these guys charge," Joan whispered a moment later when one of the men pushed a wheelbarrow past the porch.

"Who cares? You're not paying for it, right?" I said, opening the door just a little. "The trust is paying for it."

"That's not the point," Joan said. "The point is that it's wasteful and Whit wouldn't have liked it. We could do just as good a job."

"No, we couldn't," I said.

"You know, my family once had almost as much wealth as the Whitman family, and it was all frittered away by my great-grandparents, who were very extravagant with just this kind of thing."

"But it wasn't their extravagances that wiped them out," I said. "It was the stock market crash and the Depression, right?"

"Other families survived. The Whitmans thrived."

"But what good is having so much money if you never spend it?" I asked, though I knew the answer.

"Dear, the money in the trust was earned by Whit's great-grandfather, who was an incredibly brave and enterprising man. He made all the money. Whit didn't earn the money, so he didn't feel he had the right to spend it. He lived off his earnings from the banjos and some of the interest from the trusts, of course. But he wanted the interest to keep growing, as it had always grown. And, of course, he would never, ever"—here I said the words with her—"*dream of touching the principal.*"

"Go ahead and laugh," Joan said. "I'm just looking out for Perry's and Spin's children and grandchildren, as Whit would want me to do."

"I don't know what the trusts amount to," I said, though I had an idea, just from Internet research I'd done over the years. "But I think there's plenty available to do some improvements here without touching the principal. Besides, this estate is part of the trust and they might want to sell it someday."

"Perry might, but Spin would never," Joan said.

"Anyway, they have to keep it maintained, or its value will depreciate."

"Well, I have to pay for the engagement party from my allowance, since I'm throwing it."

"So, how much could it cost?" I asked. "I'll help. I've got plenty saved, I've been selling lots of articles."

"No, no, I don't need your money," said Joan, as she always did.

"It's just a barbecue, right?" I said. "Like we used to have when Whit was here. It can't be much."

"You know, I just got my bill from Anson's gas station. Spin never paid me back for the charge that Laurel put on there."

"Joan, seriously? What was it—thirty-five dollars?"

"It was thirty-eight dollars and forty-seven cents," Joan said sadly.

This was too much; I couldn't wait to tell Sally. Now that Whit was gone, Joan was the cheapest person on earth. It was confirmed.

been sort of zoned out, as she so often is when she's writing music, but now she tuned in to what Laurel was saying. "He's on the board, that's all. It's the wetlands commission. There's a group of them. It's just a two-year term. It's just, you know, community service stuff. He's a volunteer. Whit was always involved with this stuff. Joan, too. She's on Planning and Zoning."

"No, I think she's not on the Planning and Zoning Commission right now, Sal," I said. "She's too involved with the soup kitchen and the senior center."

"Whatever, anyway, he enjoys it," said Sally. "I think he just had to wrap up a lot of stuff before you guys go to Scary's."

"Sally," I said.

Laurel laughed and said, "Scary's?"

"I meant Perry's. Did I say Scary? I meant Perry."

Sally and I were both trying to keep straight faces, but Laurel noticed and said, "I get the sense that you guys don't get along so well with Perry."

"I wouldn't say that. We just don't see him and Catherine much anymore," I said.

"Don't lie," said Sally. "We don't really get along with him. We never have. He's always had a big fucking chip on his shoulder. He's always hated us."

"He doesn't hate us, Sally," I said.

"We haven't seen them much this year, which has been nice," said Sally.

"After Whit died," I explained to Laurel, "things got a little bit tense between Perry and Joan. He wanted to have people come in and replace the roof, fix things up. Since the house would someday be his and Spin's, he wanted to make sure it didn't depreciate in value. Sally, that's all it was, and you have always been after Joan to do more maintenance here, so it wasn't just him."

"Why didn't your mom want to do the improvements? Was it the cost?"

SIXTEEN

Spin and Laurel were planning to go to the Hamptons on the fifth of July, to spend a few days with Perry's family. Spin had a lot of things that he had committed to during those two weeks before they left, so we had Laurel to ourselves much of the time. One morning, a few days before the party, Laurel admitted that she was a little surprised by how much he had to do.

"I thought that once school let out for the summer, he'd be on vacation. But he's still spending so much time at the school. And then all this work for the lake and the town."

"They don't really finish all their school stuff till July," I said. "I think there's a June session or something, right? Like a summer school? Spin usually teaches some of the courses for that."

"Well, at least he gets paid for that. I just found out that he doesn't get paid for any of the work he does for the town."

"What do you mean?" I asked. "Spin doesn't work for the town—why would he get paid?"

"I mean the wetlands inspections, for one. Every time somebody wants to put up a shed or put in a driveway, he has to go inspect the site. Why isn't he getting paid for that?"

"No, he doesn't have to inspect every site," Sally explained. She had

"Partially that," I said. "It's just that she's used to things the way they are. She gets anxious when people start moving her stuff around. Plus, Perry and Catherine like the Hamptons—they almost never come here. Joan felt like every time he came here, he was doing an appraisal, trying to figure out how much he'd make the minute she died. Anyway, I think Perry got the hint. He stopped pestering her. That day he was here with Catherine was the first time we've seen him in almost a year."

"Oh, I guess that was when Spin bought him out," said Laurel. "He did say it was last year sometime."

"What?" Sally said. "What do you mean?"

"You know, when Spin paid Perry for his share of the house."

"What house?" I asked.

"Spin bought Perry's share of this house?" Sally said. "When?"

"Oh no, I . . . I thought you all knew. Spin's going to kill me. Please don't tell him I said anything."

"But I want to find out if it's true or not," Sally said.

"Please," Laurel said, "I'm sure I'm wrong, I shouldn't have said anything. Just pretend we never had this conversation. I'm probably mistaken."

"It's fine, don't worry," I said. "We won't say anything to Spin."

We were dying to get Joan alone, but when she came home that afternoon, she and Laurel were suddenly inseparable. They raked the weeds and stones from the beach for the barbecue. They hung up strings of paper lanterns that Laurel and Spin had bought. Because Sally and I were following them around, trying to get Joan's attention, we kept getting shanghaied into helping. We had to bring up the folding chairs and tables from the boathouse and hose off all the cobwebs.

"Lottie, where's the extension cord we use for the outdoor

Christmas lights? Can you run and find it? And Sally, those lights are going to attract mosquitoes. Where did Whit keep the torches? Can you look for them? And I guess we'll need to get some citronella oil."

In the midst of all this, Washington Fuentes had wandered over. Washington was now our friend. At least Joan and I considered him our friend. There hadn't been any more break-ins, but he still stopped by. Washington's a big runner, like Joan, and she told him he could park at our house whenever he wanted to do the lake run. It's seven miles; people like to run it so they know their exact mileage. He always stopped to say hello when he was finished. Joan and I usually invited him to have a drink with us on the porch.

The day we were getting ready for the Fourth of July party, Washington told us that he was heading into the city to spend the holiday with family.

"Oh no," Joan said. "Stay until Saturday. You have to come to our party." We had invited him multiple times, but I think he hadn't really taken us seriously.

"No, it's a family thing, I don't want to intrude," Washington said, his eyes on Sally. She was standing on a nearby chair, wearing cutoff jeans and a tank top, trying to hang a strand of lights from a tree branch.

Men love Sally, they always have. Even beautiful Laurel seemed invisible to men when Sally was around. I had noticed it with all the guys who had been working on the property. I'm almost ashamed to admit how much satisfaction I took in this. I had always thought the reason guys tended not to notice me was because I'm on the shy side and not as pretty as Sally. But Laurel is outgoing and very beautiful, and even she seemed to disappear when Sally was around. Everett is the only guy I've ever known who doesn't seem sexually attracted to Sally. He's always treated her more like a sister.

Sally has a lot of sex—she always has—but she never really has a steady boyfriend. The dynamic that was developing with Washington was typical, and I wanted to help him. I wanted to tell him to ignore her. Sally isn't attracted to men who pursue her; she likes to be the pursuer. When she notices their stares, she's turned off. It was too late for Washington Fuentes. She didn't like him. She didn't like his profession. And now she didn't like that he liked her.

"No, please come," Laurel said to Washington. I think she was flummoxed by the way he ignored her. She clearly wasn't accustomed to it. She took his hand in both of hers and made a sweet, pleading face. "I won't know anybody, either. We can hang out together."

Washington laughed, but he pulled his hand away. Laurel then sort of leaned her shoulder against his and looked up at Sally, who was having a hard time getting the light strand to stay on the branch. Sally was swearing like a pirate and swatting at bugs. She paused for a moment when she saw that we were all grinning up at her.

"WHAT?" she demanded. "I'm being eaten alive up here. A little help?"

Washington stepped over.

"Get down. Let me hang it, I'm taller," he said.

"No, I can do it. Just hold the rest of the lights."

"Get down. I'll hang it. You'll fall," Washington said, playfully grabbing her ankle and pretending he was going to make her fall.

"I've got this. Let—GO!" she said. She was kicking at him now, and laughing despite herself. They ended up in a little bit of a tussle, until she almost tumbled off the chair.

"Okay, careful. I'll hold the lights," Washington said. He turned and gave us a sheepish smile. I felt bad for him. It was hopeless.

"Sure, I guess I can come on the Fourth. What time?" he asked.

An hour later, we finally had Joan to ourselves. Laurel liked taking Whit's old car and driving around, exploring the area, so she had volunteered to go to the hardware store for the citronella oil. She had just pulled out of the driveway when we cornered Joan in the kitchen.

"Is it true?" Sally demanded. "Perry sold his share of the house to Spin?"

"Yes."

"Why? What happened?"

"Spin told me that he was tired of being in the middle of everybody. He loves this house. He knew that Perry would just want to sell it when the time came, so he bought Perry's share in it."

"I'm just so surprised," Sally said. "I don't think that was very smart of Perry. You're probably going to live another thirty years. By that time, who knows what the value of this house will be? Probably triple what it's worth now. And I don't understand how he could sell his interest in something that neither of them owns yet. The house is part of the marital trust—they don't get any of it until you die, right?"

"Actually, no, that's not right," said Joan. "The house is separate from the trust. The boys own it. Or owned it. They inherited it when Whit died. Now Spin owns it."

Whit had died two years before. I couldn't believe we were just hearing this now.

"What are you telling us, Joan?" Sally was concerned. I was, too.

"Whit had an understanding with the boys that I should be allowed to live here as long as I like. But he wanted to make sure it stayed in the Whitman family, so it was kept separate from the part of the trust that allocates my expenses. There were some tax considerations, too. I don't know. Anyway, Perry was hinting that he'd evict me if I didn't consent to having the whole place renovated, and I was just in a state."

"Evict you?" Sally said.

"When was this, Joan? Why didn't you tell us?" I asked.

"I didn't want to worry you. Also, I thought Perry was just being a bully. Fortunately, Spin stepped in and offered to buy Perry's share. They had the place assessed, and Spin gave Perry his half. I don't know what they finally settled on. A few million for the half share, I think. That's what Perry used to build that house on the beach in Southampton. So it worked out great for everybody."

"So now Spin owns Lakeside?" Sally asked.

"Yes."

"Do you pay him anything? Any rent or anything?"

"Of course not. No. Spin doesn't want to live here now. He loves it at Holden. It's boring for him here. The campus faculty have such a great time. When I was growing up, my parents and the other faculty had dinner parties or barbecues three or four nights a week. Spin and his group do that now. He loves it. Plus, he spent most of his money buying Perry's share. If he were to assume ownership—I'm confused, but there's a legal term—he'd have to pay all the expenses. But as long as I'm living here, the expenses for the house come out of the trust. If I were to move, or if I became his tenant and started paying him rent, the expenses would have to come out of his own money. I don't think he makes enough to pay the taxes and the insurance, to be perfectly frank. It's fine. It worked out best for everybody."

"Joan, this is very generous of Spin. He has all his money tied up in a house that he doesn't live in. And you were begrudging him the thirty-five dollars at the gas station?" I said.

"What thirty-five dollars?" Sally asked.

"It was thirty-eight dollars and forty-seven cents," Joan said, sadly.

SEVENTEEN

I had a problem: LoneStarLiza. I had managed to dissuade Liza and the others from holding an online auction to raise money for Wyatt, but they wanted to do *something*. Not just Liza but also Bigboots, Satansplushy, Martinimama, and a few others. They were all SAHMs, like me—Stay At Home Moms. But many of them used to be Work Hard in Office Moms (WHOMs, I called them), and they liked a project. They loved a cause.

The moms had decided to raise money in honor of Wyatt and to donate it to the hospital where he's being treated. Because the privacy of our children is so important to Topher and me, I explained that I couldn't reveal the name of our hospital. But, I offered, Boston Children's Hospital has arguably the foremost research team working on disorders related to myelomeningocele, which is what Wyatt has. It's a rare form of spina bifida. Very rare. I suggested that if they wanted to raise money, they could give it to Boston Children's. Within hours of my posting this, the week before, a GoFundMe account had been set up. The account was called "Team Wyatt." They explained about Wyatt and supplied a link to my blog. By the following day, there was a #TeamWyatt Facebook page and a Twitter account. It drove up my blog traffic, but it was worrying me. People were donating their hard-earned money for a child who is just my blog child. What if somebody found this out?

But, then again, what if they did? Myelomeningocele is real. It's a terrible disorder, a crippling birth defect. The money that my followers were raising would help real children who suffered from this dreadful affliction. They weren't giving it to me. I couldn't really see how this would be a problem, even for the donors, if they were to learn the truth. And, well, how would they ever find out?

While I was considering all this, I got an e-mail from Matt in Australia.

"Any more signs of Mr. Clean?" he asked.

"No, he seems to be taking a break," I told him.

"You might be wrong. He might have been in and out of a few places. Some people don't notice a little tidying up. Anyway, that's not why I'm e-mailing. I'm worried about your blog."

I had never told Matt about my blog.

"What blog?" I replied.

"This LoneStarLiza person is a fraud. She's trying to get you in trouble."

My fingers were shaking as I typed the words, "Are you a hacker or something?"

"Something," he replied.

"Aren't you afraid of getting caught?" I asked him.

"No, it's my job. I work for the government."

"Oh." I sat for a moment and then typed, "Is it the CIA?"

"I don't work for your government," Matt said. "Everything isn't about the United States, you know."

"What government do you work for?"

"Never mind about what I do. You should be worried about this new person commenting on your blog: LoneStarLiza."

"She's not new, she's been commenting for years."

"Check the spelling of the name. Gotta run."

I went back through the comments on the blog. Matt was right. I had a longtime commenter who was LoneStarLisa. LoneStarLiza with a *z* had just started commenting in the past few weeks. Why was she so anxious to raise money for Wyatt? Then it occurred to me that for all I knew, Matt was LoneStarLiza. He likes invading people's spaces. He probably liked messing up my blog and was annoyed that I hadn't figured out it was him. I logged out.

After lunch, I helped the others prepare for the party.

Everett had been more attentive toward me than usual, ever since that night I had gone off with Fuentes. Laurel noticed it, too. We were carrying some collapsible tables up from the boathouse and she said, "He can't take his eyes off you."

Everett was washing out an old livestock watering trough that we fill with ice, beer, and wine at parties. Whit had found the thing years ago at a yard sale.

"He's been watching you all day," she said.

"That's only because I went over there last night," I replied. "He's always all cow-eyed the next day. It only lasts until he decides he's bored and wants to be with, you know—her."

"I don't know," she said. "I think he's different since the other night, when you went off with Fuentes."

"Really?" I looked over at Everett. He had finished hosing the trough and had turned it upside down to dry. He was folding the end of the hose in his hand so that the water would stop, which was when he saw that we were looking at him.

"What?" he asked.

"Nothing," I said.

"Nothing? I'll give you nothing," he said, and he ran at us with the hose.

"NO, EVERETT," I screamed, dropping my end of the table and starting to run. But it was too late. He had unfolded the end of the hose and turned the spray on me and then Laurel.

I was laughing. He had gotten me a little wet. Laurel, however, was entirely soaked. And she wasn't amused.

"What the fuck?" she said angrily. She was holding her arms out and looking down at her soaked jeans and T-shirt.

Everett turned off the hose and said, "Oh, sorry. I guess you shoulda—"

"What?"

"Run?" Everett said. He was trying not to laugh, and I saw that this was further infuriating Laurel. She stomped up the steps and into the house.

Everett came over and said, "What the hell? It's just water."

"Shhh," I said, giggling. "She'll hear you." He started kissing me.

"You're so wet," he said.

"Because you just sprayed me with the hose," I replied, laughing.

"Let's go." He pulled me toward his house and said loudly, for anyone to hear, "Let's put your stuff in my dryer."

"Okay," I replied equally loudly. "You're so kind."

Sometimes, Everett and I had wild sex. Sometimes we had sad sex. We had a lot of sweet, sad sex after Whit died, but lately we had been having fun sex. That day, we had a blast. I pulled off my wet clothes before we even got into the bedroom, and he started doing a Wicked Witch of the West impersonation.

"OOOOOOH, you got me wet. I'm meeeeeltiiiiing."

The dogs were barking at him, alarmed by his strange voice and mannerisms. He chased them out of the room and then leaped onto the bed with me.

We never did put my clothes in the dryer, but I've always got a few things at Everett's, and a while later I found a pair of my shorts and put on one of his T-shirts. Spin had just pulled into the driveway, and I needed to get back to the house to help with the preparations.

"Why was she so upset about getting water on her?" Everett asked, still not able to let it go.

"I think she wears makeup," I said. "Probably didn't want her mascara to run."

"She definitely wears makeup," Everett said. "And her mascara was running."

"Well, so there you go."

"Why wear makeup around here?" Everett said. "I can see when you're going out. Or if you're older."

I knew Lisa Cranshaw was older—ten years older than Everett. I had cyberstalked her—just a little. She probably wore makeup to bed, and this thought pleased me.

"Let's go," I said. "People will be here in a couple of hours."

Laurel and Spin were in the kitchen when I returned to the house. Laurel was sitting on Spin's lap. She was freshly showered and wearing a cute summer dress. He was drinking a beer.

"Hi, Lottie," she said. You'd never have known she had been so angry. "Go get ready, I want to do your hair and makeup tonight."

"What? No, Laurel, it's just a barbecue. We don't get dressed up. I mean, what you're wearing is perfect. I might put on a little dress, but I'm not going to wear makeup."

"Just a little," she said. "I'm really good at it."

"I'm the worst," I said.

"It's because I used to model. I had to learn how to do my hair and makeup when I was starting out," she said.

"You used to model?" I said. "I didn't know that."

"Yeah, I still do, when I have the time."

I was surprised by this, frankly. Laurel is beautiful, but she's tiny. She's shorter than I am, and I'm only five-four. I assumed that she had modeled skiwear or something, but Spin said, "She's with—what's the agency, Laurel-lee?"

"Ford," she said.

"Wow," I said.

"It's boring, just catalog work."

"Just my boring fiancée. The photographer, model, writer . . ."

"Olympic skier," I added.

"*No!*" She giggled. "I did not ski in the Olympics."

"You're lucky, you don't need much," Laurel said as she put the finishing touches on my makeup. She had me facing away from the mirror, so I couldn't see myself.

"There, look," she said finally, and I turned. She had put a lot of makeup around my eyes ("smokey eyes," she called it). Lots of charcoal-colored eyeliner, some beige eye shadow (she called it "champagne beige"), and lots of mascara.

"I feel like a drag queen," I said. "I've never worn this much makeup."

"Look at your eyes, they're so green. I thought they were bluish, but they're really kind of green," said Laurel.

"I think it's too much," I said.

"You're just not used to it, that's all. Go show Sally. See what she thinks."

I did show Sally. Joan, too. They both loved it. Sally even let Laurel give her a little makeover; then we all went down together, Sally, Laurel, Joan, and I.

Just before we went outside, where dozens of people were already gathered, Joan stopped and took Laurel's hand in hers.

"Laurel, I'm so glad that you're going to be a member of this family. You feel like one of my girls already."

"Oh, Joan, that means so much to me," Laurel said.

"We all feel that way, Laurel," I said. "We're so glad that Spin found you."

And with that, we went out and joined the party.

The guests had started arriving around seven. By eight, there were cars parked all over the lawn and as far up and down East Shore Road as you could see. It was like the old days. Many of Spin's and Perry's friends from high school, as well as all the people Joan and

Whit had socialized with at the club and in town. And all the blue-grass people were there—the "pickers and fiddlers," as Whit used to call them. They came from all over New England. Everett had burgers and hot dogs going on the grill, and soon two long picnic tables were covered with salads, vegetables, homemade breads, and pies that people had brought. Somebody brought fried chicken. Somebody else brought ribs. Spin had set up a bar on the porch and he was mixing up pitchers of margaritas. Dogs ran through the crowd, picking up any morsels that had been dropped.

A couple of the old bluegrass guys grabbed Sally and dragged her over to the little deck outside Whit's shed. That's where we always played on summer nights—we turned it into a stage when we had parties. It's pretty there; the lake's in the background. And Spin had set up a microphone and speakers. The musicians were already playing, and Sally was saying hello to everybody, but she shook her head at their entreaties to play. "Later," I heard her say.

Laurel wandered through the crowd with Joan and me; Joan introduced her to everybody. Soon Perry and Catherine arrived. They were staying with friends for the weekend and had left the kids back in Southampton with the nanny.

The crowd, Whit's old crowd, made us all feel nostalgic, even Perry. He actually hugged me when I greeted him. Usually we just politely touch cheeks. Everybody mingled, and soon a large number of the guests were seated at the various picnic tables and card tables, eating and listening to the music. It was sort of a rotating group on the deck—a banjo player would leave the deck to get a drink and another would take his or her place. Georgia Devereaux, an old friend of Whit with a great country singing voice, sang a few songs. Every now and then somebody would say into the microphone, "Why aren't there any Whitmans up here? Where's Sally? Where's Spin?"

People tended to call us all Whitmans, even Everett sometimes.

I was sitting at a table with Laurel, Spin, Perry, Catherine, and some others. Everett kept bringing us food. Laurel and Catherine were excitedly making plans for the Hamptons visit. I heard Catherine tell her that they, too, were going to have a party, but it would be more intimate than this. A real dinner party.

There was a little break in the music and Joan's voice came booming from the speakers.

"Hello? Everybody? Your attention, please?"

I grabbed Perry's arm and said, "Oh no, Perry, she's making a toast or something. She's going to go on and on."

"Oh Jesus," he said, taking a big gulp of his beer.

And Joan began. She thanked everybody for coming, and then she called up Laurel and Spin.

"Spin? Spin dear, where are you? Come up here, you and Laurel both."

I was dying for them, but Spin is such a good sport that he waved, took Laurel by the hand, and walked with her up to the deck, where my mother stood.

"Here they are!" Joan said. "I hope everybody has had the chance to meet Laurel. If you haven't, you will. And, in case you haven't heard, Laurel and Spin are going to be married this summer. She's here to stay and we couldn't be more thrilled about that."

There was a lot of clapping and hollering.

"Perry," I said, "go up there and see if you can get the mike away from her."

He nodded, took another gulp of his beer, then wiped his mouth and started over to the deck.

As I've said, Joan isn't the most emotional person, so I was surprised that she suddenly had a little tremor in her voice.

"Spin, Whit was very proud of you, he always was . . . and for good reason."

People in the crowd started clapping and somebody shouted "SPINNER!"

"But I know that if Whit had been able to meet Laurel . . ." She actually paused here, because she was getting a little choked up. There were easily a hundred people on our lawn and you could have heard a pin drop. "If he could have met the beautiful, kind, wonderful young woman that you've chosen to spend your life with, I know that of all the things you've done, all the choices you've made and will make in your life, this is the one that would have made Whit the most proud."

Everybody cheered. Joan saw Perry and handed him the microphone. She looked relieved. I'm sure she hadn't expected to get as emotional as she did. When Joan stepped off the deck, Perry placed the microphone back on the stand, and the banjos and fiddles started up again. Spin grabbed Joan and pulled her into a big bear hug. They walked back to our table and Spin had one arm around Laurel and one around Joan.

"That was so sweet, Joan," Catherine said.

"Yeah, Joan," Everett said. He had started in with the margaritas a little early. He'd been drinking before the guests had even arrived, setting up the grill with Spin, and now he was feeling good.

"Spin, it's true. What Joanie said," Everett added.

"Thanks, brother," said Spin.

Everett said to Laurel, "Too bad you never got to meet Whit. He was . . . well, my dad used to tell me that other people in this town, other people in Whit's"—he raised his fingers to do air quotes—"'circle,' I guess you'd say—"

"Yeah, I guess you'd say that if you were seventy," Sally scoffed.

"Well, he was seventy when he said it, Sal, you little bitch," Everett said, giving her a playful shove, making her laugh.

"Now, wait—let me finish," Everett said. "Dad said that when most of these guys did stuff for the community or gave to local charities and shit like that, he used to say they were 'padding their obituaries.' Dad said that most people did this shit because they wanted the town to love *them*. But Whit did that stuff because he loved the town."

"Aw, Ev," I said.

"That's sweet," Joan said.

"So, I just want to make a toast to Spin," Everett continued. He stood and held his drink up high. "Spin, my brother, I see so much of your father in you, and you know I mean that as a mighty compliment. I don't think a lot of people understand what it was like for you, growing up the way you did, sort of straddling two families, but you made it one family. You made it whole. I admire the shit out of you, man. . . . You'll never know how much. You're the best friend I've ever had. . . . You're the brother I never had. I love you, man. I always will."

I wished I hadn't let Laurel put so much mascara on me; I was crying when Everett and Spin stood and hugged across the table. Sally was openly sobbing, Joan and Spin were a little teary. But I noticed that Perry had a sort of frozen smile during Everett's tipsy speech and that Laurel hadn't even heard it. She was looking at some photos on Catherine's phone.

"Now let's play some music," Spin said.

Spin grabbed his guitar from the porch and Everett went into the shed to grab a banjo. When they got on the deck, everybody cheered and gathered around. "Where's our fiddler?" Spin shouted into the mike. "And we need another banjo. Charlotte!"

"Oh Jesus," I said.

Laurel leaned across the table and said, "Lottie, I didn't know you play, too."

"She's really fast on that banjo," Catherine said. "There's a video on YouTube."

"I don't play much anymore," I said.

Sally came running over, grabbed me, and we ran up to the deck as everybody cheered.

Sally had her fiddle with her and she started playing with the guys while I went into the shed to find my favorite of Whit's banjos. It was hard to hear, but I was able to tune it before I went back outside. They were in the middle of one of Whit's old favorites, a favorite of most bluegrass nuts—"Foggy Mountain Breakdown"—and I stepped onto the stage next to Everett and started matching my banjo rolls to his.

Spin segued into another tune on the guitar, and he said into the microphone, "Here's something that Sally and I made up when we were kids. It's called 'Soggy Bottom Breakdown.'" Norm Hungerford, still an excellent bass player despite his failing memory, was on the stage with us. Craig White had his mandolin. It was like old times.

Mike Reynolds, another fiddler, got a big round of applause after a very lively solo during "Orange Blossom Special," and Sally couldn't help herself when he stepped back from the mike and motioned for her to take his place. She got up there, and at first she just did these long strokes on one string. It sounded just like the long whistle of a train. Then she plucked at another string and made a little *toot-toot* sound, and then she was off. She played the chorus and wove in melodies from other pieces, like "Flight of the Bumblebee" and the "Sabre Dance." She even managed to weave in Beyoncé's "Beautiful Liar," which only the younger people got.

When we finished the song, she was all fired up. "Here's something that my sister and I sang at Whit's memorial service," she said into the mike. "Those of you who knew Whit, which I guess would be all of you, know that he loved gospel music."

I was shaking my head no and tugging at her arm. I hadn't sung anything in ages. She ignored me. "And this was one of his favorites. Come on, Lottie."

Spin and Everett pushed me up to the mike with her and we sang "Down to the River to Pray."

EIGHTEEN

We stopped playing music when the fireworks started. Everett, Spin, Sally, and the others started up again sometime after that, but I was through. Joan and I both went up to bed a little after midnight. I woke up a few times in the night and could hear some hangers-on outside until almost dawn. The few neighbors who had declined our invitation would be politely complaining to us about this for weeks.

It was sunny and hot when I awoke the next morning. I went upstairs to check my e-mail, as I do every day, and saw that there was one from Australian Matt.

The subject line read "LoneStarLiza."

The e-mail said only: "Have you checked the children?"

I puzzled over this for a few minutes before replying: "What are you talking about?"

Then I went outside to survey the damage. It wasn't that bad. Somebody had thrown the empty cans and bottles into recycling bins. Bags and bags of garbage had been placed in a pile close to the driveway, ready for Everett to take them to the dump. I noticed that his truck was parked where it had been all night and that his window shades were still drawn. I suspected that everyone would be hurting this morning. I went back inside to make some coffee, and Laurel was standing in the kitchen, yawning. She smiled and said, "Morning, Lottie."

"Hey, Laurel," I said. "How are you this morning? Did you stay up as late as the rest of them?"

"No, I think we went up around two. What a fun night, though."

"Yeah? Did you have a good time?"

"I had a GREAT time," said Laurel.

"I'm so glad." She looked like a little girl in her cotton nightgown. I gave her a quick hug. "Sit down. I'll make some coffee."

"Let me make it. Maybe I'll make some eggs, too. I know Spin'll be down soon—he's in the shower. He's a little hungover."

"Well, you don't look so bad."

"I didn't drink much. I just got such a nice feeling from all your friends, Spin's friends. Everett took a bunch of us out on his boat."

"A bunch of you?" Everett's boat is an aluminum dinghy with a small outboard motor. He just uses it for fishing. It really isn't meant to hold more than three adults. "Well, as long as you all made it back to shore."

Spin walked into the kitchen, doing a sort of Frankenstein imitation. He was stomping along, straight-legged, with his arms out in front of him.

"HEELP MEEE!" he cried. He sat at the table and put his face in his hands. He pulled Laurel onto his lap and she started kissing his head very tenderly.

"Poor baby, do you have headache?"

"Just a little one," he whispered.

"What can I get you, baby? What would make you feel better?" she murmured.

"A full body transplant. I need a different body."

"I'm making breakfast. You need to eat something, Spin," I said.

I kept glancing out the window at Everett's. He usually likes to swim off a hangover, but it looked like he was still sleeping.

By the time I had cooked the breakfast, Joan had come down.

"Where's Sally?" she asked.

"I don't know, her car's not here."

"She gave that guy Fuentes a ride home," Laurel said.

This was interesting. I knew Joan liked Fuentes as much as I did, so I gave her a little smile, but she seemed worried.

"I hope she's okay. I hope she wasn't too drunk to drive."

And no sooner were the words out of her mouth than Sally strode into the kitchen, still wearing the clothes she'd had on the night before.

"Who was too drunk to drive?" she demanded.

"Oh, there you are," Joan said.

I was dying to know what had happened, but knew she wouldn't tell me until we were alone.

"What?" she said to all of us.

"Nothing. Sit down, eat," I said.

After breakfast, Laurel and Spin were getting their stuff organized. Joan went out for her run, and I followed Sally into the music room.

"What happened?" I asked her.

"Nothing," she said. She was setting up her recording equipment. "I drove him to Ramón's, and when I stopped in front of his house, he hopped out of the car and said good-bye. I was laughing. I had thought we were on the same page; I wanted to get some Washington Fuentes action. But he seemed like he wasn't interested. He came and stood by the car window, said how much he had enjoyed the party. I finally said, 'Cut the crap. Can't I come in?' He said, 'Sure, if you're too tired to drive, come in.' He set me up in one of the little nieces' rooms. It was adorable; I was surrounded by stuffed animals. I actually slept, Lottie. I slept really well. When I woke up this morning, he was still sleeping, so I left."

She was tuning her violin. "Man, I did a number on this last night. I called in a few favors from some of the bluegrass boys. Rick Cohen's coming over with his bass, and he's also trying to find a kettledrum for Everett to play. He knows somebody with a fucking kettledrum. I mean, who knows somebody with a kettledrum? Spin said that's what I need for this part of the score, and he's so right. He's going to play some really beautiful Spanish-sounding guitar. We're going to do a thing we worked out last night. Each night this week, I've got somebody coming. I can record everybody, then mix it and have the sample ready for the director by Friday."

"That's so great, Sally," I said.

She had stopped all her messing around with the instruments and said to me, "I wonder why he didn't want to have sex last night?"

"Were you drunk?"

"No, he wouldn't have let me drive if I had been. He seemed tipsier than I was."

"I don't know," I said. And I didn't.

I wandered over to see why Everett hadn't come out yet. He always wakes up early, even if he'd been partying heavily the night before. I tapped on his screen door and called in to him.

"Hey, babe," he called back. "I'm in bed. Come here."

The house was completely dark. I opened the kitchen shades and saw a couple of beer bottles in the sink. I walked into his bedroom and found him in bed, facing the wall.

"Oh, Jesus Christ," I said. "What happened to you?"

He just made a groaning sound.

"Laurel and Spin are leaving soon. Get up so you can say good-bye, Ev."

I turned to leave and he said, "Lottie?"

"Yeah?"

"C'mere."

"Everett, no, really, not now."

"Baby, I just want to hold you. Please? Please come here?"

He was still facing the wall. I walked over to the bed and sat down. He rolled over, wrapped his arms around my waist, and pulled me down next to him, spooning me. I felt his lips on the back of my neck. He was breathing hard and holding me so tight.

"Babe?" I said. "Ev? What's wrong?"

"Don't leave me," he whispered. "Don't ever tell me you want to leave me."

"What? Leave you?"

His breathing sounded halting. I could tell he was crying. I tried to turn over so I could see his face, but he wouldn't let me. He held me tight. "Lottie, I'm sorry."

"What?" I asked. "Why?"

"You know why. I'm just sorry. I've been taking you for granted. I'm sorry. I'll be better. I'll be better to you. Just don't ever leave me."

"Everett, baby, I won't. Why are you so upset? What is it? Is it because Spin's getting married?"

He didn't answer right away, but then he said, "Yeah, I guess."

"Oh, Ev, you know I love you," I said. "I won't leave you." I turned to kiss him. It seemed to me that some very steamy sex was called for, but he held me to him.

"Just let me hold you."

"Okay," I said.

We lay there for about twenty minutes or so, and then we heard Spin's Jeep drive off.

"Wait. I hope they didn't leave without saying good-bye. C'mon, Everett, get up."

"Okay, I'll come over in a few. I'm gonna go for a swim," he said.

Spin's Jeep was gone, but he was in the kitchen, having coffee with Sally.

"Where's Laurel?" I asked.

"She ran off to get some things at the pharmacy," Spin said. He seemed agitated. I thought it was his hangover, but then he said, "Sally, this is not your business. You really need to let this go."

"What's going on?" I asked.

"Spin just told me that he and Laurel aren't planning on having a prenup."

"Oh," I said. "Well, that really isn't our business, Sal."

"Thanks, Lottie," Spin said. He started to stand, but Sally grabbed his hand.

"Please, Spin, listen to me for one minute. I just don't understand how Jim Haskell—isn't Jim the lawyer for the trust? I don't get why he isn't insisting you do a prenup. Why you aren't protecting your-self, you know, that's all. I'm just looking out for you. I don't under-stand why Haskell isn't insisting on it."

"Oh, well, let me explain it, then. It's because I'm twenty-six, so I get to make my own decisions about how to live my life. Sally, look, I know you mean well, but you probably think I have a lot more money than I do. I don't have much that isn't . . . tied up. Laurel has money, too. She has her book deal. We discussed it, and neither of us likes the idea of a prenup."

"Spin, you won't get the bulk of your inheritance until Joanie dies. Anything that you bring into the marriage is your own money, but anything that you acquire once you're married, well, those become marital assets. Laurel would be entitled to it all. You need to protect that."

"From what? The woman I'm marrying? Laurel isn't preying on me for my money."

"So just explain it to her. Tell her that you're just looking out for any children you two might have in the future. Because God forbid something happens to you, Spin. She would likely remarry. Your money, your family's money, could end up in the hands of a future husband, a complete stranger."

"Laurel would make sure the money went where it was supposed to go."

I realized that Sally was making some sense. "You really are placing a lot of trust in her, Spin."

"Yeah, well, my dad placed a lot of trust in your mom," Spin said, his voice a little lower. "Joan never signed a prenup."

"But Whit already had come into his money at that point, so she didn't really have a claim to any of it, do you see?" said Sally. "Besides, Joan is from this town. He knew her parents. He knew he could, you know—trust her."

"Yes, she's always been so trustworthy."

I don't think I'd ever heard bitterness in Spin's voice until that moment, but it was loud and clear.

"Wait, Spin," Sally said. "Why are you mad at Joan? She's always loved you—you know that. She's always wanted the best for all of us, you and Perry included."

"I'm not sure if that's true. I don't think destroying my parents' marriage was the best thing for us."

"What?" I cried.

I looked out the window to make sure that Joan wasn't jogging up the driveway. Everett was swimming out toward the middle of the lake, but Joan was nowhere to be seen.

"I can't believe you just said that, Spin," Sally said. "Your parents' marriage was over before Joan and Whit ever got together. I mean, not legally over, but it hadn't been a marriage, from what I've always understood, for a while."

"Oh, well, I guess my mother didn't know that, or I wouldn't be here, would I?"

"What do you mean?" Sally demanded.

"Come on, don't pretend you never wondered why I was so young when you moved in here."

"Spin, really, what's the point of going back over this stuff now?" I said quietly.

"Because I'm fucking sick of acting like we're one big happy family. What do you think it was like for me and Perry growing up as occasional guests in our own father's house? A guest in my house. I'm a guest right now, aren't I? In my own house. How do you think that makes me feel?"

"Spin, no! You're not a guest. What are you even talking about?" Sally said. "This all has to be coming from Laurel. What has she been saying to you? You've never been like this. What's going on? What has she been brainwashing you with?"

"Laurel? This has nothing to do with Laurel."

"It has everything to do with her," Sally said.

"WOULD YOU SHUT UP FOR ONCE?" Spin shouted at Sally.

I burst into tears.

This was so unlike Spin. Sally was actually stunned into silence by his outburst, and he leaned across the table and said, right in Sally's face, "I am so sick of walking on fucking eggshells around you. Pretending that everything is fine, that you're fine. I defend you all the time. Everybody in this town knows you're out of your mind. What do you think it was like for me to go to Holden and hear about the legendary Sally Maynard, my own sister? I thought of you as my sister. I idolized you, and then I found out that you were the fucking whore of Holden."

Sally lunged at him and started swatting at his face, yelling, "What did you just call me? What—"

I was screaming at both of them, pulling at Spin, when the door flew open.

"What's going on?" Laurel asked. "I heard screaming. Is everything okay?"

"Yeah, let's get our stuff."

Sally and I were trying to hide our tears, but Laurel saw that we were upset and she put her hand on my shoulder and said gently, "Charlotte, what's going on? Are you okay?"

"Yes," I whispered.

"LAUREL!" Spin snapped from the hallway, and she followed him upstairs.

NINETEEN

Did you hear what he called me? Did you hear him call me a whore?"

Sally was whispering in my ear. We were lying together on my bed.

"Yes," I said. I couldn't stop crying. "I don't understand."

"I do. It's her. I hate her. I've been onto her from day one."

"Shhhh, Sally, no, be quiet."

But she carried on, her voice ranging from a whisper to a near shout and then back to a hoarse whisper.

"I haven't wanted to say anything because I KNOW nobody believes ANYTHING I SAY around here, but I saw who she was from the beginning. You can see that she's empty, there's nothing inside but black. EVEN THE DOGS DON'T SEE HER. It's because she doesn't have a soul. She doesn't have a scent. You can't tell. Most people can't. BUT THE DOGS CAN TELL. SHE DOESN'T HAVE A SMELL. That's how they can tell. How do you think she's been getting texts on her cell phone the whole time she's been here?"

I could hear footsteps out in the hall. This house is so old, you can hear everything. "SHHHHHH, Sally," I said.

"We don't have cell service on this fucking lake," Sally said, and now she was laughing, "but her phone lights up day and night with texts. She's on a different web. She's hooked up to the dark web, the deep web, the deep, dark web. I've had to keep my mouth shut this whole time."

"Those are e-mails, not texts," I whispered. "She's not getting texts."

I heard their car doors slam. Sally also heard it, and she jumped up to look out the window.

"Thank God they're going. We have to plan. We have to protect ourselves," Sally said.

"No, Sal," I said, trying to keep my voice very calm. "The things Spin said, they had nothing to do with Laurel. It sounds like he's been holding on to some bad feelings for a long time. I just don't understand how we didn't know he was so unhappy."

Now she was pacing back and forth between the two windows, looking out of each one as she ranted. "He wasn't unhappy. It's her. She's poisoned him. Have you seen how black her eyes are?"

"No," I said. "Sally, stop."

"There goes Everett. EVERETT!" she called, banging on the window.

"No, Sally, we don't need Everett," I said.

"EV! Ev! Ev!" Sally called again through the open window. I heard him asking her what she wanted.

"Come up here, quick. It's an emergency."

"Oh, Sally, don't say that."

But it was too late—he was running up the stairs.

Everett still looked a little rough, even though he'd had a swim and a shower. He stood in the doorway and I could see he knew, without her saying anything, that Sally was off. He just stood there with his shoulders sagging, watching her pace back and forth. She stopped every few seconds to peer out the window like a fugitive.

"What if they come back?" she said. "What if they come back? Let's lock the doors. Everett, run down and lock the doors."

"Oh, Jesus Christ, what now?" Everett said to me.

"The thing to do is to change the locks, Everett," Sally said. "Laurel's been brainwashing Spin. She's been telling him all sorts of lies, sick lies about us, about me."

"What kind of lies?" Everett asked. "Sally, what lies?"

I tried to get his attention. It's never a good idea to get her to elaborate. For Christ's sake, what was he thinking?

"He thinks that we've made him feel like a guest. She wants us out. She called me a whore. She thinks we're all whores. . . ."

"No, Sally," I said, and as she continued ranting, Everett came and sat next to me. I quietly filled him in on what had taken place in the kitchen. "Laurel wasn't even there, but somehow Sally thinks she was behind it."

"She was behind it," Sally said. "Everett, you know how wicked she is. She's evil; you know that. I know you know. If anybody in this house would know that, you'd know."

"What the fuck are you talking about?" Everett said. He jumped up and lunged at her. He grabbed Sally by both her shoulders, shook her, and said, "WHAT ARE YOU SAYING? WHAT ARE YOU TRYING TO SAY?"

This was as uncharacteristic of Everett as Spin's flare-up had been. I screamed his name. He let go of Sally and took a step back.

"I'm sorry, Sal," Everett said after a moment or two. He leaned back against the wall.

"It's okay, Everett," Sally said. Now she was crying, and he put his arms around her.

"Let's all just calm down," he said.

Joan walked into the room just then and said, "What on EARTH is all the shouting about?"

Joan, Everett, and I spent the afternoon cleaning up the yard and the beach. Sally had gone into the music room. She started out with the same melody she had been playing all week, and then she moved into a livelier one. She went back and forth with the doleful, melancholy tune, lilting, lilting, then suddenly flew off into the fast reel. When I recall that afternoon now, it seems like the perfect score, that chaotic melody. It lulled you into a sense of calm and then it was on fire again. When we were outside, the sound of it was very faint, but I strained to hear it, and I know the others did, too. It was like listening carefully to an erratic heartbeat so that you could tell when it became steady again.

The sky was a perfect summer blue, and the lake was dotted with sailboats. A motorboat sped back and forth in front of the house, pulling an inflatable tube that carried children who laughed and screamed as they bounced across its wake. Everett was stacking the chairs and tables. Joan and I picked up litter, empty bottles, and cigarette butts, and we shared disjointed thoughts in passing.

"He told me he was hungover. He wasn't feeling well," I informed Joan when she dropped some paper plates into a garbage bag I was holding. "I'm sure that was a big part of it."

"A guest?" she said a few minutes later as we carried some empties up the steps. "He feels like a guest?"

"He was probably still half-drunk," I said on our way back down the steps.

"How could he have felt like a guest?" Joan asked when we were back in the kitchen washing up.

"I have no idea."

Everett carried the tables and chairs down to the boathouse and then he came into the kitchen. Sally's music had become quieter; she seemed to be working out a sequence of chord changes. Joan was going through some leftovers that somebody had covered up and left on the table.

"Everett," she said. "There's some fried chicken left from last night."

"Yeah?" he said, and he sat down.

"No, guys," I said. "It's been sitting out all night."

But they ignored me.

"Tastes good," said Everett quietly.

"Yummy," said Joan. "Everett, have a beer. The fridge is filled with beer. Charlotte, get Everett a beer."

"Nope," Everett said. "I'm good. I drank too much last night. I like the sound of what Sally's got going in there, with her fiddle."

"A beer will make you feel better. Hair of the dog," said Joan.

"No," Everett said. "Listen to that. She's got this kind of Turkish, almost Arabic-sounding thing going on there, then she dives back into the hillbilly reel." He was tapping out a rhythm on the table with his fingers.

"What's the movie about?" Everett asked me.

"It's set in the nineteenth century, I think. A sort of Western. I don't know. Yeah, I see what you're saying about this tune. It's mountain music, but you could see somebody belly-dancing to it."

He listened for a few more minutes and then he got up and rummaged around in our silverware drawer until he found four spoons that he liked, then he left the room.

A moment later, we heard Sally stop her playing. When she started up again, we could hear the tap-tap-tapping of the spoons. They sounded like the little cymbals that belly dancers hold in their palms. They were just the thing. We heard Sally let out a whoop of delight.

"Joan," I said. I listened to make sure that they were still playing. "Mom, did Whit ever find out what happened to Sally?"

"That's sweet, I like it when you call me Mom," Joan said. She had now moved on to some cookies that somebody had left in a Tupperware container with a Christmas tree on it. "You girls always called me Joan. I think it's because you were so little. You called him Whit, and Perry called me Joan, so I can see where it would get confusing."

"Did Whit ever know about Sally and the boys from Holden that night? Did he find out?" I asked.

Joan looked at me then with a confused expression. "Did Whit *find out*? Of course he did. I told him that night."

"What? No, that can't be," I said, blinking hard, trying to keep the tears from coming. "I mean, I always thought that if he knew . . ."

"What?" Joan asked. "If he knew, then what?"

"He'd have gone to the police."

The music had stopped. I wasn't sure exactly when. Joan and I both held our breath, wondering if Sally was within earshot. But she started up again.

"Whit was the one who told me *not* to call the police. I thought you knew that. We had a big fight about it. I don't think I ever got over it. I thought you knew that."

"No," I said.

"I never forgave him. How could you not have known that?"

Spin was here at Lakeside that weekend; he would have been twelve or thirteen at the time. He was still living in New York with Marissa and coming up on alternate weekends. I remember that he came down to see what all the commotion was about. He had always been a light sleeper. We were all in the foyer, helping Sally; Spin was crouching wide-eyed on the stairs. The first time Joanie told him to go to bed, she used her normal voice. The second time, it was more like a scream.

We should have just taken Sally to the hospital. I know that now.

She had been really out of it when Everett and I found her. Everett had wanted to take her to the hospital, but every time we mentioned the idea, she would thrash around and scream, "I am not going to the hospital. You can't make me." She was so messed up. It wasn't just booze. Everett kept asking her what she'd taken. "Vodka," she'd mumbled.

"What else?" Sally was still on the ground, just inside the tunnel, when he asked her. She was trying to stand, but she kept slipping because the tunnel floor was wet and starting to freeze. She giggled when she slipped. Everett kept standing her up and she kept sliding.

"She doesn't have her shoes," I said to Everett. "She's sliding because she just has socks on."

When Everett dragged her out of the tunnel, we saw that her jeans hadn't been pulled up all the way. "Who would leave her like this?" I asked. That's when I started crying—when I was hiking up her jeans. "Who would leave her like this out in the freezing cold?"

I kept looking for her shoes. Sally, in her semiconscious state, heard me and started saying, "My shoes, Max, those are new. I want my new sneakers. Where the fuck are my sneakers, Max?"

Everett picked her up and carried her down the bank and back to the truck. For some reason, I thought it was important to find her shoes.

"Forget her fucking shoes," Everett shouted. "We need to take her to the hospital."

"Where are my shoes?" Sally asked. She was giggling and playfully punching at Everett's chest. "I WANT MY SHOES. Where's Max? Who are all you other guys?"

What if we hadn't gone looking for her? What if we had fallen asleep in Everett's room? What if she hadn't told me that she and Max Osborne sometimes went to the tunnel? Max was her current boyfriend. He was a day student. Sally and I had gone to preschool with Max; I'd always hated him. Now she was hooking up with him in the Holden field house and, on occasion, down in the old railroad tunnel. What if I hadn't known that? She would have frozen to death that night.

The tunnel was a frequent destination for Holden students—had been for years. It was spooky and secluded, yet not too far from campus. It was a perfect party spot. But once the nights started getting cold, nobody went there.

When I opened the door to the truck and the light came on, I could see that Sally had blood on her face.

"Everett, look," I said. "And her pants . . . I can't tell if they're wet, or if she's bleeding, or what."

"Oh man," Everett said, setting her gently inside the truck's cab. "Quick, get in on the other side of her."

Soon we were speeding along the old service road and then we were in Harwich Center.

"We need to call my mom," I said.

"We'll call her from the hospital," Everett said.

"NO! I'm not going to the hospital," Sally said. "They'll send me to jail. I'm all fucked up."

"You won't go to jail," said Everett.

"Sally, what happened?" I asked. "Who were you with? Was it Max?"

"Yeah. Where's Max? I wanna go home. I keep telling you that. I keep telling everybody."

"Who, Sally?" I said.

She was dozing off.

"Keep her awake," Everett said, elbowing her hard. "SALLY! WAKE UP!"

"I'll go home, okay?" Sally pleaded. "Please, let's take me home. I won't say anything. I don't even know you guys."

"Everett, we have to go near the lake to get to the hospital. Let's stop and get my mom. There's no cell service here."

"I'M NOT GOING TO THE HOSPITAL!" Sally sat up straight now and started wiping her mouth. "Ow, what happened?"

"Sally, do you want to go home and see what Joan thinks?"

"NO. I just want to go to bed. I'm fine."

I was relieved when Everett turned onto East Shore Road. Sally did seem improved.

When we got to the house, Everett wanted me to go in and get Joan. He would wait in the truck with Sally. But Sally had sobered up somewhat during the short drive. I mean, she was still a mess, but she seemed a little better. She stumbled out of the truck and Everett and I walked her into the house.

"I just want to go to the bathroom," she said. I helped her to the powder room next to the foyer. I tried to go in with her, but she closed the door.

"Privacy, PLEASE!" She giggled. She was alternating between silliness and anger.

I went and woke up my mom. Whit kept snoring away.

Downstairs, Joan and I persuaded Sally to open the bathroom door and let us in. She had a cut lip. Her hair was caked with mud.

"Oh no, oh my God, oh sweetie, what happened? What happened?" Joan said.

"I don't know, Mommy," Sally said. Now she was even more lucid. "I can't remember. I need to take a shower."

I pointed to the spots of blood on Sally's jeans, and Joan got very upset. It was the only time I'd ever seen my mother really cry.

"Sally? Sally? What happened."

"I want some water. I'm hot."

We followed her out of the powder room. Everett was standing by the front door, and when I looked at him, he nodded at the stairs. That's when we saw Spin. Joan sent him upstairs.

"Come in the kitchen, dear."

"Okay, Mom."

Sally was walking fine now, just a little slowly, and my mother had her arm around her.

"She seems so much better," I said.

"There's no way that was just from alcohol," Everett said.

"What do you think happened?"

"I have no fucking idea, but she didn't get that fucked up and then recover so fast just from vodka. And she didn't get to that tunnel alone. Somebody took her there. Who's this kid? Who's this Max?"

"Max Osborne."

"We have to call the police," Everett said.

We went into the kitchen, but Joan and Sally had gone up the back stairs. We could hear the water rushing through the old water pipes.

"Tell her not to take a shower, Lottie. She might have been raped. What the hell's wrong with your mother? She should know better."

I ran upstairs, and sure enough, Sally was in the shower and Joan was standing there helping her wash the mud out of her hair.

"Joan, Everett wants to call the police."

"WHAT? No!" Sally said.

188 · Ann Leary

"Shhhh, sweetie, it's okay," Joan said. Then she said to me, "Tell Everett to go home. I'm going to wake up Whit. We'll call the police."

"NO!" said Sally.

"We'll take her to the hospital," Joan whispered.

TWENTY

I had received another e-mail from Matt.

SUBJECT: Have you checked the children?
I guess you're not much of a movie buff.
Matt

I was about to respond to the e-mail, when a new message popped onto my screen. It was from Laurel.

Dear Lottie, I'm so, so sorry that we had to leave this morning with everybody so upset. Spin and I had a long conversation on the way to Long Island. He's so sad now, I can't even begin to tell you how sad he is. He and Perry went and sat on the beach for almost two hours, I don't know what they were talking about, but Spin said he'll explain it all to me later. I want you to know that the two weeks I spent with you, your mom, and Sally were two of the best weeks of my life. I felt like I found a new family with you, and I won't let a misunderstanding drive Spin, who I love more than I can ever express in words, and you guys apart. Please tell me that you are all okay, especially Sally, I was so worried about her. XOXO L

I was relieved to get Laurel's e-mail. I knew that she wasn't the cause of Spin's anger. In fact, she was going to help us sort it out. I immediately e-mailed her back, expressing my relief and gratitude. I urged her to have Spin call me if he felt like it.

Then I Googled: *"Have you checked the children movie."*

I'm not a movie buff, but as soon as I saw the results of the search, I got the reference. *When a Stranger Calls.* The baby-sitter is all alone; the children are sleeping upstairs. She gets calls from a creepy guy, who keeps asking, "Have you checked the children?" The calls are coming from inside the house. Scary as hell.

I replied to Matt: "HAHAHA regarding the movie reference. If you could see the state of our house, you'd know that Mr. Clean doesn't live here."

Everett e-mailed me in the middle of this.

SUBJECT: Can you come over?

That was it. Nothing in the body of the message.

He was out on his porch with the dogs. When I walked up, he took my hand and kissed it. It was the sweetest thing he's ever done. He just held my hand there, kissing first the back of it and then the palm.

"Isn't it buggy out here?" I said. "Let's go inside."

He got up without letting go of my hand and followed me inside.

I remember that when Whit died, our lovemaking was really intense for a while. *Intense* isn't quite the word. It was especially passionate, I guess. There was the same kind of passion the night that Spin and Laurel left. We both seemed to be grieving, for some reason.

Everett usually goes right to sleep after sex, but that night he didn't. He just wanted to keep cuddling. I was starting to doze off when he said, "Charlotte?"

"Yeah?"

"I'm not gonna be seeing anybody else anymore. Just you. I'm sorry. I didn't realize how much I was taking you for granted."

I pulled his arms tighter around me.

"Really?"

"Yes."

"But why? What brought this on?"

"Nothing. It's just how I feel."

"Did Laurel have something to do with it?"

Suddenly, Everett stiffened up.

"What do you mean by that?" he demanded.

"Nothing, why?"

"Why did you bring her name up?"

"She's been talking to me about our . . . setup. She has lots of advice, seems to know a lot about relationships. She's been talking to me about you. I thought she might have said something to you, that's all."

"No, she didn't say anything to me."

I realized that he was hurt because I assumed that somebody had influenced him.

"I'm sorry, babe," I said. After a few quiet moments, I said, "Everett, Joan told me today that Whit knew about Sally. About the night in the tunnel."

He didn't answer.

"I don't know why that's making me so sad. He used to make jokes about Sally and me sneaking onto campus, long after that. Why would he tease us about that if he knew about that awful night? We never went back after that. It's so surprising. Aren't you surprised?"

"Not really. I mean, I guess I always thought that he probably knew."

"You did? Didn't you hate him when you got arrested? You couldn't go back to college because of the charge. Why didn't he speak up?"

"I guess he felt that he didn't really know what happened. None of us really knew. It would have been bad for Sally to go through a trial."

"*You* had to go through a trial."

Now Everett sat up and leaned against the wall.

"It was a hearing, not a trial. Why is this important now? Who cares about something that happened more than a decade ago? I hated college. Remember how I came home every weekend? I was homesick. I missed it here. I missed you."

"You did?"

"Yeah."

"Why didn't you tell me?"

"I must have," he said, lying back down. "I feel like I must have told you hundreds of times."

"Oh," I said. I lay there and listened as his breathing finally slowed. He was asleep.

I always thought that it was Joan's idea not to go to the police. I always blamed her.

When Sally got out of the shower that night, she went straight to bed. By the next morning, our mother's sadness had turned to anger. I heard them in Sally's room. The door was shut, but I listened from the hallway. "Why were you drinking in the woods? What did you think was going to happen? Who else was there? . . . Well, why did you think three boys wanted to go in the woods with you?"

Joan took Sally to her gynecologist. Apparently, Sally told the doctor that she had gotten drunk with her boyfriend and that they had had unprotected sex. I guess he gave her something to help prevent STDs. A morning-after pill. When they got home, Sally's face was swollen from crying and she went up to her room. I went in to talk to her.

"What happened?" I asked her.

She went and threw open the door and looked out into the hallway, then she shut it and came back to her bed, where I was sitting.

"Shhhhh—listen, do you hear that?" she said.

"I don't hear anything, Sally." Sally could be a little paranoid, especially when she was tired. She thought people were listening in on conversations sometimes. This had started long before the night at the tunnel.

"I don't remember much," she whispered. "Max and two of his friends, Sam—a kid from Westchester—and another boarder. . . . I can't even remember the name of the other guy. They wanted to go to the tunnel. We were gonna get high. I had some weed. The kid Sam, he had vodka in a Starbucks thermos. It was mixed with orange juice and it wasn't that big, so how much could we have drunk?"

"What do you mean?"

"I don't know how I got so fucked up so fast. I only remember having one cup of the stuff."

"I thought you were drinking out of a thermos."

"No, they had these cheap paper cups. The kind they have on tennis courts, the kind they have in the field house at Holden. We each had cups. I only remember drinking one. And then I was driving up to the house with you and Everett. And then this morning, when I saw my lip . . ."

"Sally, you weren't just bleeding there."

"I know."

"So what'd the doctor say?"

"What do you mean?"

"Did he examine you?"

"Yeah." Now she was crying, and I hugged her.

"What did he say?"

"He asked me if it was my first time. I said yes. I lied and said it was. He was so old and mean-looking."

"Oh Sally, stop crying. We have to tell Joan."

"Tell her what?"

"That you were drugged. That they had sex with you when you were . . . They raped you, Sally."

"I told her, Lottie. I did. I told her, but she didn't believe me. She said that she knew about us sneaking onto campus. She reminded me that Whit's a trustee. I said that Max Osborne and his friends forced me to go to the tunnel, but she said nobody would believe me. He's the fucking class valedictorian, Lottie. He's already been re-cruited by Amherst. Who's going to believe me?"

Her voice was slowly rising, and I begged her to lower it, but I was becoming enraged. It was just like Joan to worry more about her rep-utation than about Sally's welfare. I was certain that she hadn't told Whit; I knew that he'd be enraged if he found out what had hap-pened to Sally.

"I'm going to talk to Whit," I said. "They left you there, Sally."

"NO," Sally said. "I don't want Whit to find out."

"Sally, he'd want to know. He'd help. He'd be on your side."

"No. I begged Joan not to tell him, and I'm begging you. I don't want . . . I would die if he knew. And Spin's here. What if he heard about it?"

"But you didn't do anything wrong."

Everett was furious. "This is insane," he said later. "We should have taken her straight to the hospital. We should have called the police. I hate that whole Osborne family. His brother, Clod or Clay? He was on my Little League team, always hated his fucking guts."

"Well, Sally's not going to see him anymore."

"Oh, is that a fact? Now that he and his buddies gang-raped her, she's calling it off?"

"Everett. She doesn't remember anything. She just remembers coming home."

"Well, I remember what shape she was in. You remember. She could have died."

"She seems okay now. Let's forget about it. Sally has. She watched *Gilmore Girls* all morning, now she's out playing with Whit and Spin. Whit just finished a new banjo, they're playing music. I could hear her laughing on my way over here, all the way from his shed."

It was the following weekend when Everett caught up with Max Osborne. His uncle Russ was the head of security at Holden and he told Everett there was going to be a dance on Saturday night. That meant that the dorms would be open late, until eleven. Everett waited in his truck a little way down the road, about halfway between the Holden gates and the Osborne house. The Osbornes' house is almost on the Holden campus. Everett told me later that he wasn't at all surprised to see Max pull out of the gate in his dad's BMW.

"Yup, he took Daddy's car to drive across the road," he said.

Everett watched Max pull into his driveway. He drove up behind him. Max got out and walked toward the truck, sheltering his eyes with his hands. He was blinded by the headlights; he couldn't see.

"Hey, who's that?" Max called out.

Everett turned off the headlights and jumped down. "Max?" he said.

"Yeah?"

"It's me. Everett Hastings. I'm a friend of Clay's."

"Oh, hey, man, what's up?"

Apparently, it was Max's screams that had the police there so fast. His parents had awakened when they heard the commotion. They looked out the window and saw that Everett was giving Max a pounding. Just with his fists. Everett was booked on a first-degree assault charge. He really messed up Max's face. He had followed Max and attacked him, unprovoked, I guess that's why it was considered first-degree assault. It was considered unprovoked.

In the end, Everett got a year of probation. Max's family didn't want a trial. Everett didn't want a trial. The prosecutor made a deal with Everett's lawyer. But Everett was expelled from UConn. He moved back to the caretaker's cottage and the timing worked out; Bud had been diagnosed with Parkinson's that year. He and Betty were going to move down to a retirement community in Florida. Now Whit wouldn't have to find somebody else to move into the carriage house. Everett would live there and do the odd jobs. Everett was like a third son to Whit; Whit had always said so. Whit had even helped Everett with his legal fees, we found out later. I remember thinking that was so generous of Whit and so like him to do so without telling anybody.

TWENTY-ONE

Sally seemed to be back to herself the day after Spin and Laurel left. I was worried that she had stopped taking her mood stabilizer, but if she had, she would have ramped up quickly into full-blown mania, which, in the past, had meant a complete break from reality. She thinks, for example, that cars have reptilian brains, that Joan works for Al-Qaeda, that she has the ability to read people's urine and predict the future—stuff like that.

What happened that night in the tunnel didn't make Sally sick, it didn't cause her disorder. I know that now. I learned everything I could about bipolar disorder after she was hospitalized the first time. The tunnel incident, the rape, didn't even trigger her first manic episode; that happened months later.

Sally, I learned from her doctor and from my own reading, has an imbalance in her brain. It's physiological. You can see the differences in MRIs of bipolar patients. Her moodiness as a child, her intense times of joy, her dark fits of rage; later, during adolescence, her insomnia, her hypersexuality—these had all been signs. Nobody knew what it all meant at the time. Joan had a sense that something was wrong, I had heard her talk to Whit about it over the years, but he had always laughed off her fears. Sally was an artist, a *true* artist, ac-

cording to Whit. He had always considered her a wildly gifted musician, a sort of prodigy, and he chalked up her behavior to youthful
high spirits.

"She'll outgrow this," he said to our mother. "She'll end up dull
and resigned to life like the rest of us." That didn't happen, but she's
been very successful when she stays on her lithium.

The Monday after the Fourth, Sally was up very early. She'd been
working on a thing called a Loop Station. A "Looper," she calls it.
She's able to record tracks on her violin, the piano, other instruments
and vocals if necessary, and then mix them. It's not recording studio
quality, of course, but she was using it to create a sample for the film
director.

Matt responded to my e-mail:

> I didn't mean Mr. Clean. Hope I didn't freak you out. Was trying to be
> funny. But LoneStarLiza has the same IP address as you. She, or he, is
> there. In the house. Is it you? Is she your sock puppet? Be careful.

He had to be wrong about this. I'd never told anybody, not even
Sally, about my blog. So there's no way anybody in the house could
be commenting on it.

Rick Cohen came over after lunch. Rick's a retired electrical engi-
neer and a kick-ass bass player, an old friend of both Sally and Whit.
He had agreed to play the bass for her score, and I could hear them
playing, talking, and laughing from where I was working in the attic. That evening, I was surprised to hear Sally say that she couldn't
wait for Spin to get back. She wanted him to play some Spanish guitar. Everett can play blues guitar, rock and roll, bluegrass, but Spin is
really the better guitarist.

Sally had a great idea about a solo for the guitar and banjo for one
of the sequences in the film. I'd wandered into the music room to see
what she was trying to score, and she showed me this sequence of two
men driving a herd of cattle over some arid country. This is where she
wanted the Spanish music. I played the banjo part and as I was playing,

she kept saying, "This'll be where Spin comes in" and "Maybe Spin will do something there." I was glad she was preparing a project to work on with Spin. It would help everybody move on from that argument.

It was Tuesday afternoon when Washington Fuentes drove up. I was sitting on the porch, watching Everett and Sally work on her score. Everett had somehow borrowed three enormous kettledrums and set them up on the deck next to Whit's shed. Sally played the stuff she had already looped, the melody he'd be accompanying, and then they started recording.

Everett really loves making music, but he had never played kettle-drums before, so he spent a good hour messing around with them while Sally set up her equipment. After they'd played the piece through a couple of times, he convinced Sally that they needed a snare and a cymbal, so he brought these from his house. Now, with the ac-companying bass and backup violins that Sally had blasting from the Looper, Sally and Everett's drum and fiddle sounded quite amazing.

"Brava, Sally!" I shouted when they took a break.

"I can hear the wind, it's too much. The rain, I'm afraid it's about to start," she fretted.

They had started up again by the time Washington drove up our driveway. Everett and Sally didn't hear him, they were so absorbed in their work, but I gave him a big wave and he joined me up on the porch.

The air was humid, the breeze was hot, and Sally's hair was damp with sweat. She was wearing shorts and a bikini top. She had the vio-lin tucked under her chin and was tapping the beat with her bare foot as she fiddled. Everett hit the giant drums at this point and they re-sounded with a *Boom! Boom-boom-boom BOOM!*

"Wow," Washington said.

"She's composing it for a movie," I told him.

Sally stopped suddenly and shouted, "Jesus Christ, Ev, I told you, the second fucking phrase, you came in too soon."

"No, that's not what you said. But whatever," he said, laughing.

They started up again.

"She's probably going to be doing this for a while. Did you come to see her?" I asked.

"Well, yes, but I also wanted to talk to you. Is anybody inside?"

"No," I said.

"Can we go inside and talk?"

"Sure," I said. I held open the door. Sally was facing Everett and didn't see us, but Everett did. I think it distracted him, because when we got inside, I heard Sally shout, "STOP, STOP, STOP. Go back. Start again."

I offered Washington a drink and he declined. He seemed a little uncomfortable. I suspected it had to do with Sally.

"What's up?" I asked.

"I'm worried about you," he said.

"Me?" I asked. "Why?"

"You have an enemy."

The reports were anonymous. They'd started almost immediately after Washington came to our house to talk about the break-ins. Somebody was sending letters to the local barracks. They were printed in plain block letters and were addressed to Trooper Fuentes. They were about my blog. They knew it was mine. They knew that Washington knew me personally. They wanted me to be investigated for fraud. Washington showed me copies of the letters.

I just listened. The first letter accused me of starting the Go-FundMe account for Wyatt's disorder. He tried to hand it to me, but I didn't want him to see how much my hands were shaking, so I just kept it clenched in my lap. He placed the others on the table.

"So, I know it's your blog, because I had somebody at headquarters track the IP address," he said.

"Okay," I said. We heard the fiddle and the *BOOM! Boom-boom-boom BOOM!* carried in through the open windows.

Finally I said, "So, are you here to arrest me?"

Washington said, "No! Of course not. I mean, I'd shut down the blog if I were you. Somebody might investigate it, but not me. Not state police. Tell your sponsors. Hopefully, they'll just terminate your contract. They don't want this to get out any more than you do. You need to talk to a lawyer. You should have just been happy with the income from the sponsors. When you started this fund-raising drive, well, that's considered fraud."

"Wait, what do you mean? The fund for Wyatt? I didn't start that. I've been trying to stop it. It was this LoneStarLiza person."

Washington looked at me sadly. "I had our tech guy trace that IP history, too, Charlotte. It's been coming from here. If not your computer, another computer that shares your Wi-Fi."

That's what Matt had told me. *Have you checked the children.* LoneStarLiza was coming from inside the house.

"Washington, I swear, I've been trying to make it go away. If you've read the blog, you must have seen that."

"Who would do this?" Washington asked. "Who would want to set you up like this? Make you look like you're scamming for money on your own blog?"

"I have no idea. I just posted the other day that any money should go to a hospital. Did you see that? I haven't received a penny from that blog except what the sponsors are paying me. Maybe somebody has hacked into our Wi-Fi and they're making it look like it's coming from here. That's possible, right? I actually know some hackers."

I was thinking about Matt. Maybe he was playing some kind of sick joke. Why had I even become involved with him? He was clearly unstable, an admitted criminal and hacker.

"I don't know. I'm not an IT expert, but it looks bad, Charlotte. Close it down before people start looking into this. Maybe it'll all go away. It would be bad for your blog if all your followers learned that you don't have kids, right?"

"Yes," I admitted.

"Anyway, the thing that worries me is that you have somebody who really wants to hurt you. Read these letters again. There's a threatening tone. This person hates you."

Just then, Sally came in. "Officer Fuentes!" she said, and she actually blushed a little. He stood up and they hugged. It was awkward, in a sort of adorable way. Everett had followed her inside and was getting himself a glass of water.

"Hey, Everett, how's it going?" Washington said.

"All right, how 'bout you?" Ev was licking the little arc between his thumb and forefinger. It seemed he was getting a blister from the drumsticks.

"Either of you ever heard of somebody named LoneStarLiza?" Washington asked them.

Everett just took a sip of water. He seemed lost in thought, and then he realized the question was being asked of him.

"Lone star who?" Everett asked.

"No," said Sally.

Washington was watching them carefully. He could see that it wasn't either of them.

"It looks like somebody's been using one of your computers."

TWENTY-TWO

In a perfect world, Washington Fuentes wouldn't have dropped this bomb in front of Sally. But he didn't know her history. He didn't know that when she's on edge, as she had been ever since the night of the hornet spray—ever since Laurel had arrived, come to think of it—that it's never a good idea to confirm her paranoid ideas. Just a few days ago, she had been carrying on about Laurel having some dark, evil Internet dealings, and now Washington had announced that somebody had been using one of our computers.

Washington hadn't quite believed me when I said that Sally and Everett knew nothing about my blog. When he saw their confusion, he looked at me apologetically. I decided just to give them the one-liner.

"I have this blog, it's a mommy blog. It's kind of—huge."

"What?" Everett said. "A *mommy* blog?"

"Yes, it's actually a famous mommy blog. I've picked up some sponsors this past year. One big one. They pay me a lot. I guess I'll have to pay them back. They might sue me."

I do this thing sometimes when I'm nervous. I giggle. I've done it since I was little. In situations where I might be expected to cry, I often laugh. "Paradoxical laughter," it's called. I had been giggling when I started with my little confession, but now it was getting out of control.

"So," I laughed, "these mommies, some of my really loyal . . . mommies . . . they started a fund."

I had to keep pausing to gasp for air. "And now Washington's involved!" I was bent over, I was laughing so hard. "Because it's illegal."

"What?" Everett said. "Baby, what the fuck is going on?"

"I can't," I cried. "I'm going to wet my pants."

Now Sally was laughing, too. "I can't understand anything you're saying," she said, choking with mirth. "You joined a mommy fund? What is that? I don't even know what that is."

"Washington, tell them what's going on," I said. "Tell them the whole thing." And I ran to the bathroom.

Nobody was laughing when I came back into the kitchen.

"It's her," Sally was saying. "It's Laurel. I knew it. She wants to hurt us." Sally kept looking to the window, as if she expected to find Laurel walking up the driveway.

"No, Sally," I said.

Everett said, "Hey, Sal, it looks like it's starting to rain. We gotta get those drums inside. I borrowed them from Holden, I can't let them get wet."

"She must have gone into the attic, Lottie, when you were asleep."

"My laptop's password-protected. She'd never have figured out my code."

"Or she went into your house, Everett, when you weren't here. Or maybe when you were asleep," Sally said.

"I doubt that," Everett said. "Anyway, I'm moving those drums." He went outside. I didn't blame him. It was clear that Sally was just getting started.

"Sally, this has nothing to do with Laurel," I said.

"I've known it all along, Washington," Sally said. "She's not who she appears to be. She's a fucking fraud; I've known it all along."

I caught Washington's eye and gave him a look. Unfortunately, Sally saw me.

"What the fuck was that look about, Charlotte? See? Nobody trusts a thing I say, but we'll all be sorry when she's ruined us."

"Sally," I said, "Laurel doesn't even know about my blog."

"HA! That's what you think," Sally said. Then she grabbed Washington's hands and, looking into his eyes, whispered, "Washington, nobody believes me. Nobody in this family believes a thing I ever say, but this is the truth: Laurel Atwood isn't who she seems to be. She's some kind of devil. I know you don't believe me, but she's fucking evil. . . ."

Washington said, "I believe you."

"She's a predator. She's got something wrong with her."

"I know. I believe you."

Sally paused and stared at him, blinking. "What? What did you say?"

"I believe you, Sally."

"You do?" she said. Now she was blinking back tears.

"Yes."

"How much have you made on the blog?" Everett asked me later, when we were alone at his house. "I mean . . . just a ballpark figure."

"Oh, you know, maybe around two hundred thousand. Roughly," I said. "This year. So far."

Everett howled. "Are you KIDDING ME? Let me see what's so great about this blog. And, by the way, you need to talk to a lawyer before you fold it. I don't think what you're doing is illegal. What's it called, anyway?"

He was about to enter the name on his computer, but I told him not to.

"We don't want this hacker to know. They might be watching your online activity."

"Charlotte, there's no hacker. Sally's right. It's gotta be Laurel."

"What?" I said. "Not you, too. Based on what? Why would she do that?"

"Okay, babe, listen." He closed his windows and then pulled me close and said quietly, "I was going to tell you this. I was sort of waiting for the right time. The night of the Fourth, after you went to bed . . ."

"Yeah?"

"I was drunk, okay. And a few of Spin's friends wanted to go out on the lake. I took them out. I didn't even know them. They were guys from Holden. We smoked a joint, Laurel was with us. I was really messed up. It wasn't till we finished the joint that I realized how completely wasted I was. I wasn't even gonna try to dock the boat. I just turned off the outboard, pulled it up, and we drifted onto the beach. Spin was on the beach, laughing really hard at us. We almost flipped the thing getting out of it."

"Okay, yeah, so what happened?"

"Most people had gone home. Spin and Laurel went in the house and I went to bed."

I could see where this was going.

"I was asleep, I don't know for how long, and then she was in my bed. I thought it was you at first. . . ."

"OH, GIVE ME A FUCKING BREAK!" I shouted. "You thought she was me, RIGHT!"

"Babe, I swear, it's all a blur. I was wasted. She had been sort of flirting with me all night. On the boat, I admit . . . maybe I was flirting back. Just a little."

"You expected her to come over here."

"No."

"I think you did. You told her to."

"Babe." He tried to hug me, but I pushed him away.

"You thought she'd come over after the boat ride and then you were surprised to see Spin on the beach."

"Charlotte, not in a million years would I do that. Why would I lie about this?"

"Don't touch me. I have no idea who you are."

"I was drunk."

"I don't care how drunk a person is, he doesn't do what he wouldn't do sober."

"That's not true."

"Could you murder Spin? Could you stab him in the heart or bash his head in with a brick just because you were drunk?"

"No."

"So I think you could have thrown her out of your house. You could have told Spin. You could have told me. Oh, now I understand why you've been so loving and caring ever since. It wasn't because of your feelings for me. It was guilt. It was because of your guilt about Spin. You said he was like a brother to you. Even Perry wouldn't do a thing so low."

"You know what I don't understand right now?" Everett said.

"What don't you understand? Basic human decency? How to be honest? What? What is it?"

"I don't get why you're so upset for Spin. I'm sorry that I did that to Spin. But I'm more sorry about doing it to you. I'm not drinking. I'm not smoking weed anymore. I'm doing this for you. I hate myself for what I did. But not just what I did to Spin, it's what I did to you."

I opened the door to leave.

"I have to tell Spin," Everett said.

"Everett, no." I turned to face him. "Take it to your grave. I'm serious."

"Charlotte, I'm telling you, Sally's right about her. She's evil."

"Oh, *she's* evil. Maybe she was drunk, too," I said. But I don't drink, and I hadn't noticed that she was in the least bit tipsy that night.

"I've been thinking about this a lot. I mean pretty much nonstop since they left. It wasn't just a drunken thing. She e-mailed me. She sent me a selfie . . . she and Spin on the beach."

"What?" I said.

He logged on to his computer. "I couldn't figure out why Snacks lets her pick him up, why the dogs are so casual around her. I think Sally was right. Dogs bark at strangers because of the smell of adrenaline that people, almost all people, emit in new situations. Dogs smell that. It alarms them, they bark, and the person pumps more adrenaline out for the dog. She doesn't have that."

"Everett, I don't even know what to say. The dogs? What on earth?"

"Nobody's hacking me from a remote location. She was sneaking in here. The dogs wouldn't have even barked at her. It would be like if you or Sal walked in. Look. Look at what she sent me. She's trying to scare me."

I looked at the screen.

TWENTY-THREE

Sally's car was gone when I awoke the next morning. She had left us a note. She knew a guitarist in the city who could play Spin's part. She needed it done that day. She planned to stay with friends and deliver the music to the director the next morning. She might stay in the city for a couple of nights; she would let us know.

"I think it's the best thing right now," Joan said while we drank our morning coffee. It was raining out, a hard, steady summer rain.

"Yup," I said. It was hard to talk, I was so depressed about Everett.

Spin and Laurel arrived home around two o'clock that afternoon. The rain had eased up, but the sky was still dark, more showers were expected. The lake was as still as glass; it had taken on the color of the sky, so when I looked out from my attic window, there was no horizon, just a wall of gray. I heard Spin and Laurel drive up and then come inside. I heard them chatting with Joan in the kitchen. Then I heard Joan let out an excited scream.

"LOTTIE!" Joan called out. "Lottie, come downstairs quick!"

I ran down the back stairs to the kitchen and found Joan hugging Spin. She was actually wiping away a little tear from her eye.

"Tell Lottie," Joan said.

Spin and Laurel looked at each other, grinning.

"Well?" Spin asked Laurel.

"You tell." She giggled.

Spin took a deep breath and said, "Laurel and I got married yesterday. In Southampton. Right on the beach."

I was able to make my tears look like happy tears. I ran over and hugged them both.

"What? How?" I asked. "Oh, how exciting. Congratulations to both of you."

I made coffee while they gave us the details. My back was to them, so they couldn't see how shaky my hands were. They realized they didn't want a big wedding. It wasn't just the tension with Sally. Marissa was also being crazy, trying to go all overboard with the plans. They just wanted to get married. They went to a justice of the peace. Perry and Catherine and the kids were the only attendants.

"It was spur-of-the-moment and very romantic," Laurel said, hugging Spin.

"I want to see pictures," Joan gushed. I knew she was happy for Spin and Laurel, but I suspected that her real joy sprang from the realization that there wouldn't be a wedding at Lakeside.

"Laurel-lee, get your phone. Let's see the photos," said Spin. *Laurel-lee.*

We had coffee and some stale cookies that Joan had kept from the Fourth. We looked at the photos of Laurel and Spin on the beach in front of the setting sun. Laurel wore a lovely white summer dress, not a wedding dress, just a lovely slightly sheer dress that was blowing around her knees. Her feet were bare. So were Spin's. He wore a pale linen suit, the trousers rolled up above his ankles. In some of the shots, they were standing in the surf. There were shots of them together and with Perry, Catherine, and the children. Perry and Spin seemed to be wearing almost identical suits. Laurel had a delicate bouquet of white and blue flowers. Little Emma carried a smaller bouquet and had white and blue flowers woven into her blond curls. It had all been thrown together on a whim, and somehow, it was more perfect than if they had planned it for months.

After we had admired all the photos, Spin and Laurel went upstairs to unpack and I went up to the attic to finish my work. About a half hour later, there was a gentle knock on the attic door.

"Come in," I said. Laurel walked in first, followed by Spin. Spin always has to duck to get through the door to this room. It was framed up over a hundred years ago, when most men weren't six-two like him.

"Oh, guys, hi," I said. I closed my computer and pointed to the little twin bed. "Sit down."

Spin came over and gave me a big hug. "We wanted to talk to you about the other day. With Sally." He held on a little longer than normal. Then they sat on the bed.

Spin said he was sorry about the way he had shouted at Sally that day. I assured him that we had all lost our tempers with her at various times over the years. Me, Joan, Everett. Even Whit on occasion. It wasn't Sally's fault; it's just exasperating for family members.

"It's like living with an alcoholic," Laurel said. "My best friend's mom was an alcoholic. It's really a similar dynamic. It's like walking on eggshells."

"Yes, those were exactly your words, weren't they, Spin? Walking on eggshells?" I said.

"When?"

"When you were so angry at her the other day," I said.

"I can't even remember. I was so furious."

"I know," I said. "So tell me more about Southampton."

Laurel showed me some photos she had taken of Perry and Catherine's beautiful house. "Look how cute that little Emma is," she said, pointing to a photo of Emma holding a kitten. She held the little kitten against her chest, both of her arms crossed over it. She was being so careful not to drop it.

"I keep telling Spin, I only want daughters."

"What's wrong with sons?" I asked.

"Yeah!" said Spin. "Not even one boy?"

"I hadn't really thought about it until this weekend, but now I know I want daughters. Three or four. Just like Emma."

"Emma worships Laurel," Spin told me.

"No wonder she's so fond of her," I said, but added quickly, "Perry and Catherine are lucky with their two kids. That's what I'd want. A little girl and a little boy. I mean, in a perfect world."

We talked about the weather forecast for the next few days. It was supposed to be gloomy. I was amazed at how I was able to maintain a calm demeanor. I had been crying on and off all day. Now when I sniffed and got teary, I complained about my allergies. The pollen count was out of control that week. They planned to go into the city in a few days and spend some time with Marissa. She was upset that they'd eloped. Now she wanted to really get to know Laurel.

Finally, they went downstairs and I e-mailed Everett. I had been trying to reach him all day. He didn't respond to my calls or e-mails. He'd left with his dogs in the early-morning hours. I had told him I'd be happy never to see him again.

I had several e-mails from Washington. They were cryptic. Just: "Is it done? Did you end it?" He really wanted me to close the blog. I knew he was looking out for me. I knew it had to be done.

I opened the administrator's log-in for the blog. There was no reason to look through any of it again. I had read through hundreds of posts the night before. I hadn't read the early entries in ages.

I started the blog a couple of years ago, when I happened upon a Web site for mothers. I found it enthralling. I've always loved the idea of being a mother; I look forward to having children of my own. When I read the sometimes funny, often poignant accounts of new mothers, I started to fantasize about what Everett might be like as a father—what our children might be like. So I started the blog.

LoneStarLisa (with an *s*) had actually been commenting for two years, almost since the beginning. She had three sons; she was a homeschooler from Austin, Texas. She had posted a link to photos on her Facebook page. In fact, she and I had become Facebook friends in 2013. Well, she and Susan had. Susan is my mommy name. I guess I can reveal it now—my blog is called Lazy Susan.

My name is supposed to be Susan Fields. Initially, I just posted funny stuff about how lazy I am as a mother; that was my whole gimmick. It was easy. I would post the opposite of the veiled brags I saw other moms post on parenting Web sites. Apparently, conscientious mothers limit the amount of time their kids watch TV and play computer games. I bragged that I limited my kids' screen time to their waking hours. The minute they went to sleep, electronics off! I asked my followers if six months of age is too young for sleep-away camp. I did one controversial post about how I was so exhausted from lack of sleep (Mia was very colicky as a baby) that I watched *Rosemary's Baby* and thought, Some moms have all the luck.

In the beginning, I used to just take ordinary aspects of mothering and turn them into humorous anecdotes. But soon I started writing about more serious stuff, like my postpartum depression after Mia's birth. That had been what prompted me to start the blog. The loneliness. That horrible loneliness and despair I felt after she was born. So many people could relate to that. It was after that entry that the blog really took off. There was no reason to scroll through the entries again now. I had done it the night before—all the birthday parties, all the school trips and bake sales. Mia's first steps. Wyatt's first words. The way their warm bodies felt when they crawled into bed with us at night. The way that Wyatt's cowlick was exactly the same as his father's, and how I loved to trace the swirl of it with my fingers. They were beautiful, my children. But they weren't real, and when I typed in the commands to take the blog off-line, I was fine. It was when I went through the steps of deleting the blog completely, using some tricks I had learned from some online friends to try to wipe it from the Internet entirely, that I became sad. I needed to remove the URL from the most common search engines; I couldn't remove it from the entire Internet, but I did the best I could. Later I went down to help Joan get dinner ready.

Laurel came in while I was cutting up peaches for a pie.

"Hey, has anybody seen my phone?"

"No," Joan said. She immediately started looking around the kitchen.

"You had it when you were in my room. Maybe you left it up there," I said.

"No, I had it after that. I had it in our room. I took a nap. I just don't know where I put it before the nap."

Spin shouted down from the second floor, "I've got it, Laurel! You left it in the bathroom!"

"Oh, thank God," Laurel said.

I put the pie in the oven and checked on the roast. Spin and Laurel set the table for dinner and then came into the kitchen.

"Is Everett coming?" Spin asked.

"No," I said. "He's not home."

"Should I set a place, just in case he shows up?"

"No," I said. "He's not having dinner with us tonight."

When we all eventually sat down to dinner, Joan asked if they'd had any traffic on the way home from Long Island.

"It was a little slow when we first got on the Hutchinson Parkway, then it eased up," Spin said. Riley was sitting next to Spin's chair, wagging his tail. Spin could always be counted on to slip him treats from the table, something Everett and Whit hated. Suddenly, Spin stood and looked out the window.

"Now I know what's strange. Where are Everett's dogs? They didn't come out when we came home. And they didn't bark. The house is so dark."

"Everett might be moving," I said.

"What?" said Spin, laughing. "You're joking, right?"

"No," I said.

Joan said, "Charlotte, what do you mean? What's going on?" She went and looked out the window at Everett's dark house.

"We had a fight," I said.

"What happened?" Joan asked. "He took the dogs? Where?"

I couldn't talk without crying, so I just ate my food. I really didn't feel like getting into the whole thing. I just wanted to eat my food and watch Laurel. She gave me a little sympathetic smile and cut into her meat.

"Sweetie, what happened?" Joan persisted.

"I found out last night that I have no idea who Everett is. He's not who we thought he was."

Again, Spin laughed. "Is this a joke?"

Laurel looked from him to me with an air of detached concern.

"Don't be ridiculous, Charlotte," Joan said. "I've known Everett since he was in kindergarten. He's not perfect. He could be a little more . . . industrious, maybe."

"I don't want to talk about it," I said.

I finished my dinner but told them I didn't feel like dessert. I went back up to the attic. Now that the blog had been taken down, I needed to close Susan's social media accounts.

When I started accumulating a lot of followers on the blog, I had Susan join Facebook, Instagram, and Twitter. She started a Pinterest page. Susan had five thousand Facebook friends, the maximum allowed, and over a million Twitter followers.

I have thirty-one Facebook friends as myself. As Charlotte Maynard. Mostly people from town, old friends from school, some friends of Sally and Spin.

Spin, Laurel, and Joan watched a movie, then Laurel came up to talk to me before she went to bed.

"I just wanted to make sure you're okay," she said.

"Yeah, I'm fine."

"What happened? With Everett?"

"He ended up in bed with somebody on the night of our party. She was somebody I know, somebody I considered to be a friend." I looked her dead in the eyes as I said this. Her calm, sympathetic demeanor made my heart race. I wasn't angry, though. The rush of adrenaline, my hot face, my shaking hands—they weren't caused by feelings of rage. I wasn't angry. I was afraid.

Feelings aren't facts, I reminded myself.

"Oh no," Laurel said. "How horrible for you. Well, I see why you two can't stay living so close. I think it's for the best. Once he moves his stuff out, we can get somebody in there who really wants to work. It always drove Spin and Perry crazy that he was living there rent-free. And Everett's whole slacker persona? It's an act. I've known guys like him. That glib charm. He takes advantage of others. He's taken advantage of you and he's taken advantage of Spin's good nature for years."

"I see that now," I managed to say.

I needed cell service, so I waited until everybody was asleep and then I pushed my old bike across the lawn and onto the road, just as Sally and I had done all those nights in high school. All those nights at Holden. I rode up to the beginning of East Shore Road and looked at my phone. Three bars. There's a little grassy area there at the intersection, and if it hadn't rained all day, I would have sat on the grass, but the grass was soaked. So I stood, my bike leaning against me, and tapped out Everett's number. I got his voice mail.

"Everett," I said. "I'm sorry. Come home. We need you to come home. You were right about Laurel. She and Spin"—fitful sobbing and snorting here, I was really losing it—"they're . . . married. Where are you? Come home. Please come home, Everett."

I shoved the phone back into my pocket and was just about to get on my bike when I saw a car approaching. I could tell by the headlights that it was a Jeep. A lot of people have Jeeps around here, but I knew it was Spin's. I pushed my bike over to the passenger door.

"Oh. My. God. I was so worried about you." It was Laurel. I knew it would be Laurel.

"Why?"

"Because I heard you leave. I looked outside and saw you riding off on your bike."

"I like to ride my bike at night," I said.

"It's dangerous, though. Put it in the back, I'll drive you home."

I heaved the bike into the backseat of the Jeep and climbed in.

TWENTY-FOUR

Whit loved the idea of survival. He had a romantic fascination with the idea that you might overcome any trial offered up by nature or fate, as long as you were prepared. He took every opportunity to teach us children survival skills. We learned how to make a fire without matches; how to collect drinking water from dew; which forest plants are edible and which are poisonous. Navigation was what he loved most—navigating without instruments—and we all knew how to tell which direction was north or south without benefit of a compass or cell phone. On hot summer nights, floating on our backs in the lake, he taught us how to find Polaris. We all tried to be the first to see it.

Polaris. The North Star. It's right there at the end of the Little Dipper, right there at the tip of the handle. If you face Polaris, you're facing north. The most important thing to do, if you're lost at night, is to find Polaris. Pick a landmark while it's still dark. When the sun comes up, Polaris will be gone. Pick a distant hilltop, a cluster of trees; hopefully, you'll see something that's directly below Polaris. That's true north. You can navigate from there.

We live in Connecticut in the electronic age. What scenario could he have possibly fathomed that would involve our needing to know which direction was true north?

Whit showed me once the way a female duck will swim erratically, feigning a broken wing. We were out fishing in the old skiff when we saw one do this. "Watch this," Whit said. He paddled after her, and suddenly she shot into the sky, as healthy and sound as could be.

"She's got ducklings in the cove. It's an instinctive defense against predators. She was making herself look vulnerable, so we'd go after her and away from her offspring. Then she flew off once we weren't a threat."

I often wondered why Whit didn't travel more. Why didn't he go on treks in Nepal or Tibet? Why no trips to Antarctica or safaris in Africa? Joan would have been game; she loves anything involving exercise. But he never really left town much after we moved up here. He just built his banjos and made music.

"You're so clever," Laurel was saying as she pulled the Jeep back onto the road. "Here I thought you were a total shut-in, and instead you're out riding your bike all over the countryside in the middle of the night."

There's a driveway right there at the end of East Shore Road where you can turn around and drive back, but she just paused at the stop sign, then took a left.

"I thought we were going home," I said.

"Let's drive around the lake, I hate backtracking," said Laurel. "I always prefer going forward."

"Oh," I said.

"Don't you feel the same?" she asked. "Like when you're hiking, wouldn't you rather make a loop than backtrack?"

"I don't really hike."

I looked up at the stars. The road straightens out for about a half mile before you turn onto West Shore Road. We started going very fast. A lot of people speed on that stretch because it's so straight. The top was down, so I tilted my head back and looked up at the sky. Where was Polaris?

We sped past the turn onto West Shore Road.

Now we were on Housatonic Road. There are woods on both sides and you can't see much sky there, just the treetops spinning past.

"What's going on, Laurel?" I managed to say.

Each fraction of a mile, each turn of the wheels was tearing at me. We were getting so far from home. I tried to maintain a casual tone.

"I just thought we'd chat," she said.

She slowed down slightly and veered off onto a dirt road. It was Hunt Hill Road, a steep incline that leads from the lake to the neighboring town of Wakefield. She drove up the road a short distance, until we came to an open field, then she steered the Jeep into the field and turned it around. I thought she was going to take us back to the road, but she stopped the car and said, "Wow, look at that view."

You can see the lake from there. The storm clouds were rearranging themselves, and for a brief moment we saw the moonlight, pearly and muted, slanting across the lake's glistening surface. Then the wind shifted, a dark cloud settled over the moon, and the lake was lost in the gloom.

"I know you took my phone this afternoon. I know you read my texts and my e-mails."

I was silent.

"Do you have any questions?"

"Questions about what?" I whispered.

"About what you found on my phone. Don't lie, don't even apologize. I admire you, Lottie. You and all your little sneaky life hacks. So go ahead, ask me anything."

There was nothing to ask, really. I'd had Matt do some Internet sleuthing that afternoon. He had provided me with information that I hadn't been able to piece together from her phone. Laurel wasn't from Sun Valley. She never had a sister. She had grown up in Breckenridge—that's why she was such a great skier. But she wasn't on any ski team. Her mother was a pothead who cleaned motel rooms. Laurel had been arrested twice, from what Matt had seen. Once for soliciting as a minor, once for extortion. She was thirty-five, not twenty-seven.

She had been married to a man named Craig Henley. Matt wasn't able to find out anything about him.

"Why Spin?" I asked finally.

"Why did I fall in love with Spin? He's very lovable, you know that."

I heard the hollow cry of an owl.

"I don't think you love him," I managed to whisper. "I know about you and Everett. I know what you did the night of the party."

"Oh yeah?"

There was the owl again, calling out into the dark.

"I downloaded all the texts and e-mails on your phone. I have them. I can prove to Spin that you're not who you say you are. That you're a user and a fraud. That you slept with his best friend."

"I don't think you should do that, Charlotte," Laurel replied. Her tone was casual and breezy. "I think we should all be friends. We're so alike, you and I."

This made me laugh. "Alike? In what way are we alike?"

"Almost every way. We're both good people, but we're smarter than most. It's unfair that some people are given things in this world that smart people like us should get—like college degrees. So we find a way to get them. I think you love holding court on your blog from your little perch in the attic. I think the whole reason you don't like to leave the property is because you can't face honest people, you're such a fraud. . . ."

"I've never taken advantage of anybody. I've never lied to anybody about who I am—anybody I know in real life. Does Spin know that you were married before? Does he know how old you are? I downloaded everything on your phone, all your texts to your friends, making fun of Spin—making fun of all of us. I'll show them to him."

"No, I don't think that would be a very good idea. I'm married to Spin now. You live in our house. I think you should be a little bit more gracious."

"Why did you send the letters to the police? I liked you. I don't get why you would come in and sabotage everything. You didn't have to fuck Everett. We could have all gotten along."

"Spin is stuck. I wanted to move things along, get you and your mother to move along. This town is dull. I've made Spin see that. Now he wants to move, but we can't afford it. All our money is tied up in the house."

"*Our* money?" I blurted out incredulously.

"Yes," Laurel said.

We were silent for a minute or two. Then I said, "I won't say anything to Spin. About you and Everett. About any of it."

"I know," Laurel said.

"Not because of you, but because it would kill him. I wouldn't hurt him that way."

"I know."

"Let's go back home, okay?"

"Whose home? Do you have a home now? Did you and your mom and sister finally find a place to live so you're not freeloading off Spin and me anymore?"

"No, I guess I meant Spin's home."

We sat for a moment.

"Your home," I said.

Laurel started up the Jeep and drove us to Lakeside.

It was the third day of rain. I waited in my room until I smelled coffee. When I went downstairs, I found Joan pacing around, waiting for it to finish brewing.

"My tennis got rained out," she said.

"Sorry," I said.

"I need to run. I can't sleep if I don't run, but it was thundering a few minutes ago."

"It'll let up," I said.

She was very still for a minute, then she pulled me close and said,

"They're finished painting all the residences at Holden. I wonder when they're going back? It feels a little crowded. I mean, I'm not used to having company for so long."

"I don't think they're going back, Joan. I don't think they consider themselves company."

"What do you mean?" Joan asked.

"I think Laurel would prefer to live here."

"No," Joan said. "They can't live here. Why would they want to live here with us? It's much more fun living on campus with the other couples."

According to Laurel, she already did live here. When I'd gone into her phone, the day before, I'd seen the e-mails to the architect in New York. He was the architect Perry and Catherine had used for their house—I recognized the name. She and the architect had made a date for him to come up and look at the house for the "renovation project." He was coming up the following Thursday. They had several back-and-forth e-mails. Spin was CC'd on all of them.

We heard their footsteps on the stairs and we both made ourselves busy—pouring coffee, putting bread in the toaster.

"Morning!" said Laurel.

"Good morning, dear," Joan said. "Who wants breakfast?"

Joan made us scrambled eggs, and as soon as we sat down, Spin began. "Joan, Charlotte, we wanted to have a talk. I think this is a good time, while Sally's still away. You know, Laurel and I have discussed this a great deal. We just don't see living on campus. Laurel's not going to take the teaching position. She needs to finish this manuscript. She's not going to be able to teach until her book is finished."

Her book. She wasn't writing a book. I had been up all night. Matt had found out more about Laurel. She had never been to college or graduate school—that's why she'd suddenly decided not to apply for the teaching job. All of it, everything she had told us about herself, had been fabricated.

Joan said, "Spin, are you trying to tell us that you want to stay on here? With us?"

"I'm really sorry, Joan," Spin said. "Laurel and I've talked about this. I've talked about it with Perry. There's no way that would work. That's too much of a strain to put on a new marriage, sharing a house with—family."

"Besides," Laurel said, "we're going to have some work done on the house, and we know how unsettling that would be for you, Joanie."

"Nobody calls me Joanie," my mother snapped. Actually, we often call her that. We children do—her children and stepchildren.

"They want to sell the house, Joan," I said.

"No," Joan said. "Spin, that's not true, right? Why would you sell it? Where would you live?"

"Anywhere, Joan. Anywhere I want. I'd like to live someplace that I choose, not a place that was chosen for me."

And there it was again: the quiet rage I had heard that day with Sally.

"I could live anywhere I want, if I got my assets out of this place."

Joan took on the stern maternal voice she had used when scolding us as children. "Spin, I didn't ask you to buy Perry's share of the house. If you hadn't done that, you'd have plenty of money."

"You have plenty of money. You could live anywhere," Spin said. "Joan, one of the reasons Dad kept the house separate from the marital trust is because you always complained that all your friends went to Florida in the winter. He thought that you might want to move there and he didn't want you to be burdened with the house. I remember having that conversation with you, Perry, and Dad."

"Yes, that's true, Spin. But I didn't expect your father to die when I was still relatively young. I can't move to Florida now. This is my town. I've lived here all my life. Your father meant for me to live *here,* in this house, as long as I want. I'm not planning to move anytime soon."

Laurel stood up and said to Spin, "This is uncomfortable for me. It's family business. I'm going upstairs, sweetie."

After she left, I said, "Spin, listen, before you met Laurel, you were so happy at Holden. This lake project with Yale was really important to you. Now you want to abandon all that? You just met Laurel—"

"I'm calling Jim Haskell. Then I'm calling my attorney," Joan interrupted. She stood up shakily. "Your father would be so disappointed in you right now, Spin."

"He was *my* father, Joan. I'll have to reconcile that with myself, but it has nothing to do with you."

Joan stormed out of the room. I started to go after her, but Spin put his hand on mine and whispered, "Wait, Lottie. I shouldn't have said that to her."

"Let's go out on the porch," I said.

He followed me outside and I sat on the old porch swing. He stood there, staring out at the lake.

"You know, Lottie, I thought I loved Holden, but what I really loved was that I had a neutral place to live when I was a kid. That's why I spent so much time there before I even became a student. My mom always resented the time I spent here; my dad resented the 'influence' he thought Mom had on me. They were both happy when I was at Holden, because I wasn't with one of them or the other."

"I get that," I said.

"Shove over a little," he said, and he sat next to me on the swing. "Holden was more of a home to me than either of the houses that I grew up in. My mom's house was really her husband Peter's house. This house was yours—Sally's, Joan's, and Dad's."

"How can you even say that, Spin? Whit always made this a home for all of us. And you've always been so involved here. What about the lake study? The task force?"

"I'm just telling you the way I experienced it. When I finished school, I had no idea what I wanted to do with my life. It felt comfortable to go back there. But now I want to move on. I'm almost finished with the lake survey. The results are going to be published, my name will be on it. Laurel and I want to travel. Use my schooling and experience with inland waterways in parts of the world where clean water is a matter of life or death for the people living there."

We could hear somebody, either Joan or Laurel, walking around upstairs.

"Spin," I said quietly. "I get it. I really do. And I'm sure there's some way that we can work something out with the trust so that you can get your assets out. The trust should be able to purchase the house back from you, right? Or maybe, with Joanie's money, and some money I've saved, we can lease it from you."

"No, we're selling Lakeside. We're going to do some renovations and then we're selling."

I said, "What if things don't work out with Laurel?"

"Not this again," Spin said.

"She's not who she pretends she is. I have proof."

Spin turned to me angrily. "Proof of what, exactly?"

"She wasn't in an accident, she never had a sister who died."

"I know you think that's shocking for me to hear, but I've always known that."

"You have?" I asked.

"Well, I've known it for several months, yes. She told me before she moved here. She was trying to write a novel. It turned into sort of an online writing experiment. Maybe a little bit like your fake blog."

I said nothing.

"Yeah, Laurel told me about it—about your whole weird virtual family."

"That's not really what my blog was."

"That's true, your blog is different. Your blog is about getting money by deceiving people."

"No," I said. "It wasn't that. Anyway, it's gone now, the blog."

"Well, Laurel didn't profit from what she was doing online. And you're wrong about the other stuff. She did go to college and graduate school. She was on the U.S. ski team."

"How do you know?" I asked.

"Because she told me," Spin said, his voice trembling with rage again.

Why hadn't he ever told us he was so angry? All we'd ever done was love him. How could he be such a fool?

Fuck him.

My sudden anger gave me relief. He was right. He was an adult, he could make his own decisions. He deserved her. I had Everett. It was time for all of us to move on.

I put my hand on Spin's arm and squeezed it gently, then I went up the back stairs to the attic.

TWENTY-FIVE

I was sitting in the dark when I heard Everett's truck pull in. I peered out the window and waited until he turned on the little lamp next to his kitchen window—the signal we'd used for years—inviting me over.

I pulled on a pair of jeans and a T-shirt, then opened the door and peeked out into the hallway. I walked down to the second floor. It was dark; there was no sound coming from any of the rooms. Riley, who had been asleep on the floor, rose and wandered over to me, his tail thwap-thwap-thwapping the wall as he came. I grabbed his collar and we made our way down the stairs together. Then we both crept out through the dog door. The front door is creaky; I didn't want to wake anybody.

Everett met Riley and me at his front door. He pulled me into the house, into his bed. He hadn't been gone a full day, somehow it felt like years. Afterward, we went down to the lake. The rain hadn't cooled the air, it had only made it thicker, soupier. Everything was sodden. We dove into the cool water and swam out to the float. We needed to be away from the land, Spin and Laurel's land. Away from our houses, the houses that belonged to Spin and Laurel. We lay on our backs on the float, just as we had done so many times when we were children.

I told Everett everything.

"Spin needs to know," Everett said.

"He doesn't want to know," I said. "Let's get out of here. Let's move. We can both work anywhere. Let's move to California."

Everett sat up and grinned at me. "Who *are* you?" he asked.

"I'm serious," I said. "Would you want to do something like that?"

"Hell yeah," Everett said. "I could get a lot more business if we were someplace where I could work outside with dogs year-round. Maybe Southern California. I can't believe you're even considering this. Let's do it."

The idea terrified me. The idea terrified and thrilled me.

"Or the San Francisco area," Everett said. "I have a cousin there. In the meantime, let's get out more. I can't look at the two of them together. You're right: There's no point in telling Spin. He won't believe us."

"Right," I said.

"Let's go to the diner for breakfast tomorrow," he said.

"Okay," I agreed.

We did go to the diner. I didn't feel the dread when we pulled out of the driveway. I felt free. Free of Laurel and Spin. Free of Lakeside. We drove through town. At the diner, I saw an old friend from high school, Hailey Borden. She has a baby now. A little baby girl. She let me hold her as we chatted. On the ride back to the house, Everett and I talked excitedly about our plans for the move. Sally could come with us if she wanted. There would be more access to the film community in California. Joan would likely stay here in Harwich. She could afford to buy or rent anyplace that was a reasonable size. It would be good for her to move into a smaller place. She wouldn't be so overwhelmed.

Spin had married Laurel, we kept reminding each other. Nobody had forced him. He was an adult.

"He made his bed, now he can lie in it," Everett said.

Lakeside belonged to him. He could do what he wanted with it. It was time to get on with our lives.

Spin was standing ankle-deep in the lake when we returned to the house. He was frowning at something in the water. He leaned over and plucked out a long, spirally weed and examined it.

"Look at him," Everett said, chuckling.

"I know," I said.

Spin turned and gave us a smile.

I never held a baby before Spin was born. Sally and I loved to help the nanny care for him and play with him. The nanny's name was Camilla. She was English, and she had a degree in early childhood development. When Spin started smiling at us—real smiles, not those newborn grimaces—Camilla explained that babies start smiling around four or five weeks of age. That was nature's way of ensuring that the mother/baby bond remains strong.

"At first, the mum is just awash with love for the new baby, but after a few weeks, the constant feeding and caring becomes tiresome. The mum—well, most mums without help are exhausted. But then, a miracle! The baby starts to recognize faces. And when he sees a face, it makes him smile. This is just when the mum needs it most, because that smile does something to her chemistry, to her emotions. It's just nature's way of ensuring that she keeps caring for her little one."

Sally and I spent hours pressing our faces close to Spin just to get him to smile. Later we did it to get that delicious giggle of his. It's not just a baby's mother who has her chemistry changed by the smile of an infant.

"I have to tell him," Everett said after a moment.

"I know," I said.

Spin wandered over to the truck and leaned in on Everett's side. "Hey, bud, you wanna give me a hand this afternoon? I have to do a final reading for this lake survey. You wanna come out and give me a hand for an hour or two?"

"Sure," said Everett.

"Great," Spin said. He managed to give me a forced smile. "I just have to run over to Holden and grab my meters and some other equipment I left there."

"I'll tell him when we're out on the lake," Everett said to me when Spin was gone. "That way, Laurel won't be able to interfere. I'm just going to tell him about the night of the Fourth. I'll let him find out the rest on his own."

TWENTY-SIX

The other day, I came across another video Spin sent me during that week in Sun Valley, that week he first met Laurel. He couldn't have shot it on the same day as the one he shot with Laurel, because that day had been snowy and gray. The day of this video, the sky is blue, the snow is fresh and untouched. He's at the top of another peak, only this time he's alone. What I love about this video is that you can see his shadow for most of the run. From the moment he pushes off until he reaches the bottom of the mountain, almost seven minutes later, he doesn't stop, and you can see his entire shadow the whole way down. For the longest time, I thought it was lucky footage, I thought the sun just happened to be hitting the mountain at exactly the right angle. Spin has always had a gracefulness. I know that's not a word often used to describe men, but it's the perfect word to describe Spin's lithe, silent shadow in that footage—the shoulders and hips moving up down, up down, just barely, just the right amount to coast down the mountain. He made everything look so easy.

I thought it was just luck that his shadow was captured on that video. I thought it just happened that the sun was at the exact angle at that time. The other day, though, something occurred to me. I watched it again. I called Sally. She was in a recording session. She called me during a break.

"Look at the other Sun Valley video," I said. "Not the one with Laurel, the other one."

"You know what?" Sally said. "I have to go, I'm not talking to you about these videos. Please stop watching them."

"Just watch it when you get home."

"No," Sally said. "Lottie, delete them. You're making yourself sick."

When we hung up, I watched the video one more time, and now it was so clear, so obvious. Spin had deliberately tried to capture his shadow. He had chosen that exact time to do that run, had angled the camera just so. The other video had shown what it was like to ski from his perspective; the camera was angled out at the scenery. In this video, Spin wanted to see himself. He wanted to see what he looked like. Maybe he wanted to see what the big deal was, what it was that everybody—our family, his friends, Everett (especially Everett)—thought was so great.

I try not to think of the specifics of that afternoon very often. I had to recount them for the police and the attorneys too many times, and now I try to avoid thinking about the actual incident. But I do think of that drive Spin took to Holden Academy to get his notebooks and his meters that day. He would have gone down Maple Hill Road and past Harwich Center, another quarter mile, then turned left through the main gates of the Holden campus. He would have driven past the playing fields where he had run around every summer since he was five—first at soccer camp, later lacrosse camp, and then preseason football. He would have parked in front of the field house named for his great-grandfather and walked past the headmaster's house, where my grandfather lived for twenty-five years. All the men, all the coaches, all the knowledge that Sally and I imagined we had been missing, they had all been there at Holden. The education that we felt had been denied us—this had been Spin's birthright. Somehow, in our minds, he was carried aloft into a bright homeland of community and belonging when he moved into his dorm there. Acceptance, enlightenment, knowledge—it would all have been ours there, too. At least that's what we once believed.

I was up in the attic when Everett and Spin pulled away in the little skiff. They pushed it from the beach and then hopped inside. Everett lowered the engine and gave a quick tug to the pull cord and they motored off. I watched them glide across the still water until they were around Whitman's Point. There they disappeared from view.

There's a tree there at the end of Whitman's Point. It's a sugar maple, hundreds of years old. In the winter, her rough branches reach out above the ice like ancient, pleading arms. In the summer, she regains her youthful beauty, her full green skirt rustling and swaying over the lake's edge. When I was little, I loved paddling our old canoe into her shade on hot afternoons. I loved to drift there. When I pressed my ear to the floor of the canoe and closed my eyes, I could hear the clacking of crayfish as they scuttled beneath me. At least I thought I could. If I held my breath and listened hard enough, I thought I could hear the minnows play.

Everett was going to tell him about the night with Laurel and just allude to the fact that there were other secrets she was keeping from him. We thought there might be some way that Spin could get the marriage annulled if he moved quickly enough. We were sure that Spin would believe Everett. Everett had nothing to gain by telling Spin. He knew what he was guaranteed to lose—Spin's friendship, forever. It was worth it to Everett, to save Spin from Laurel.

They were out for so long. An hour went by. I took an old pair of binoculars from the top of the fireplace mantel in our living room and went out on the porch to see where they were. Two kayakers came close to our dock. In the distance, a motorboat pulled a skier. I heard Laurel walking down the front stairs. I snuck through the kitchen and up the back stairs. A few moments later, she drove away in the Jeep, as she did every day. Driving off to the side of the town where there's cell service. She said she needed contact with the "real world."

Finally, I heard the dogs barking down by the lake. I looked out the window. Everett was still at the tiller, steering toward shore. Spin was laughing and calling to the dogs. Snacks raced to the end of our dock and soared through the air into the water. It was his thing; we all loved it when he did that. He swam out to the boat and then swam alongside it as Everett pulled up to the dock. What had happened? Spin was so jolly. Had Everett told him? Was Spin possibly relieved? That thought actually occurred to me at the time. Perhaps Everett had laid it all out for Spin and he was happy to know the truth.

Spin jumped onto the dock and tied up the skiff. He grabbed his meter and his notebook and waited while Everett made some kind of adjustment to the engine. They walked back along the dock together, and when they came to the end, I could hear Spin say, "Thanks, man. Hey, you wanna head over to the tavern later? You, Laurel, and me? Get a burger and a beer?"

Everett had been facing his house when Spin said that, but then he turned and said something that I couldn't hear.

That was a big deal with the police later. They insisted that I should have been able to hear what Everett said. I had heard what Spin said, about going to the tavern, so, according to the police, I should have been able to hear what Everett said. I couldn't. He said it quietly. And he was looking down.

I think Spin must have had trouble hearing him, too, because he walked over to where Everett was standing.

Everett was still looking down. I couldn't hear what he was saying, but my heart raced when I saw Spin's posture change. He had been standing there barefoot on the lawn, leaning over and patting the dogs, and then suddenly he stood ramrod straight. The clipboard and meter were tossed on the ground and he just rushed Everett.

By the time I got to the beach, they were sort of entangled in a wrestler's hold. Spin was punching Everett's sides with his fist. I was screaming at both of them to stop. The dogs were snarling and biting at them, and finally Everett managed to trip Spin. Spin fell back, he landed on his side, and his head bumped the corner of the dock hard. I've never heard a sound like it. The dogs sniffed at him. Everett leaned over and said, "Spin? Buddy?"

I heard him say that. I was almost next to him then and I was calling Spin's name, too.

Spin was just lying there blinking. Everett leaned over.

"Spin, you okay?" Everett asked.

Spin closed his eyes. After a moment, he opened them and propped himself up on his elbow. He reached around and felt the back of his head.

"Fuck, man," he said to Everett, who was now kneeling next to him. Then Spin said, "My fucking head."

He started to sit up, but Everett put his hand on his shoulder and said, "Don't try to stand. Don't get up too fast. Let me see your head."

"I'm okay," Spin said. He sat up slowly and squinted at Everett.

"I'm sorry, man," Everett said. He was teary now; I was, too. "I'm really sorry," he said.

"Your head's bleeding, Spin," I said. "Let me look at it."

Spin bowed his head down and we saw that there was a steady trickle of blood coming from the back of his scalp. Everett whipped off his T-shirt, wadded it up, and then pressed it against Spin's head. I sat next to Spin and held the shirt. Everett knelt in front of us, looking into Spin's eyes.

"Spin, I'm just . . . sorry, man."

"It was an accident," Spin said. He was wincing, but he also managed to smile. "Stop making such a big deal of it."

"It's not bleeding much," I said to Everett. "Head wounds usually bleed a lot. It's barely bleeding."

After a minute or two, the bleeding had almost stopped, and we asked Spin if he wanted to go inside, but he was distracted. We thought he was trying to process what Everett had just told him. Spin seemed content just to sit there and stare out at the lake, so we sat there with him for a few moments.

"You should wash that cut," Everett said finally.

"Yeah," Spin said.

"Do you want to come in my house? I think maybe it's best," Everett said.

"No, I want to see Laurel when she gets back. We're going to the tavern tonight. Wanna come?" Spin asked.

I remember feeling in that instant that my heart had stopped.

Everett said shakily, "Spin . . . do you remember what just happened?"

"Yeah, I hit my head."

"Do you remember what we were talking about?"

"Yeah, the lake survey," Spin said. He looked quizzically at the blood on his fingertips from when he had touched the back of his head.

"Go call an ambulance," Everett said. There was a terrified urgency in his voice, but also, I sensed that he felt relieved. I felt it, too. Spin must have had a concussion. He seemed to have forgotten what Everett had told him.

I jumped up, but Everett grabbed my wrist and whispered, "I'm not telling him again."

"No, no, I know," I said, bursting into tears. I can't begin to describe my relief. Telling Spin had been a mistake. We were being given another chance! We couldn't bear to have Spin hate us; nothing was worth that. I ran to the house to call the ambulance.

When I came out, Everett and Spin were sitting side by side, staring out at the lake. I sat next to Spin.

"Do you want to go in the house?" I asked. "Let's go inside, Spin. Let's clean up that cut."

"Okay, in a minute. Let me just sit," he said. He rested his head on my shoulder.

We just sat there, the three of us. A motorboat sped across the lake. Its wake formed huge furrows that spiraled outward and then rolled up onto our beach. I pushed my feet forward to meet the cool froth of the little waves.

"Love this hour, right?" Spin said.

"This hour?" I asked.

"It's so shiny," he said, and it was true; it was that time in the afternoon when the sun glints off the lake and you see everything through a sort of silvery filter.

"It's the slying now," said Spin. "It's the slinge."

I pulled away and looked at his face.

"Spin?" Everett said. "Buddy?"

"Yeah?"

"Are you okay?"

He just smiled.

"Yeah."

"Let's go inside," I said. I took his hand and stood, but he just sat there gazing out at the water.

"Come on, let's go," I said.

"Wait for Dad," Spin said. "Less wait for Whit."

"Whit?" I said, my heart racing. "Come on, Spinny. Let's go inside."

"Juss Whit," he said. "Whit for Whit."

"Spin," I cried. "Can you stand?"

"Is small," Spin said. His words were slurred. He walked between us now, his legs moving in small shuffling steps. "Iss a small song, sweet, swing it again."

"What song?" I cried. I let go of him for a minute so I could open Everett's door, and he cried out, "No, come back, Lottie."

"I'm right here," I said, and as we moved him across the threshold, he said, "Was that song?"

"Where the fuck is the ambulance?" Everett said. "Where is it?"

It was a subdural hematoma. When people talked about it later, people here in town, they always referred to the famous actress who died after the skiing accident. One minute she was joking with the paramedics, the next minute she was dead.

Spin didn't joke with the paramedics. He died before they arrived. Everett and I sat him down on the sofa, and he just closed his eyes. We kept telling him to wake up. I kept pushing him, calling his name. I knew he shouldn't be allowed to go to sleep. He never opened his eyes again. The cut that we had seen on the back of his head was nothing. There was another lesion, on the inside. His brain had crashed against the back of his skull when his head bumped against the dock. It was bleeding, but the skull was intact. There was no place for the blood to go. Maybe if we lived closer to a hospital, he would have made it. Maybe if we had gotten him to a hospital sooner, they would have been able to drill a little hole in his skull and relieve the pressure.

Everett went in the ambulance with Spin. Laurel arrived home while they were gone. I saw her walk into our house. Well, it wasn't our house anymore. I guess it never was ours, really.

"Hello?" Laurel called out, I could hear her from Ev's. She must have been standing in the front hall. All the windows were open. I could hear her from where I crouched next to the window in Everett's kitchen. I was huddled there with Riley and Snacks. I led them into Everett's room and closed the door. It was dark in there; he had his shades pulled down. Laurel knocked once on Everett's front door, then walked in.

"Hello?" she called.

When I heard her footsteps approaching the bedroom, I backed up into his cluttered little closet and closed the door. I smelled Everett there. I would have been happy to stay there forever, to be honest. I could smell his skin and it reminded me of hundreds of days in the sun. I could smell his musky, familiar sweat, his hair, his breath. I felt him all around me. His presence reassured me. Spin would be fine. Ev was with him.

When Laurel came into his room, she didn't open the closet door. I heard the dogs' excited feet on the old wood floor as they skittered up to her. I heard her say to them quietly, "Fuck off." Then I heard her leave.

TWENTY-SEVEN

Joan and I stayed in the house through the fall and winter. The estate was all tied up in probate and we were allowed to stay on until it was settled. Spin, of course, had no will. What twenty-six-year-old has a will? Perry and the trustees tried to get his marriage to Laurel annulled, but it was impossible. You should have seen her cry at his memorial service. Her lawyer was the husband of Everett's old girlfriend, Lisa. That's how small the world is up here. He had his arm around her as she sobbed during the church service. He had his arm around her in a photo I saw online recently. They were at a fund-raising gala for Memorial Sloan Kettering Cancer Center. She's been all over the Internet lately: She's about to star in a reality show about New York "society" women. She's the "hot widow," according to one of the promos I watched.

Joan and I have to be out by tomorrow. Once the estate was settled, we were given a month to pack and leave Lakeside. Laurel gets everything—the house and Spin's savings, which were more than he had let on. (He was always thrifty, just like Whit.) When Joan dies, Laurel will inherit the rest. The Whitman stocks, all the old Whitman steel money that had been preserved so carefully by Whit, Whit's father, and his father before him.

We've been given one month to make the last twenty-seven years go away. Truthfully, most of the stuff in this house is Whitman stuff. It all belongs to Laurel now, so there isn't a lot to move. Everybody left us alone at first, but these past few weeks, Laurel and that architect have been driving up here and walking all over the place. Joan manages to exchange curt civilities with them. I never come down when they're here. I've heard them whispering, more than once, that they know I'm in the attic, "hiding."

Once, when Laurel and the architect were talking about me, I wasn't in the attic at all, I was in the little crawl space behind a closet in the master bedroom, the same room that they were in. I know all the hiding places in this house. It's satisfying knowing that I'm still able to fit into my favorite hiding spots from when I was a little girl.

One morning last week, I was up in the attic when Riley started growling. I told him to hush. I had been teaching him not to make noise when people come in, but that morning, he kept growling.

I opened the attic door a little. The footsteps in the foyer were heavy—slow and unfamiliar. I closed the door and waited. I peeked out the attic window but didn't see a car in the driveway.

The person was in the kitchen now. Joan had gone out for her run. Neither she nor I had gotten around to doing the dishes from the night before. I was planning to do them when I finished what I was doing on the computer. Now I heard the water running and the dishes clattering. That's when I realized who it was.

Mr. Clean had lain low for most of the winter, but in April, he had hit two more houses. He was taking more risks, showing up when people were only out for a few hours. Washington was on the local news one evening, urging residents to lock their homes and never to open the door to strangers.

So that morning, when I heard the commotion in the kitchen, I tiptoed down the back stairs. I was barefoot and made my way down so slowly. I know every floorboard that creaks in this whole house.

When I arrived at the bottom of the stairs, I peered into the kitchen. Mr. Clean's back was to me, but I recognized his stooped posture. It was Norm Hungerford. Whit's old friend, Mr. Hungerford. I watched him for a few minutes. I was afraid of surprising him, afraid he might have a heart attack or something. Finally I just walked into the room and said, "Mr. Hungerford?"

Mr. Hungerford looked at me quizzically. "Yes?"

"Hi, I'm Charlotte, Whit's daughter."

"Oh, well, hello, dear," he said.

"What are you doing?" I asked.

"Helping Betty with the dishes. Run along now."

Old, senile Mr. Hungerford had been Mr. Clean all along. His fingerprints matched those taken in the other houses. He never tried to evade being caught. Washington loved this. He said that's how it happens sometimes. When you try not to get caught, you usually do. When you just go about your business, you can get away with a lot.

Sally found a sublet in Manhattan, but she comes up here on weekends to stay with Washington. They're together now. The film-maker loved her score and she's spent much of the winter recording it. Now she's helping us pack up our things. Joan is staying in Harwich, renting a lovely house right near the club. She can walk to the tennis courts from there. I'm going to stay with her. Just for now. She has an extra room. It's just a temporary setup.

Everett has to be out of his house tomorrow, too. He has a friend with an old barn, and that's where he's storing his stuff until he moves. He's going to Vermont, not California. He's been to Vermont, but he's never been to California. That was his reasoning.

After Spin died, Everett and I still talked about moving someplace together, but our grief and remorse got in the way. We never talked about it, but our plan to move on was too enmeshed with Spin and his death. Maybe it would be forever, there was no way to tell. Those first few weeks after Spin's death, we had to keep reassuring each other that it was an accident, that it wasn't our fault. We never lied to the authorities. It was Washington who questioned us first, and we told him the truth. We told him about the night of the Fourth, and about the argument on the beach. About how Spin had charged Everett first, but that Everett had tripped him, causing him to fall. It was an accident.

Laurel, of course, disputed this. She called Washington's superior to say she wanted somebody else assigned to the case. She told him that Everett had a violent history, that he had been arrested for assault in the past. She knew this from Spin.

Why hadn't Whit let our mother go to the police when Sally was raped? Everett would never have been arrested if he had let her do that. He never would have attacked that Osborne kid if Whit had done the right thing.

"You're allowed to be angry at Whit," Sally's therapist had told her. "You're allowed to hate him."

Laurel claimed that I was a known liar. She told the officer who replaced Washington on the case about my mommy blog. Fortunately, old Ethel Garner had been sailing past our beach in her Sunfish that afternoon when Spin died. She had seen the entire incident and confirmed our version of what happened. The death was determined to be an accident, but everybody in town now thought of Everett as Spin Whitman's killer. There was lots of commentary on the *Harwich Times* Web site about the whole thing. Here's a sample:

> **ELW**: Sad about what happened to Whit Whitman's kid.
>
> **LUCYDUECEY**: I feel bad for Ev Hastings. They were best friends. Sucks. I hear that the chick who married Spin is selling the house. No more Whitmans in Harwich.
>
> **HORSEGAL**: End of an era.
>
> **BILLFEN**: I don't feel bad for Hastings. I think there's more to this story than meets the eye. I heard the new wife was forcing him to move out. He might have wanted Spin gone?
>
> **GARDENIA**: What a horrid thing to say!
>
> **JS**: @BILLFEN WTF is the matter with you? You suck.
>
> **TMK**: Whit's wife and daughters are still at Lakeside, no?
>
> **LUCYDUECEY**: Second wife. Stepdaughters. They've all moved on,

I think. Sally used to come up here a lot, but I haven't seen Charlotte in years.

ALI: Not true, Charlotte's still here. I see her all the time.

BIRDDOG: I've only seen her on Facebook in recent years.

ALI: Huh, I guess that's the only place I've seen her, too.

JAMESP: I went to Holden with Spin. He's a great guy.

BILLFEN: "Was" a great guy, huh, Ev?

JAMESP: Moderator? Can you please delete the outrageously disrespectful comment above?

You get the idea.

I heard from Matt a few days after Spin died. He sent an e-mail with his condolences. I have no idea how he knew about the accident—it only made local news, and there was no mention of me or Sally, since we're Maynards, not Whitmans. I asked him how he'd heard about it, but he didn't say. He likes to be invisible. He somehow snuck into our family via the Internet and had a look around. I know it sounds creepy, but in fact, I find it comforting to know that at any given moment, when I'm at my computer, my friend might be watching me.

We've been going out for drives every day, Ev and me. We still talk about possibly getting back together. We like to assure each other that this is going to happen, but who knows? We need time. Sometimes we get out of the truck and walk around. I'm much better about this now. I still don't like open fields or places where people are walking around, but I like quiet country lanes and wooded paths.

On the first warm day of spring, about two weeks ago, we actually took a walk along the old railroad bed. Everett had three dogs he was training and we needed to exercise them. We ran along the path with the dogs—they were young and we wanted to tire them out. The dogs raced into the old tunnel, but I hesitated before going in. Everett was surprised when I told him I hadn't been there since that night we found Sally.

Later I told Sally that we had been to the tunnel.

"So?" she said. "Washington and I walk there a lot. It's so pretty this time of year. I've been back there a bunch of times."

I've started a new blog; it's another mommy blog. The diaper company has worked with me to develop it. I have two children again, but neither of them has special needs; that's where I ran into trouble the last time. Theo, my three-year-old, is a tyrant; he just got expelled from preschool. Poppy, who's seven, is small for her age, but she's very bright and has a big heart. She's the kindest person—an "old soul," as my followers often comment. She takes after my brother, Cole.

Cole's death was the reason I started the blog; it was a way to deal with my grief. I was surprised that the diaper company wanted me to start up a new blog, but they had been angry that I terminated the old one without consulting them. Now they know the deal; they know it's not real. That was never really an issue for them. They're really only interested in the numbers. I've had this blog up for only six months and I already have more followers than Lazy Susan ever had.

Tomorrow, Laurel's contractors will start "gutting the place" (their words). I recently heard the architect talking to his assistant about a screening room and a gym. These things are very attractive to buyers, according to him.

I don't like thinking about what Lakeside will look like later, after we're gone. I'm glad I'll never see it. Yesterday, Everett took away the banjos Whit gave Sally and me. He took some books and photographs that are ours as well. This afternoon, the appraisers are coming here to do an inventory. We don't have any way of proving the banjos were gifts. But they were. Everything else will be sold or demolished: Aunt Nan's floral bedspreads and gilt-edged mirror. Joan's heirloom irises. The old scarred butcher-block countertop. The little swale in the floorboards in front of the old porch swing. Sally and I helped wear the wood out there with our bare feet. Whit probably started the little groove when he was a boy, swinging on that same swing. I heard the architect say that the floorboards on the porch had dry rot, all of them, and would have to be replaced. He warned his assistant not to sit on the swing. "Look how rusty that chain is," he said. "Accident waiting to happen."

I'm focusing on my blog now. I like to write about my kids. Today I wrote about how sweet they smell after their baths. Theo has a little cowlick in the same place as his father's. I like to trace it with my finger when he's falling asleep. The only time he'll hold still long enough for me to really cuddle him is when he's all drowsy in those last moments at the end of a long summer day. He still likes to curl up in my lap and listen to stories. He still sometimes sucks his thumb when he's falling asleep. He works his jaw in little circular motions and his big brown eyes gaze thoughtfully at the air in front of him.

What does a three-year-old think about? What does he remember? Who will this little person be, in the end? I love telling him about his great-grandmother, who thought her sweater was a cat. And about her own mother, who killed a rabid raccoon with a book, and ate her pie from a plate like a dog. The stories are familiar; he's heard them many times and he smiles at his favorite parts, even as his eyelids grow heavy. Soon he'll be asleep. Soon it'll be dark enough to walk outside and go for a swim.

The moon is almost full now. Each night this week, the sky's grown brighter and it's harder to see the stars, but not impossible. I'll still be able to see Polaris tonight. Someday, I'll show it to my children. It's at the end of the Little Dipper, right there, at the tip of the handle. Once you find Polaris, you've found true north. You can navigate anywhere from there. Find a landmark, I'll tell the children. You have to find a hill or a house or a tree while it's still dark; that way you'll be oriented the next day, when the stars are gone. Kids find it comforting to learn stuff like that—how to find your bearings, how to get where you're going, what to do if you're lost. I remember resting my head on Whit's shoulder one night when I was very small, so I could follow his calloused finger as it dropped from Polaris to the ridge below. The second ridge in the row of hills across the lake was our true north. The sky's fading into a watery pink now. The lake's turning iridescent and dark. In a little while I'll swim out to the float. I'll look for Polaris, then find the ridge below. I'll remember it, though there's really no need now. Tomorrow we'll all be gone.

ACKNOWLEDGMENTS

I wish to thank my brilliant editor, Brenda Copeland, and my wonderful agent, Maria Massie.

Many thanks also to the great team from Macmillan/St. Martin's: Sally Richardson, Stephen Morrison, Laura Chasen, Meg Drislane, Olga Grlic, Brant Janeway, Michelle Ma, Jessica Preeg, Lisa Senz, Laura Wilson, and Dori Weintraub.

Finally, much gratitude to my mother, Judith Howe, and my sister, Meg Seminara, who read the many drafts as they morphed into this book, and to my husband and children, who suffered through my writing it.